D0877422

TWO WEEKS
Until the Rest of My Life

Harold T. Fisher

Rosefogg Books

All Rosefogg Books' titles are available at special quantity discounts for bulk purchases for sales, promotions, premiums, fund-raising, educational or institutional use.

ISBN-10: 0-9844200-0-2
ISBN-13: 978-0-9844200-0-1

Library of Congress Control Number: 2010902473

Printed in the United States of America

Cover and Interior Designed by
The Writer's Assistant
www.thewritersassistant.com

Acknowledgment

This is my first novel. It was never really meant to be a book. It started as a dream, a poem and then a short story. All of that happened on December 15, 1992. I was living in Huntsville, Alabama at the time, trying to find my way as a young TV news anchor and reporter. By the time I sat down to write on that day, it was an idea that blossomed into a novel. Believe it or not, I was writing by hand on a yellow legal pad.

I am a man, one hundred seven percent, I have always joked. However, this book is written from, what I hope is, an accurate woman's voice. In my short lifetime, I have seen some of the finest black women alone, lonely and unhappy with their love life. Today, not much has changed. Often they are consumed with family and careers, not taking time out for their love needs, wants or desires. Few of them ever take the opportunity to indulge their fantasies, whatever they may be. I hope this will give you an opportunity to do so.

While this book is about what women deserve and should avoid in their lives, men should read it too. Guys, you never know, you just might learn a little something.

Anyway, this book is dedicated to my mother and father, Helen and Harold. They've always said education is the way, formal and otherwise. Thank you for your love and support. It is also dedicated to "The Fellas." Ron, you are the calm one, the thinking one who never moved too fast even when I suggested that you should. To Butch, who never takes life too seriously. That's something I am still trying to learn. Finally, to Dexter, I met you first. You have had so much pressed against you and still you have survived and thrived. I have never, EVER stopped believing in you.

To the reader, I can only say this. I hope this book will take you away, make you smile, make you think and make you believe love can be found in the strangest places and at the strangest, most wonderful times of your life. Don't ever pass it up. If you do, you will miss something.

I love you all.

Harold T. Fisher aka *Rosefogg*
Baltimore, Maryland
June 3, 2009

TWO WEEKS

Until the Rest of My Life

Prologue

This may sound funny to you, but I'm feeling like a man. No, not as if I want to make it with a woman. I am a woman, and I love men. But it's the kind of powerful, hard-pressed desire men always have. It's a mental thing, a physical thing. Yes, I admit it; I'm horny. It's not the usual sistah-needs-some-lovin'-c'mon-hold-me-gently kinda thing. That would be nice. Yes, that's very true. But, it's like, like... (Sigh!) It's like a brooding, thick, and thorny growth of bittersweet weeds. It's sprouting and blemishing the manicured lawn of my body. I can't get rid of it. I can't think of anything else. It's getting in my way! All of a sudden, I just want to find a nice, hard, healthy piece of a man and just sit on him. No! Jump on him, grind on him, work my hungry hips, and make him cry out—wear him out. Make him tired while he's trying to knock the bottom out of me. Damn, I really feel horny...like a man!

$\mathcal{O}_{ne}$

This office is beautiful, despite the desk, pockmarked and chipped as if no one cared about it. Seven years ago, did I ever think a black woman would ever sit behind this desk? Would Denise Younger get a shot at running the Federal Procurement Office? There are a lot of black folks in this office, at least black women. There are plenty to choose.

Maybe you deserved this promotion more than you first thought. Too bad you had to fall into it because of someone's mistake.

Mr. Stansky got caught in the act of screwing his secretary on this very same antique walnut desk. What a way to go out. Going and cumming at the same time.

I guess I know how you feel, Stansky. Sometimes you gotta get it when you can, but not at work, stupid!

Here comes Bruce. Back to work.

"Did you say something, Ms. Younger?"

"No, Bruce, whatcha got?"

Bruce Russo is a fit tall, slender thirty-year-old white guy just out of graduate school. It was difficult, if not impossible, to get him to call me Denise, so I settled for Ms. Younger. I hired him as an assistant because he probably would have starved to death if he hadn't found a job soon. Washington, DC isn't as bad as some think, but without a job, this city can eat you alive. Bruce quickly showed me that he's deputy material. He's good at deciphering government contracts that read like Chinese trigonometry. He's friendly enough and even cute for a white guy.

I guess.

He's very kind but also kind of strange. Every time he comes into my office, he always seems to have a slight sheen of perspiration on his face, and there's always a nervous energy that I just can't pin down. His hands tremble ever so slightly. It makes me wonder if they had professional black women in his town of Perry, Florida, or any of us at all.

"I have some good news and some bad news. Which do you want first?"

I look at him and give him my best imitation of Evilene in the musical *The Wiz.* "Bruce, don't nobody bring me no bad news!"

That always breaks him up into a stitch of nervous laughter although I seriously doubt if he had seen the Broadway production or the movie for that matter. Yes, he *is* actually rather handsome in a rugged kind of way, nice body too—tall, lean with a flat stomach. He does have a few pockmarks on his cheeks, kinda like my desk. When he laughs, they form together and remind me of the photographs of the moon in my high school science books. But he also has those pinched crow's feet in the corners of his eyes. The only time most people see those cutesy-wootsy facial details are on the airbrushed perfection of *GQ* magazine models. I'm sure the twenty-something Georgetown barflies think he's cute, and he probably wouldn't have a problem taking home a big-boobed blondie for the horizontal hoedown after a happy hour.

"Okay, let's have it, good news first."

He leans over the front of the desk. His red-striped Republican tie licks at my desk blotter. "Well, the good news is the Fellows

Cellular Phone Corporation is cutting the initial bid for all its packages in half. The original bid of $300,000 for the staff is down to $147 grand. That's the lowest bid by a long shot, and you get yours free with the deal. Mr. Jason from upstairs gave yours a thumbs-up. No conflict of interest!"

"Well, isn't that something?" I say almost to myself.

Isn't that something indeed? Fellows Cell Phone Corporation had the best equipment on the market this year. But the rep they sent to me was a real slug. He tried so hard to sweet-talk this plump thirty-five-year-old chocolate ass between the sheets. Who the hell did he think he was? Sometimes white men think all black women are born whores. Maybe his reduced contract price is an apology. Well, I never give up any pussy for work, a contract, and for the last seven months, not for dinner with a nice, warm maple-syrup-colored brother. Maybe that's why I have this manly feeling trying to invade my stuff.

"The bad news is that you have to leave for New Orleans tomorrow. There's a two-week conference on public/private partnerships. Mr. Jason can't go. His wife broke her leg in a car accident earlier this week, and he has to stay home with her for the next month or so."

I lean backward in my high-back leather chair. The gears creak and whine like a door in an old haunted house movie. Damn! New Orleans, I've never been, but always wanted to go. Still this is July, and I know it's hot as hell down there. Besides, I am supposed to hook up with Saundra on Saturday to catch a drink and hear about her latest man adventure. For the past seven months, I've been kind of living vicariously through her escapades ever since I found out Joseph, that creep I was dating, smoked weed and Lord knows what else. I may drink a little too much now and then, but drugs are out. None at all, and I don't deal with those who do. I guess Mama and Daddy succeeded with the big drug scare for me.

Bruce is just standing there waiting for me to say something. I can feel him looking, and then trying politely *not* to look at my breasts. I guess I don't blame him. If I were a man, I would look at me too, especially at the thimble-sized nipples trying to tear through my silk blouse. Even in the warmest weather, they don't want to behave. I make no attempt to cover up. Today, I just don't care. I blew out a long breath.

"What time is my flight?"

"Um, 6:35 tomorrow night."

Well, at least that gives me a chance to get my clothes out of the cleaners and go shopping for something nice and feminine to sleep in. I'll have to call Saundra and ask her to take me to the airport. Lord knows I don't want to pay for two weeks of airport parking at Washington National. It's a good thing the eagle flies tomorrow too. I won't have to stay in some cracker-box hotel room for two weeks either. I can tack on some of my money to the travel allowance if I need to and upgrade to a small suite. Bruce is still standing, sweating, and staring. I look back at him. If he had chosen a different career path, he probably would have made a pretty good-looking matinee idol.

Or maybe the cute axe murderer in a B movie. Now that's *just mean and mischievous.*

"Bruce, is there something on your mind?"

"Uh, no. No, ma'am."

"Don't call me ma'am. I'm only thirty-five! Besides, the last name is Younger, remember?"

"Sorry, Ms. Younger."

Humph, no laughter. That was supposed to be a joke. He didn't get it.

"There is something I want to ask you, if you don't mind." He folds his hands palms up just below his belt line. "Every time you come in to see me for anything, you're sweating or at least looking distracted, as if I were going to shoot you or something. Do I make you nervous?"

"Ms. Younger, you, ah, well kinda."

"Why? I'm not going to bite you. You are one of the best members of my staff in the office. I've told you as much. I know things were rough before you got this job. But you have it now. You've always been very respectful, if a little stiff. I'll have you know, when I leave this job, whenever that happens, you would be the person I would recommend to replace me. Don't worry, your job is quite safe."

"Ms. Younger, if I may, that's not exactly what I mean. I mean, uh, well, it's just that you are very uh…"

I lean forward on the desk, put my chin in my hands, and let a quizzical look invade my face.

"Attractive!" he sighs with exasperation.

My mouth falls open, and Bruce rattles off like a gerbil running on a cage wheel. "I've never really met anyone quite like you. I mean, your hands are very pretty, kinda long, graceful. Nails are always done. Most women with a short 'fro like yours look kinda manly—"

Did he say 'fro?

"Yours is real feminine. Every day you smell wonderful. You always wear nice colors. They're rich and vibrant, alive even. Sometimes, when you move across the room, it's as if the wind is blowing just for you. You know I did graduate school rather late. A whole lot of the women just seem to let themselves go after undergrad. But you really look like you're trying to take care of yourself. Oh my, God, I've said too much already. This is going to get me in trouble with Human Resources."

"Go on, Bruce. You seem to be doing a really good job so far," I say, soaking up the compliments like an old dry sponge.

"Well, your waist seems so teeny, you've got to be working out. It's almost invisible. Your face always looks so clean and fresh even with the makeup. Ms. Younger, can I be totally honest with you?"

"You mean you haven't been so far?" I say with a chuckle.

"Well, you're pleasing to look at, hard not to. I don't want to seem lustful or leering. I also don't want to seem inappropriate although I guess it's too late for that. I know I've probably said too much and will probably get in trouble for this. I just really enjoy working with you. You're not like the women—the black women—at home."

I knew it! I don't think there is a lot going on for sisters where he's from!

"The men I grew up around didn't always say nice things when they spoke about black women. Where I come from, there just aren't many black people to begin with, so you're kinda one of the first black women I've worked with this closely. I've learned a lot about black women, just being here for a little while, and I've learned it mostly from you. You're a really good role model for black women, hell...for all women."

I am shocked. Not like a slap in the face, but more like I think the world is flat and someone told me its round and has proof.

"Ms. Younger, I don't want to upset you or have you thinking I am trying to come on to you. I have a lot of respect for you. I know you're a hardworking woman. You *did* ask me, and I thought you should know what I think of you as a person."

I close my mouth and regain my composure. My tongue is bone-dry. I guess I look like a schoolgirl after her first surprise French kiss. "Well, Bruce, thank you for sharing your thoughts with me. It's, well, flattering that you would see me in that way. And don't worry about being inappropriate. I'm a big girl, and I believe you're sincere about your thoughts. Besides, I've always expected everyone in the office to speak their minds when we have one-on-one chats. Here's the proof in the pudding."

I look at my Rolex; I am also looking for an out from this conversation. I find one. "Damn, look at the time, it's 3:30. I have to call Saundra about a ride to the airport tomorrow. Bruce, can you finish up the cell phone stuff? I've got to leave early if I'm going to get my clothes out of the cleaners."

"Yes, ma'am."

"And call Mr. Jason and tell him I won't be in at all tomorrow. I will be on that flight!"

"Yes, ma'am."

I grab my purse and stretch my long legs toward the door, but I do a quick stop and turn just outside my door at Bruce's desk.

"One more thing, Bruce—" His cutie-pie face looks into mine. "I really appreciate your kind observations. We can keep that between us, okay?"

"Yes, ma'am."

"Bruce, don't call me ma'am. The last name is Younger, or did you forget?"

"Yes, ma'am, uh, Ms. Younger."

I can feel Bruce's sweet smiling eyes on my backside, as I walk out of the door and down the long hallway leading away from our offices.

There is a little more swing to my hips. I imagine that slow-motion breeze he spoke about as I left the office behind. The smile on my face is surprising. I am even a little embarrassed.

Two

I get to the garage where my Volvo is parked. I was so proud of that car when I bought it new in '89. The pearl gray finish is so…middle class. I have arrived. Now all I can do is look at it and think about the drive through the early rush hour traffic. Damn, New Orleans in July, *DC* in July is bad enough. I can already feel the sweat running down my sides, even in the relative cool of the underground garage.

Man! You got a lot to do in a day. Okay, let's see: dry cleaners, call Saundra, get stockings, go to the bank, and pack your stuff. You got a lot to do!

I pull out of the garage with the AC blowing full force, but the ninety-plus-degree heat seem to fight the cool air tooth and nail before it hit me in the face. Lucky for me, I put all those clothes in the cleaners last week. I can get them now before I leave tomorrow.

※

As I step into the house, the air conditioner chills my sweat-soaked silk blouse.

I collapse on the sofa thinking about Bruce. If he weren't white, if he weren't so thin, if he didn't have those pockmarks and…and…and if I didn't work with him, I might give him a little taste of these thick legs and big hips.

Ha! That's a lot of "if he weren't." Damn! I bet you wish there is someone around you could give these hips and legs to. You're feeling that man-feeling again, aren't you? Did the feeling ever really leave? Don't you just want to grab a brother, throw him down, and make him scream with some soulful hip twists? This feeling is making me sweat even with the ice-cold air-conditioning blowin', and it's getting on my last nerve.

The answering machine is flashing. I press the "play" button. It's Saundra talking about how good this man is in the sheets.

Hey, save some for me, girl, I can use a stiff one.

It's another message: Daddy, checking on his little girl. He has really been lonely since Mama died in the car accident three years ago. I'm surprised he hasn't fallen into deep depression from grief. They were so close.

Check out Saundra first.

She always picks up the phone on the first ring. "Whel-loh?"

She also tries to act as if she's asleep in case she doesn't want to talk to whoever it is.

"Girl, stop trippin', it's me."

"Hey, hey! What's happenin', Ms. Thang? Ready for this weekend?"

"No, no. I gotta go to New Orleans for a conference for two weeks, and I need you to take me to the airport tomorrow at 5:30. This is a real drag."

"You got it! I'll just save you the juicy, greasy details about David for when you get back. And it was juicy too, girl!"

"Was it greasy?"

"Gree-zzzee!"

"Slimy?"

"Slippery!"

We both scream into the phone.

"Wait a minute, Saundra, I have one question. Did he say 'Look out below'?"

"Denise, you so nasty! But, yes! He ate the groceries as if it was

Thanksgiving dinner, and you know I said, 'Thank you, thank you!'" We scream again into the phone.

"You did use a condom, didn't you?"

"Honey, I used a condom, a Jimmy, a James, a Jethro, a John, a Jack, and anything else you want to call it. I don't play that Magic Johnson stuff! Listen who's talking, you don't use condoms."

"I don't need to. Ain't nothing going on down here right now. Why bother? I have birth control pills anyway."

"Denise, you never know when you might bump into some stuff you want to get with. At least you should keep a fresh box on you or a little three-pack. Besides, you don't wanna get with someone and then have your pussy explode."

"Dang, Saundra, do you have to be so severe? I hear you already. Look, I gotta

"Say, how is Mr. Fine doing? Y'know I still think you got the finest-looking father this side of the Potomac River."

"Stop trippin' and back up off my daddy. He don't want no parts of your cookies and cream. He's all right, I guess, a little lonely still. I want him to get out there and find another woman, but he is still stuck on Mama."

"Well, maybe he'll come around soon. Give him time. Ha, ha! And

that will give me some time to get some gray hairs."

"Stop trippin', you're older than I am, and you are still too young for him. The only reason I let you hang around my daddy is because I know you're not serious."

"Don't talk to me about age. You aren't as young as you used to be, Ms. Thang."

"Look, my assistant told me today I was beautiful, striking, glamorous, one of the most beautiful women he has ever seen. He just turned thirty, so I'm still pullin' 'em and turning heads."

"Yeah, and you're getting a big head, but not the kind you really need. Are you talking about that scrawny white boy Bruce? Let me tell you something. A one-legged dog would look good to him. Besides, he's just telling you that because you handed him that job on a silver platter. Don't be fooled, sis!"

"Saundra, look, Bruce is a nice guy. I like him, he's a loyal employee, and he's not scrawny. He's very fit and probably has a nice tight six-pack. You just like your men with a little teddy bear thing going on. I'm through with you for now. I gotta check on my dad before it gets too late. Don't forget, I have to get to the airport tomorrow by 5:30."

"Okay, okay, you can count on me. I'll be there to pick you up by 4:30. Give your dad my love."

"You got it, bye-bye."

I really love Saundra. She's been hanging in there with me since our days at Howard. I guess after two failed marriages and two kids I would play the field too. I wonder, though, would I also be playing bouncing booty roulette even with a condom the way she does? Maybe that's another reason why I've been hanging out with my electric boyfriend for the past seven months. God! It has to get better than this! *Anyway, call Daddy.*

He picks up the phone on the fourth ring. "Younger speaking."

His voice still fills me with memories. So deep, thick, and strong, even at sixty. I guess I'll always be his little girl.

"Hi, Daddy, it's Denise."

"Hi, baby, how is the busiest gov'ment worker in DC doing?"

"Oh, you know same old same old. I'm going to New Orleans tomorrow for a conference, two whole weeks."

I can hear him smiling on the other end of the line. "Ah yes, New Orleans, Louisiana. Y'know, that's where your mother and I spent our honeymoon, did you know…?"

"Yes, Daddy, she was still a virgin, and you did right by her at the only hotel that would accept Negroes back then."

"Have I told that story one too many times?"

"I've heard it a few," I say with a smile.

"Well, I'll try not to mention it again. Hey, you heard from Joseph lately?"

"Daddy, I told you, Joseph and I aren't together. Things just didn't work out. You know, that's how it goes."

Daddy really liked Joseph. They even went fishing on Joseph's little boat. I never told him about the drug thing. I'm not sure he would understand. I'm not so sure he understands why I can't get married sooner, or why I'm having sex without being married. Things have obviously changed since he and Mama met.

"Daddy, are you doing all right? I worry about you."

"Now, now, gal. Don't you worry about ol' Jacob Younger. The Lord is watching over me."

"Well, Daddy, I'm just concerned about you being over there by yourself and all."

"Baby, I'm really fine. Y'know Ms. Jackson at the church wants me to go on the bus trip to Atlantic City next week, and I'm thinking about it."

"Really, Daddy? That's wonderful, but you don't gamble."

"No, I don't, but I've been thinking about your advice about gettin'
out. I think the trip will be fun, and Ms. Jackson and I get along okay."

I am beside myself. This is the first time my father has mentioned another woman since Mama died. Ms. Sadie Jackson of the second pew, right side, is sixty-five years old and looks every bit of it. I never think of my father as the young-stud type, but if he enjoys himself, maybe he can end this mourning period and get on with his life.

"Denise?"

"Yeah, Daddy?"

"You don't mind my going with Ms. Sadie, do you? I don't know much about courtin' these days. I mean, it's the first date I've had since your mother...well, you know."

"Daddy, go and have a wonderful time. I want to hear all about it when I get back from New Orleans. I love you."

"I love you too, dear, always and forever."

Daddy is always so sweet. I guess he'll be okay. I need to get by to see him more often. I need to get those burly arms around me. Who can ask for a better parent, parents...?

Mama...you still can't believe she's gone. God, she loved Daddy like no other. All their love combined was just for you, the only child. It must have been wonderful to have a man to sleep next to, to support you, to love you for all those years. You can't seem to get it right for a minute, Denise.

Enough of this depressing stuff, bed will be so good right now.

A man would also most certainly be good right now...Stop it, Denise! You keep this up, and you will end up being addicted to your little electric boyfriend in the bottom of your dresser drawer. And we don't want that tonight, do we?

Yeah, after a day like today, we certainly do.

Three

Saundra pulls her Caddy into my driveway. She's always on time for everything. But she needs to be. It takes that General Motors monster forever to get around corners.

Boy, if those backseats could talk!

But she's my girl. What would I do without her?

"Hey, hey! Are we ready to go to Naw-lins?" she crows.

"Yeah, I guess so," I say without enthusiasm.

Saundra picks up my bags and waddles out to the huge brown trunk of the Sedan de Ville with her broad round rump swaying. I kind of chuckle at the sight of the two wide trunks there together—one of flesh and one of metal. What did they used to call those cars back in the day? Low riders? Even with her few extra pounds around the middle, I can see why the brothers are always trying to get in her stuff. She was always a little thick, but that chipmunk cuteness and that come-on-in-and-sit-a-spell personality always melt the coldest heart.

"Denise, come on, girl. It's twenty minutes to five. You got everything? Drawers, fuck-me pumps, condoms?"

"Saundra!" I say, exasperated but also slightly amused. "I have my three *and* four-inch heels as always, but what do I need condoms for? This is a business trip. There will be no stiff stuff down there for me!"

"Ho, ho, you ol' ho! You're gonna get down there, hook up with some Creole brother, and never come back…but I'm sure you will cum!"

"Hey! Your mouth is off the hook today! Get in the car, woman, and take me to the airport. I don't have time for your mess."

Saundra plops her brown roundness into the driver's seat, and I get in on the other side. She has a smirk on her face as she backs the whale of a car out of the driveway, but she doesn't say anything. We are well on our way to the airport when I remember what I forgot to pack.

"Damn, girl! I knew I forgot something."

"What? The condoms, right? See, I told you!"

"No, stop trippin'. I forgot my new pack of birth control pills, and I forgot my lingerie. I have nothing to sleep in."

"Okay, so buy something when you get there. The conference starts when, Monday, right?"

"Yeah…" I say slowly.

"You have the entire weekend to shop, so chill. I'm sure they have a place where you can buy pajamas or lingerie. I wouldn't know. I sleep nekid! Hee-hee-hee! Anyway, about the birth control pills, you said you weren't going to be doing anything anyway. So I wouldn't worry. How many do you have left?"

"Three, I think." I'm beginning to get an attitude with myself. All this daggone rushing isn't my thing.

"Look, just deal with it when you come home, unless you want me to get them from your house and send them to you while you're down there."

"No, that's okay. I'll do without. Like I said, ain't nothin' happening but work for me down there."

God, I hate not having my lingerie. I can't sleep without it. It's a big femininity thing for me. High-heels, perfume, manicures, and something nice to sleep in—they all go together for me.

Shoot! By the time I get to Atlanta for my connecting flight and *then* to New Orleans, it will be too late to pick up anything.

�֎

As usual, National Airport is a great big toothache. Everybody is in a hurry to go nowhere. Ethiopian cab drivers are yelling at the Nigerian cab drivers. White folks and black folks pull up in Mercedes, Jaguars, Jeeps, and other less-recognizable cars. Hugging and kissing each other hello or good-bye. Saundra maneuvers her brown Caddy like a pro and drops me off at the Delta Air Lines terminal. I kiss her good-bye and had the skycap grab my bags. He holds out his calloused hand for a tip. I slide him a few dollars. I feel guilty. But you know what? Some folks give him more all day long. You can go broke tipping folks these days.

The plane is running on schedule, so I step up to the line to go through the metal detector. My costume jewelry sets off the alarm, so I almost have to disrobe to get through. I get my stuff and squeeze through the airplane door past first class to a window seat. I have my carry-on in my hand and plenty of "excuse me's" on my lips, trying to put on my best apologetic face for a hefty white guy already sitting in the center seat.

"Where ya goin', miss?"

"New Orleans, for a conference."

As if it is really any of your business. Instead of asking me where I'm going and getting in my business, why don't you help me put my carry-on bag in the overhead?

No such luck. I lift my carry-on, tuck it into the overhead compartment, and slide into my window seat.

"New Orleans, New Orleans. It's a great town, been there a few times m'self."

Yeah, I'll bet. He looks like the type who goes just to hook up with the whores I've heard so much about down there. Please, mister, don't try to talk my head off all the way to Atlanta, I'm really not *in the mood.*

"Jim Hildreth, pleased ta meetcha." He reaches out his meaty, moist hand. I don't want to shake it and don't feel like giving my name. I do anyway.

"Denise Younger."

"Well, Denise, let me tell you about a few places you just need to visit when you get to New Orleans, if you have the time…"

Luck just isn't with me today.

Four

Mr. Jim Hildreth *does* talk my head off all the way to Atlanta. He is a senior VP in some Fortune 2000 company that manufactures widgets for somebody else. He is friendly enough—if you want to be friendly. I, on the other hand, am thinking about my lingerie and the pain-in-the-ass-conference thing most of the flight.

The pilot flying out of Atlanta must have been breaking some kind of airspeed record. The plane touches down in New Orleans at 11:00 pm Central time, and I am off the plane and into a cab by 11:15 pm.

As the cab cruises into the French Quarter, I feel like I am in some kind of old black-and-white movie from the '40s. This city, even at night, looks like a slightly worn, but still fine, antique.

Just as I thought, the intense humidity has me sweating despite the frigid AC in the cab. The cabbie pulls up into the cab port of an elegant old hotel. It's the biggest antique building on the block and just a few blocks from Bourbon Street and the rest of the French Quarter happenings. I check in at the desk and upgrade my room reservation to a small suite. The young girl behind the desk has cocoa brown skin and a dripping Jheri curl that threatens to turn her uniform collar into a greasy rug. The accent isn't thick, but it is noticeable, slipping out from behind a gold tooth every once in a while.

Man-oh-man, I haven't seen a gold tooth in years.

"Ya got roohm sex-sex nyun."

I crane my neck trying to understand the accent. "Pardon me, I didn't quite catch that. What room?"

"Sex, sex, nyun, see."

She hands me the key and calls for the bellhop. The key has 669 on it.

"Oh, I see, okay thanks, thanks a lot. Say, you wouldn't happen to know a good place to get lingerie tomorrow, would you?"

She leans forward as if to tell me the last secret in the world. Her gold tooth flashes me a smile reserved only for black folks, I guess.

"Yes, yes, I can fihnd whatcha lookin' for. Now I know you jus' got to Nawlins, but if you got a rush tonight, you might fihnd the store called Nightie-Night open now. I'll call you de cab. You get dere in plenty of time."

It is late, but I am so happy. I pull a five-dollar bill out of my purse to give to her. She pushes it back to me and leans forward.

"Dhey'll make sure you're back in good time and condition, even if they have to bring ya back dhemselves. They've done it before."

She flashes her gold tooth at me and calls the doorman to hail a cab. The bellhop disappears into the elevator with my bags, and I am off to shop for lingerie in the middle of the night, in New Orleans.

I hope this Nightie-Night place has what you need. Maybe New Orleans won't be too bad of a place to stay, if you can keep yourself out the crazy heat.

Five

At first, the cab driver does a slow creep out of the French Quarter, barely missing slow-walking tourists, drunk or sober. This part of New Orleans seems a lot like New York, a city that never really sleeps. Once we steer out of the Quarter, he zips onto St. Charles; and I begin noticing huge stone and brick mansions. They sit back off the road like old sages, waiting for something to happen, waiting to record history as they watch from within their hundred-year-old walls. They are beautiful and elegant, even at night. They also look haunted, if not with ghosts, at least with memories I can only imagine or read about in history books.

"The doorman at the hotel says you're going to Nightie-Night."

The cabby's voice startles me out of my late-night sightseeing. "Yes, that's right. Do you know where it is?"

"Yes, ma'am, I do. But it's late. They stay open late as many places do, but only for a taste past midnight. They have a soft spot for tourists though. We'll get there, right before closing. They'll stay open 'til you're done with your shopping. Do you want me to wait for you while you shop?"

Humph! Wait and get charged up the ying-yang?

"No, thanks. I'll call another cab to take me back to the hotel."

"Suit yourself, lady, but you may have a bit of a wait."

Either way, I'm going to have to spend the money, but I don't want to feel rushed.

"I'll figure it out, but thanks for offering."

The cab turns down a side street and pulls into an extremely wide driveway of a Greek Revival–styled mansion. Several cars are crowded at the end of the driveway. Massive columns stand along the front of the building, which is brightly lit with a rich, warm glow from the first floor. I can't tell if it is the right place, but I can see a lot of movement inside.

"Is this the right place? I don't see a sign," I ask.

"Yes, ma'am. This is Nightie-Night. There's no sign! City ordinance for the Garden District, y'know."

Makes sense, why will anyone put a big flashy neon sign in the middle of all this grandeur?

I pay the cabbie, step out into the pea-soup humidity, and walk to the door. Two women, an attractive tall brunette and a not-so-attractive shorter blonde, walk out of the high twin doors. The shorter woman holds the door open for me with one hand while clutching a huge shopping bag with the other. The words "Nightie-Night" and a blue-and-yellow crescent moon logo are on the side of the bag. A *very* air-conditioned breeze blows around my face from the door and carries with it a slight scent of cedar and a stronger scent of very expensive perfume.

Even at almost midnight, the store is surprisingly active. A dozen women browse and search the long wooden antique tables with carefully folded silk, satin, and lace underthings. The glazed hardwood floor speaks a heavy, hollow echo beneath my feet as I walk toward a second room, separated from the first by a broad arch. Soft piano jazz drifts above my head from a speaker in the corner of the ceiling. Standing below the speaker is a slender black woman at a cash register. Her skin is very, very fair and very, very beautiful. She reminds me of a black Greta Garbo, looking well past her middle fifties, but there is a regal sex appeal about her that will turn the head of a man of any age.

"May I help you?"

Oh my god! What is this?

I stand there, frozen in the middle of the store, slightly startled, forgetting where I am and why I'm there. Peering down at me, almost leaning over me, and invading my space is . . .

Beautiful, drop-dead-gorgeous my-brother, my-brother! Tall, masculine, Hershey's chocolate brown, mustached, lean muscled, even through his formal French-cuffed ivory shirt. Baby boy, my god! How you *doing fine!*

"Ummm, umm, yes, ah what am I looking for...?" I stammer, trip over my words, and smile stupidly, still looking at him as if he were some kind of newly discovered art form.

Yes, he is.

"I just got into town, and I need something to sleep in. I left all my sleepwear at home."

"Ah yes, you are staying at the Hotel St. Margarite in the Quarter. The desk clerk called about you. Ms. Younger, right?"

"Mmm-hmm."

Fix your mouth, Denise.

"Welcome to New Orleans. We are happy to have you. Since this is your first time at Nightie-Night, my name is Tyriq, I'm the manager, and I'm here to serve you."

I bet you are! Serve me, honey!

Stop it!

"So, Ms. Younger, what *exactly* are you looking for?"

"Um, I'm looking for something comfortable, with a silky or satiny feel, long or short, it doesn't matter. I want it simple, not too frilly or ornate."

The manager curls up his bottom lip and nods his head. "I think I have just the thing for you. Did you have any particular price points in mind?"

"No, just don't go crazy on a sister."

He laughs, and his deep-set eyes twinkle. That's when I notice they're gray.

How strange, how spooky, and how sexy.

"I promise I won't. Follow me, please."

We walk to the back of the store/mansion. The place is beginning to thin out a little. Only a few customers left. I glance back at the cash register and am surprised to see Ms. Black Greta Garbo staring at me. Maybe it is my imagination, but the look does not seem friendly.

The back of the store obviously used to be a sitting room or parlor. Along the walls are several large antique armoires with glass fronts. Each one displays gowns or teddies, baby dolls or slips, long and short, satin, silk, lace, cotton, and polyester. They are black, white, black-and-white, and multi–candy-colored rich hues and subtle tones.

All I could say is, "Wow! This stuff is gorgeous."

"Yes it is, isn't it?" He opens one of the doors and pulls out a graceful long number colored in a Caribbean blue. He cradles the gown as if it's fine porcelain and stretches it out on a well-waxed table in the center of the parlor. His hands brush across the gleaming satin as if he is feeling it for the first time. "Is this the kind of thing you were looking for?"

"Wowwww!" I say. "This is incredible material. I could get lost in this color. I like, I like. How much is it?"

"We can work out something on the price!" he says with a raised eyebrow.

I can feel my lips and my credit card twisting and stressing at the same time.

"Whoa! Hold on, Mr. Workout Something. It's nice, but I have a few things to buy. I'm new to town, but not new to the planet. How much is it?"

"It's $68, but since you are staying at the St. Margarite, we can do $48. Is that reasonable?"

"Yes, that's fine. What else you got?"

"Before we look for anything else, let's talk size. You're a 6, right?"

How does he know that? Most men barely know their *own* sizes, much less the size of a woman they've never met.

He's probably gay.

"I take a 6, normally. There are times when my hips won't allow it, but a 6 should do just fine."

"Great," he says. "How about trying something short and a little sassy?"

I watch him move to the next armoire. He moves like an athlete. I wish Saundra could see this man's body. He is like the one-hundred-yard sprinters we used to admire and lust after at Howard U.

Tyriq pulls two baby doll slips out from behind the glass. The first is emerald green satin, with a sheer mesh midriff. The other is black lace. I'm not crazy about lace, but it is, in a word, beautiful. I run my hand over the material as Tyriq holds it in front of me.

"This is nice too, and I'm not a big fan of lace, but this works."

"I'm glad you like it," he says. He seems to study my face and then looks over my shoulder.

"I hope you are finding everything to your satisfaction."

That voice is a little too close, a little too loud in my ear, and it has a subtle but uncomfortable formality to it that I can't put my finger on. Is it British, maybe or even Caribbean? I glance to my left and discover the woman, who was at the cash register, standing at my shoulder. The rich perfume scent I smelled when I first came in is strong and pleasant. That is the *only* thing pleasant about her. She looks at me without smiling. One arm crosses at her chest. The other elbow rests on it with her hand gracefully touching her cheek. I turn around to face her.

"Everything is just fine. Your manager has been more than helpful."

"I'm glad to hear that," she says.

No smile from this heifer. She's dripping with attitude and acts likes she needs to get laid. Shoot, so do I, but I hope I don't come off like that.

"Tyriq," she speaks to him, and her face immediately softens. This sister is beautiful. I can only imagine what a killer she was when she was my age or even younger. "It's getting late, my dear. It's time to close shop as soon as you finish here."

"Yes, ma'am," Tyriq says.

When she turns back to me, the softness disappears. "Thank you for patronizing my establishment."

"Yours?" I ask.

"Oh, of course, dahling. Didn't Tyriq tell you? I'm Clara d' Beaux. This is my shop and my home."

"Well, everything here is exquisite, very nice." I look around and refer to the clothing, but finish my glance at Tyriq. "*Very* nice."

She sniffs, raises an eyebrow, then turns on her heels, and glides toward the front of the store. She looks over her shoulder at my feet.

"Nice shoes."

I glance down at my wine-colored, high-heeled sandals and my little pedicured toes peeking out from beneath the straps. When I look up to thank her for the compliment, she is already well out of earshot.

Bitch.

"What's her problem?" I ask Tyriq. "That's no way to treat a customer, especially a tourist."

"Oh, she's just tired. It's been a long day. We *are* called Nightie-Night, but we open at eleven in the morning and stay open until midnight, Thursday through Saturday. She's here all day, every day."

How gallant that he comes to his boss's defense. As well he should. I'll let it slide. I don't expect that I'll be doing a lot of lingerie shopping while I'm here anyway.

"Well, Mr. Tyriq, it's late and I need to call a cab to get back to the hotel. Can you pick a few other things really quick, but keep it all under $200 please."

"Ms. Younger, I can do that, but about that cab. At this hour, you may be waiting for a while. It is quite dark in the Garden District, and safety could be an issue. I can drop you off if you'd like."

Drop me off? He is fine, but he could be an axe murderer for all I know. He might chop me up and dump me down in the Bayou, or whatever they call it.

He looks at me as if he read my mind. "I'm not an axe murderer. We do it quite a bit, especially for tourists and visitors."

I sigh and look at him as he picks out a gold-colored chemise from another armoire.

"Can I use the phone first?"

"Absolutely," he says. "There's one on the wall near the cash register. I'll bring your things up to the front in a few minutes."

"Thanks," I say and walk to the front of the store. I dig around in my purse for a hotel brochure and find the phone number. When I dial, the same sister who sent me here answers the phone.

"Hotel St. Margarite, how may I help you?"

"Oh, thank goodness. Hi, this is Denise Younger, remember me? I'm at Nightie-Night, and the manager has offered to drop me off at the hotel so that I don't have to wait on the cab. I don't know him. Am I going to get there in one piece?"

The clerk giggles pleasantly on the other end. "Oh yes, Ms. Younger. Tyriq is a fhine young man and more than respectable. I understand your worries and all, and you should when you travel, but not with him. You'll have no bothers with him at all. We've had a good relationship with him and Ms. d' Beaux for years."

I feel a wave of relief wash over me. Tyriq is walking to the cash register with several pieces of clothing draped over his arm. The boss lady is on the other side of the store straightening the bras and panties browsers had trolled through during the day. Her eyes are on me, and a thick cloud of *I-don't-like-you-leave-my-store* hovers around her like Pig-Pen in a Charlie Brown cartoon. I guess she's trying to make sure I don't steal anything. Tyriq rings up my stuff, and I flip him my American Express card.

"Thank you, thank you. I feel so much better now," I say into the phone. "I was a little concerned."

"No problem, ma'am. I spot you when he brings you in. Did you need anything?"

"Actually, I could use a drink, something sweet, strong, and fruity. Surprise me."

"Already done, good night."

"Your total is $193.44," Tyriq says and hands me a pen to sign the receipt. His hands are as beautiful as the rest of him—large, thick, strong, not manicured, but clean and unscarred. I sign the receipt and hand the pen back to him.

"Clara, I'm going to run Ms. Younger back to the St. Margarite."

Clara looks up from a neatly folded pile of expensive panties and thongs and then pauses as if to select her next words with the care of a chef picking fresh fruit at a roadside stand.

"You will return posthaste to finish closing up, will you not?"

"Of course, I will," Tyriq says with a confident smile, but underneath there is tension, something I can feel but not identify.

It's none of your business. You got what you came for. Come on, Mr. Man, take us back to the hotel. It's been a very long day.

Tyriq opens the door for me, and a rude wall of oppressive heat and humidity immediately assault me. I've been in the air-conditioning of the store long enough to forget about the weather. He opens the passenger-side door of a gray Mercedes sedan that looks almost twenty years old, but very well preserved. I sit on worn oxblood leather seats that are surprisingly comfortable. He shuts the door, gets in on the other side, and away we go. The car floats across the trolley car tracks and cobblestones of New Orleans's main thoroughfare. Tyriq doesn't speak but gives me an occasional glance and smile. I pretend not to pay attention, but find him hard to ignore. We are at the hotel before I know it. I hop out of the car before he can get around to opening the door for me. I hand him a five-dollar-bill. He just looks at it. His forehead crinkles, slightly annoyed.

"It's a tip for you," I say. What's his problem?

"Ms. Younger, it's not necessary. This was a courtesy. Maybe you'll come back to the store another time."

The annoyance is gone, replaced by a pleasant but not quite identifiable look.

"I don't know about that. How much lingerie can a woman buy?"

"You tell me," he says. "You said you needed it to sleep in. I'm sure you sleep at least once a day, every day."

Touché, Denise. He got you there.

"Well, sir, it was nice to meet you and thank you for not being an axe murderer and getting me back to the hotel in one piece."

He laughs out loud, his gray eyes twinkling in the busy lights of the French Quarter. He salutes me with two fingers and drives off.

I walk into the hotel with my bags.

Damn, that man is fine.

Six

It is just after ten in the morning when I finally get up. I usually don't sleep past nine, even on Saturday. Daddy always says half the day is gone by then. The little suite is nice, although I have to figure out where

I am. Waking up in a strange bedroom is not something I usually do. The king-sized poster bed is soft but not saggy. The separate sitting room isn't bad either, balcony overlooking the street three stories below, a wet bar, large step down bath tub with a phone.

Not bad, Denise, not bad at all.

Man, I still have a lot to do. I have to find out when registration is for this conference foolishness. Maybe I'll try waltzing around the lower French Quarter today, but first I need to wash off yesterday's dirt. There is still stickiness about my eyes as I step into the huge bathroom. Must have slept hard. I don't know what was in that drink room service brought to me last night, but it knocked me out.

When I look into the mirror, I smile. Not a bad body for thirty-five. I notice another sign of the same thirty-five years. A gray hair. Short and curly, just like the rest of the jet-black hair on my head, but quite gray just the same. Oh well, wisdom and long life will beat out vanity any day. Besides, the lingerie I bought from the shop last night will keep any man's eyes away from a little sign of creeping age.

Yeah sure, if you had one around to see it.

✦

It is almost noon by the time I finally get dressed, do my nails, and find the information about the conference. Maybe I deserve to step out on these quaint old streets and explore a bit. I walk out of the door with my purse and immediately gasp. The humidity in the hallway is enough to chase me back inside the room, but I am determined to see some of this city no matter what. Down in the lobby, a light-skinned black woman is asking questions about the city. I overhear her say she is here for the same conference. There is no one else around her, so I assume she is traveling alone. Maybe I'll introduce myself. It'll be nice to hang with another sister while trolling through these cobblestone streets.

"Excuse me, I'm Denise Younger. I am here for the public/private partnership conference. Is that what you're here for?"

"As a matter of fact, I am. I'm Bonnie Scott, out of Baltimore. I just got in today. Can't stand the heat, girl."

"Who are you tellin'? But I was going to venture out in it anyway. How about checking out New Orleans with me later?"

"The heat is going to be here to stay, so why wait? Let me put my things in my room, and we can go now if you're game."

"Great, great. I'll meet you back here in the lobby in, what, thirty minutes?

"Fine, see you then."

Bonnie comes down as we agreed. She is *very* pretty. Lighter and taller than me with long thick dark brown hair. I would have put her at about forty-five, but she doesn't look a day over thirty-nine. I do notice a crescent-shaped scar on her left cheek, despite her makeup.

It is about one o'clock, so she suggests that we get a bite to eat. We weave through the crowd of tourists and city regulars looking for a place that serves Cajun food, but not too expensive. As we move down Bourbon Street, little black boys dance shoeless. They have hats or pans filled with dollars and coins, mostly coins. I stick my hands inside the pockets of my linen dress and grab all my change, tossing it in one of the hats. A raggedy, dirty boy with a sleepy right eye thanks me in a Southern accent that is strange to my ears. At the next corner, more of the dancing prepubescent boys, Bonnie tosses in some coins too.

Bonnie had been to New Orleans once before for a few days. It seems every store and restaurant we pass is more concerned with air-conditioning the space just outside the open doors than the inside, but we're glad to get out of the steamy, swampy air. She picks out a corner restaurant with wooden tables and lots of young people. She says the food was good the last time she was here and suggests I try a real Mint Julep. It's cool inside although the doors are open.

Bonnie is the head of public relations for WTSQ-TV in Baltimore. She says the station had been number one since Moses parted the Red Sea and that her salary is embarrassingly high for the cake job she has. How she came about it wasn't so easy. She used to be a TV anchorwoman until a demented *fan* tried to rape her and take her face off with a switchblade in the TV station's parking lot. He busted up her face, and she spent several months getting reconstructive surgery, but couldn't get rid of the scar on her cheek. Baltimore viewers loved her so much, and the management felt so responsible for not providing more security that they put her in the PR slot, gave her six figures, and a job for life. Now she's trying to turn her misfortune into a boon for the community. She hopes to get in on the public-private ticket and start a communications' program for minority college students in the city. Her biggest regret, she says, is that she never got married. It was always a TV career first, a man third or fourth, or whenever she had time to look for one, which wasn't very often. Now, all she says she wants is occasional company and maybe someone to go with on a trip to the Bahamas from time to time. By the time I start sharing a little about me, I'm working on my second Mint Julep, and our food arrives. Jambalaya for both of us.

"So, Denise, why aren't you married, or why don't you have some kind of steady boyfriend in tow?"

"Marriage? I guess I just haven't met Mr. Right yet. I had a boyfriend until just after New Year's. He was smoking weed and who knows what else. I found out, I dumped him."

"Amen and hallelujah. Just say no, you got to go. Y'know, all my years in the TV business I never touched the stuff. Our news director was busted for cashing bad checks. He was hooked on coke. He lost everything—wife, kids, and a nice home. Everything."

"I never said I didn't smoke a joint or two back in college," I confess. "I mean, it was an everybody-was-doing-it thing. But by the time my junior year rolled around, Howard University was starting to kick my ass. It was straighten up and fly right or go home..."

"Denise, are you okay?"

My heart skips a beat, and I don't know why. But my eyes are telling my heart how to act. I see him, sitting in the corner of the restaurant. The guy from the lingerie shop is talking with two other guys, both of them look very young. He's smoking a cigarette and has an intense expression as he explains something to them.

Damn, his is sooo fine!

"Bonnie, I had forgotten to pack my nightclothes, so I went to a little shop in the Garden District. You see that man with the cigarette over there?"

Bonnie discreetly glances over her shoulder as if she is looking the place over. "Yeah, I see him. He's a cute young thing."

"Yeah, well, that cute young thing is the manager of the shop. He drove me back to the hotel when I kind of got stranded up there."

"And you got in the car with a stranger? Just like that?" she scolds me with her question.

"Yes, I know. It wasn't a smart thing to do, but the hotel desk clerk said it was okay and that he was safe."

"Okay, if you say so. You are here now."

Bonnie looks at me as if she just hears a real good, dirty joke. "Listen, he does look like a dark special chocolate bar. Y'know, creamy, semi-sweet?"

"Bonnie, he's a baby! He can't be any older than twenty-seven...and look at those boys with him. They look even younger. He just seems like a fine young man, handsome and all that, but too young. Besides, I'm here to do this conference thing and go home."

"I can see that. That's why you haven't taken your eyes off him since I thought you were having a mini heart attack a minute ago."

I roll my eyes at Bonnie and slide them back to Tyriq. He curls smoke from his full lips and delivers quiet little karate chops on the table as he talks to the other two. They hang on his every word. He reminds me of the young Canadian Mist scotch model without the big Afro. He leans over a bit and squints in my direction. Slowly those pretty teeth peek out from behind sexy full lips when he recognizes me.

"Oh no, he sees me. What am I gonna do?"

"You're asking me? You said he's just a baby, remember? So offer him a nipple." Bonnie laughs and rests her scarred cheek on her fist.

Tyriq gets up from the table and works his way through the maze of tables toward me, smiling all the way.

Seven

"Ms. Younger! How are you? It's really good to see you again so soon." Tyriq puts his hand over mine and gently rubs across my lacquered nails.

I feel pleasantly uncomfortable. It's a tingly, wonderful sensation. "I'm doing fine, just kind of looking over your city, checking it out,

y' know."

"Who is the lovely lady with you? Two beautiful women in one spot, I don't know if I can take it." Tyriq flashes a beautiful smile at me and then at Bonnie. The rich, warm, inviting scent of sandalwood only adds to his overwhelming charm. I try not act too impressed with him. That's *not* an easy thing to do.

"This is Bonnie Scott. She's here for the same conference. We just met, so we're hanging out."

Tyriq shakes Bonnie's hand and covers it with his left hand. He gives it a firm stroke and shake. Bonnie looks like she might have to change her panties when this is over. "Tyriq Austin, nice to meet you, I hope both of you enjoy your stay. If you find the time, please bring her by the store, and I'll see if I can work out a special discount bargain for you."

"I'll make sure she does. I can always use a few extra pieces of lingerie," Bonnie chimes in with a mouthful of teeth.

Tyriq returns his hand to mine.

God, he is a beautiful man. When they were handing out handsome faces in heaven, he must have been standing at the front of the line.

"Well, it was a pleasure meeting you, and it was *very* nice seeing you again, Ms. Younger. I have to get back to my friends. Take care."

He walks back to the other side of the restaurant and sits down. He gives me a quick wink before turning to his friends. They both look briefly over their shoulders and then go back to talking.

"Girl, girl, girl, that's a man and a half. So smooth, so polite. It must be a Southern thing. How do they say it down here? He looks like he might be sweet on you, Denise."

"Bonnie, please. He's just a baby. What would I do with somebody like that? I admit he is handsome, and he smells nice, dresses nice too. However, there's much more to a man than the outer package. Besides, he's just being polite. He probably is like that with everyone, and even if he wasn't, he probably has a girl, and I repeat, *girl*, for every day of the week."

"Denise, I can think of quite a few things you could do with him, but I would probably get arrested for indecent exposure just talking about it. Okay, I'll leave you alone about him. You probably won't see him again anyway. New Orleans is a very big city."

"Bonnie, can I ask you something?"

"Sure, go ahead."

"Have you ever dated a younger man? I mean, someone *that* much younger than you?"

"To be honest, only once, and it was wonderful. I mean, there were differences, but the differences weren't anything I couldn't overcome."

"So, how was he—God, I don't believe I'm asking you this—in bed? Didn't you have to teach him things?"

"Girl, let me tell you. It was quite unlike anything I've ever experienced. Gentle, patient, with the stamina of…who knows? It's hard to describe. You see, he was a paralegal in a top law firm in Baltimore. I had my reputation to protect, so I really was against it at first, but he approached me and assured me that discretion was just as important to him. I wanted to go out publicly, so we decided that we would go to a few functions just to test the waters. No one really said anything, not that I would have allowed anyone to. I really liked the guy. He had a deep mind, and we kind of fit together like hand and glove. It was wonderful for about a year."

"Why did it end, if it was so wonderful?"

"Well, he got accepted to an Ivy League law school on the West Coast, and he left…simple as that. Yes, it was kind of painful when he left. I think I may have been falling in love. I was already in lust, he was just…a great guy, y'know?"

"How young was he?"

"He was twenty-nine. I was thirty-eight. Goodness, that was six years ago. I really hadn't thought about that in a while."

Bonnie's eyes focuses on the air above my head. He must have been something else, but I could never date anyone that much younger than me. It just doesn't seem natural. When I look at Bonnie again, she is dabbing her eyes. I decide not to delve any deeper into her personal life. Some things are better off left alone, I think.

We finish our lunch and left. We go on a two-hour-long walk around the French Quarter, visiting the shops and art galleries.

I try not to think about Tyriq and younger men and sex and relationships and love. I succeed, for the most part.

Eight

I wake up early Sunday morning finding my chest heaving and my lungs gasping for air. I sit up in the bed realizing that the oppressive Louisiana heat and misting humidity have outmatched the low setting of the air-conditioning. I step over to the control on the wall and turn it up full blast. The vents immediately begin to blow cold, dry air. My breathing eases enough for me to think about what I wanted to do on the last day before the conference. I want to go to church but don't know where to go. This city is so big. By the time I decide where to go, what to wear, and how to get there, I probably won't feel like going. I need to call Saundra to see how she's doing and to let her know that I'm okay.

"Hey, girl, what's shakin' down there? See anything interesting?"

"Oh yeah, this is a beautiful city, but it's hot as hell down here. I met a sister named Bonnie out of Baltimore. We did some hanging out yesterday, a little drinking, eating, and walking around. Didn't do much shopping…oh, I did pick up some lingerie when I came to town, nice little shop. So what's up with you?"

"David and I took the boys to the movies to see *Malcolm X*. I figured it's time they got a chance to see what really happened back then, at least from one perspective. The movie is too long for words, girl, but the boys sat still through the whole thing, I'm surprised."

I haven't seen the movie yet despite all the hype about it. Maybe I'll go when I get back home if I can convince Saundra to go with me and sit through it again.

"So what did you think about it? Was it as good as everybody says?"

"Personally, girl, I loved it. I remember reading the book back at Howard."

"Yeah, I remember most of what I read."

"Well, the movie sticks pretty close to the book. I mean, that little Spike Lee had to put in his two-cent's worth with that weird shot of Denzel at the end. Y' know how he does in almost all his movies where the character looks like he's standing still and the world is moving around him? That's really weird. I don't like it. He also had a whole bunch of kids shouting, 'I'm Malcolm X!' at the end. I think the movie could've done without that too. Other than that, Denzel was his usual fine, sexy self. That man could make me take a pilgrimage to Mecca any day."

"Saundra, you are just too wild. You know that?" I laugh.

"Yeah, I know, but, hey, you love me and wouldn't have me any other way. Ah, ha."

"Speaking of men, isn't it a little quick to have the boys go out with you and David? I mean after all, you just met him."

"Y'know, Denise, it's kind of funny. I was thinking the same thing. After I got back from taking you to the airport, David called and asked me out to the movies. I told him I couldn't go because I didn't have anyone to keep the boys. Greg is fifteen, and Gene is eleven. That's old enough to leave them at home alone, but I'm still a little cautious about doing it. So like I said, I turned him down. Then he got a little quiet on me and asked me if I minded bringing them along with us. I didn't know what to say at first. In all these years of dating between marriages, no man has ever wanted to take me *and* the boys anywhere unless he was dropping the boys off so he could take me somewhere and drop my drawers. I asked the boys if they wanted to go to the movies with a friend of mine. They said okay, so we went."

"Okay, so what happened after the movie?"

"Not much, I mean not a whole, *whole* lot."

"Saundra, I can tell when you're lying. What happened?"

Saundra sighs on the other end of the phone and clicks her tongue. I can tell she is walking to the hallway just outside her bedroom to see if the boys are within earshot. Then, I hear her bedroom door close.

"Denise, am I a freak?"

Her voice is quiet and reflective, almost pleading. I can tell she's looking more for reassurance of our friendship than an answer to the question.

"Sometimes, Saundra, I think you move a little too fast with men, but that doesn't make you a freak. I mean, you know, it's like, well...I don't know. Everybody needs somebody sometimes. Some needs are more intense than others, and we just have to deal with each situation as it comes along. But a freak? No, I wouldn't say that. I never liked that word anyway. I would say you have a *very* healthy sexual appetite."

"Look, Denise," Saundra's voice dips quickly into anger. "Don't give me that *Essence* magazine bullshit! Playing with myself just doesn't get it. I don't like doing without a man, a real man, not just for me but also for my boys. I'm not getting any younger, and sometimes you wonder what it is that keeps men around these days. So I'm doing for me, and I'm doing for them for as long as I can."

"Saundra, calm down. I'm not accusing you of doing the wrong thing, sis, I do understand. Besides, who am I to tell anyone what she should or should not do? All I am saying— and I guess I should have said this a long time ago—is that you should just be careful. Lord knows we all should be. Love, sex, or both, diseases are very serious issues, but if the heart gets sick or hurt, it's the hardest thing to heal."

"Denise, I'm sorry, sometimes I think I'm not setting a good example for the boys."

"They didn't see anything, did they?"

"No, no, they didn't, but I just don't want them to. You know how it is. I talk to them all the time about girls and pregnancy, but I don't want them to get the wrong idea about their mother."

"Well, just be careful. That's all I can say. Anyway, what happened?" Already, I can feel Saundra's voice perk up. She doesn't get depressed or angry often. Even when she does, it doesn't last long.

"Well, after we got back to my house, I invited David inside. He came in, but said he didn't want to think about staying too long. He told me he thought the boys had seen enough of him for the first time. I thought that was nice. It kinda goes back to what I was saying about the boys getting the wrong impression about me. Anyway, the boys went straight to bed, David stayed downstairs in the living room. We talked for a little while, and then he started looking at his watch as if it was time for him to go. I didn't want him to leave, so I started letting my fingers do the walking across his zipper, and of course, I dialed the right numbers to make him stay for a little while."

"Saundra, you didn't!"

"Hey, what's wrong with a little head for the road? It was the least I could do for the first man who ever offered to take out me and my kids. I must say learning how to roll my tongue in those Spanish classes back at Howard sure comes in handy."

"You are too wild for me, girl."

"Now, wait just a minute. Ms. Thang, you have tasted more than your share of cum in your lifetime, so don't hand me that Snow White virgin stuff! Don't play me like you're some kind of prude!"

"Guilty as charged, guilty as charged. It's been awhile, but you know some things are just buried deep in my mind."

"Well, the thing you need to be concerned about is getting a man buried inside you. Maybe I'm getting too much, but, Denise, I'm afraid you might be growing vines up there in your stuff from lack of use, girl."

Now, I'm the one getting depressed. I look at my watch. Man, we've been on the phone for almost an hour. "Saundra, look, I've got to jump. This phone bill is going to be hell. I'll call you later on this week, okay?"

"You got it. Look, take care and make sure you stop off at one of the Cajun grocery stores and buy me something spicy."

"Will do, later, sis."

Vines? She's got to be kidding.

I may be a little lonely sometimes and a little horny many times, but I'm no born-again old maid. I'll do my thing when I'm good and ready and not before. I don't care what Saundra says. Besides, I haven't been doing too badly by myself. Nope, not at all.

Nine

Monday morning is rough. I oversleep and know it when I hear Bonnie knocking on the door at eight o'clock. I get up and answer the door, looking like the last rose of summer. Bonnie is standing there in a purple raw silk suit. For a minute, I think someone has plastered a big *Vogue* magazine poster in my doorway.

"Girl, let's get it together," she crows. The conference starts in forty minutes. You need me to do anything?"

"No, no, I guess I hit the sheets pretty hard last night, and I forgot to get a wake-up call from the front desk. I hope the rest of the day doesn't go like this. My hair is nappy, and I *feel* nappy. What did you do yesterday?"

"Not a whole lot. I sat in and tried to square away this business-apprenticeship program for the TV station. I hope I can do a little recruiting while I'm here. These college kids just aren't as ready as they used to be. So I hope I can find a good candidate. I really would like to get a black male into the program, but the pickings are probably slim. I might end up with some dizzy girl. Either way, I'm sure I'll get someone for the thing."

I take a quick shower and try to whip my "do" into some semblance of shape. Bonnie calls downstairs for some coffee for both of us. It arrives quickly, and I take a couple of sips between putting on makeup and stockings. We hit the door and catch a cab to the Marriott on Canal Street by quarter of nine. The humidity is already crawling into the French Quarter. My sunglasses steam up before we get to the hotel.

The main ballroom is packed with people. Most are corporate fat cats standing around talking, sipping coffee, and stuffing their faces with beignets they don't need. We decide to slide into the nine o'clock session on government funding for new programs. That's a mistake. The presenter does little more than bash the federal government for an hour because of cutbacks in public-private partnership funding. It sounds more like a lackluster political rally against conservative Republicans than something meant to help someone. Most of the time, we sit there talking about how fat, how funny, or how bored some of the people look.

There is a short break before the next session. While I try to figure out what to do next, Bonnie bumps into a friend in the main lobby, some guy who works for the mayor of Baltimore.

"Darryl Murphy, this is Denise Younger. She runs procurement for the feds out of DC. Darryl is a special assistant to Baltimore's mayor. He gets the mayor anything he needs that can't be gotten through front door politics. He also runs down the Maryland legislature and strong-arms politicians when they try to slice and dice state-funded programs in the city."

I shake his hand and give him my courteous hello. He's not bad looking though I am not partial to fair-skinned brothers. I guess he is about forty and a little short. He has a little scraggly mustache. For a high-profile government aide, his hands feel as if they've worked construction all his life, like sandpaper. He offers to take us to dinner. I want to beg off, but I do not want to hurt Bonnie's feelings, so I agree.

The next session is much more interesting. There is a sparkplug of a black woman talking about how she cut through government red tape to get infrastructure funding for small rural communities. Apparently, many private companies and federal government agencies don't deal well with small towns that are short on resources. I've never been to a really small town. I take a few notes, but thoughts of home distracts me. Daddy is on my mind a little bit. I wonder which hotel he and Mama stayed in so many years ago. It's probably not around anymore. He always thought he was going to die first and had always provided for Mama and me. Mama took care of us very well too, but it was Daddy who always held me. He always told me that the world was my oyster and that I should be ready to crack it open. At a time when most fathers were taking their boys to football or baseball games or just not being around at all, Daddy took me to ballet classes. He was always there for my plays or recitals. Squeezing his big frame right down front where we could see each other. Mama was there too, but she was usually along for the ride. I really think Daddy enjoyed these little rites of passage. He cried when I came home during my junior year at Howard and told him I was pregnant. He had warned me about boys, but I was in love and just lost my virginity. He wanted me to keep the baby, but I was stubborn—like him. I did not want to be tied down. He paid for the abortion, and we never spoke of it again. Mama never knew.

"Denise, are you okay?" Bonnie has her hands on mine. She is looking at my face. I can feel the wetness of tears on my cheeks. I have been lost in the world of Jacob Younger. Time to come back to reality.

"Yeah, I'm okay, I just...I don't know. I was thinking about things going on at home."

"Hey, girl, you want to go back to the hotel and skip this thing for today? I mean, we have two weeks, the first day really isn't that important."

"No, really. I am fine. I was just thinking about my father."

"Is he sick? Is there anything I can do?"

"No, he is not sick," I say, smiling and drying my eyes. "He's just wonderful. I miss him sometimes, and we are very close. I was just remembering some old things, that's all. I'm really okay." Bonnie looks at me as if she does not believe a word I've said, but she leaves me alone.

Ten

When I open the door for Bonnie to come in, I have to do a double take. She is quite a sight, no...two sights and a half, wearing a clingy red silk dress. Her cleavage is so deep anyone looking probably will drown in it. The split up the middle of her skirt is so high, if she sits down, you can see what she ate for breakfast. She *does* look really good, though.

"What's the deal with the dress, Bonnie? I thought we were just going for a little dinner."

"Didn't I tell you where we were going? We're going to Arnaud's. Girl, you had better throw on something spicy. This is the grande dame of French Quarter dining, baby."

I am not dressed yet, and I am *not* going to try to outdo Bonnie, but I guess I have to put on the dog. God, I really don't feel like doing this, but it probably is going to be the most exciting thing I would experience during this trip.

She comes in and gracefully sits in one of the chairs in the suite. I pull out a man's black *pimp*-striped, double-breasted suit I had cut to fit and a matching black bustier to dip down into my cleavage just a little bit. What little bit I had.

"Bonnie, you look like you're fishing for something, and I don't mean salmon."

57

"Well, you never know what you might find in the sinful streets of the French Quarter."

"Why not Darryl? He seems nice enough, he's from your city, and you two are already friends so why not go for it?"

"Girl, Darryl isn't my type. We've worked together in the past when I was reporting on the city beat. Besides, to tell you the truth, he's really kind of digging on you. That's why he insisted on taking us out tonight."

"Oh, Bonnie, I *really* wish you hadn't. I mean, I appreciate your good intentions and all, but he isn't my type either."

"Why not?"

"Oh, I don't know. He just seems frumpy and, well, old. I don't know, he just doesn't make me tingle when I look at him, y' know what I mean?"

"Well, do me a favor. Humor him, be nice to him, and after tonight you won't have to deal with him, okay?"

"Okay, okay, but just for tonight. I've got too many other things on my mind to be worrying about some man I just met."

"You're not mad at me, are you?" Bonnie's voice softens. I look at her from the bathroom hallway where I am getting dressed.

"No, no, hey look, I'm sorry. I hope I didn't hurt your feelings. It's just that I'm not in the habit of having other people play cupid for me, that's all. Besides, this *is* a business trip." I pull the pants up over my hips and slip the jacket over the bustier. "I'll go and have a nice time. I'll be charming, gracious, and maybe even a little sexy. How's that?"

Bonnie's face lightens up. "Maybe we can go dancing afterward, if you're game."

"Hey, why not? I haven't had a chance to shake my round brownness in a good little while."

I spray some perfume into my cleavage and check my makeup in the mirror. I look *really* good. We go out the door, down into the lobby, swinging our hips like pendulums in an old grandfather clock.

⚜

We met Darryl in the lobby of Arnaud's, a fabulously huge restaurant. It's done in the authentic, rich antiquity of the French Quarter design. I try not to look around like a ghetto girl who has never been anywhere, but it's not easy. Darryl made reservations in a quiet corner. We sit down and order drinks, appetizers, and a main course. I am truly impressed with the place and told Darryl so.

"So, Denise, I know everything there is to know about Bonnie, so why don't you tell me something about you."

"Wait just a minute, my dear Darryl." Bonnie leans forward on the white linen tablecloth with her elbow. Her long painted fingernail waggles in the air. "You don't know everything about me. So don't go giving Denise the wrong impression."

A sly smile sneaks out from under Darryl's scraggly mustache, and he looks at Bonnie out of the corner of his eyes. "Now, Bonnie, you don't want me to start telling any tales about you working the city beat back in the old days, do you?"

"Darryl, darling, you can tell any tale you want to. All that is ancient history. I wasn't ashamed of my carefree young days, and you shouldn't be ashamed of yours, sweetheart."

They are looking at each other like brother and sister sitting at the breakfast table wondering who is going to get the last piece of bacon. There is also something else going on, but I am not so sure what.

"Okay, I'll leave it alone, kiddo. No use digging up old skeletons."

"Better my skeletons than yours, Darryl. Mine may still have skin on them, but yours are still living and walking around." We all get a good laugh out of that.

"So, Denise, back to you. What's a beautiful woman like you doing without a husband?"

I put on my best blush, but it feels phony. I don't think he notices. "What makes you think I *have* to have a husband?" *Chill out, girl. Don't bite his head off. He's just making conversation.* "Oh, I don't know. I guess I haven't found Mr. Right or Mr. Nice. There are just too many slicksters out there with bad manners, bad breath, and bad credit. So I'm just kind of working and doing my own thing."

"Yeah, some of those guys are friends of mine," Darryl says. "Sorry to say, but we're not all bad, at least not all the time. I hope you haven't given up on the brothers though, or trying to hop to the other side of the fence. So many sisters are these days."

"No, oh no. Not me. I mean, I can tell you when a white guy looks good, now, and there are a lot of them around DC, but I think I'll continue to take my chances with the brothers for now. Besides, even at my age, I couldn't bring one home to Daddy. You know what I mean?"

Bonnie holds up her hands as if she's caught up in a good, down-home Baptist sermon. "Amen to that, sister!"

The food comes with decorum and a bit of flare. We talk about New Orleans, the conference, and politics in Baltimore and Washington.

After dinner and a few more drinks, Bonnie is well on her way to getting sauced. She is laughing and joking about TV news stories in Baltimore, and we are laughing right along with her, but I can see she isn't going to be able to do much more hanging out tonight. I am quite ready to go in, though. The only thing on my agenda for tomorrow at the conference is a session and mixer for college students.

"Bonnie, how are you feeling? You look like you've had enough to drink."

"Denise, I've had more than enough to drink. I'm drunk as shit, and you better believe it."

"Well, maybe we better get you back to the hotel. What do you think?"

"I'm a hundred percent with you. Darryl, old friend, you feel like carrying me out of here?"

"Bonnie, you aren't that drunk. Besides, this old friend couldn't carry you if he tried."

Darryl pays the bill, and we all get up. After a few unsteady steps from Bonnie, she gets herself together, and we hail a cab.

The three of us hop out of the cab at the hotel and walk Bonnie up to her room. Her full, perfect breast implants bounce and flirt with the edge of her dress. Several men walking through the lobby of the hotel seem to forget the women they're with. They watch Bonnie's boobs, hoping the playful perky bouncing will treat them to more than eye-candy cleavage. She has already sobered up some and seems to enjoy the attention, but remarks that she is ready to hit the sheets. We say good night at her door, and I tell her not to oversleep. Darryl walks me to my room down the hall and pauses at the door.

"Well, I guess this is good night, Denise. It's been nice. I'm glad I met you."

I think for a moment. I'm still wide- awake, and it is just after nine. I want to have someone to talk to for a little while longer, but I don't want to give Darryl the wrong impression. "Look, Darryl, it's still early, and I'm not really ready to turn in yet. If you are of a mind, let's walk around the French Quarter or something."

"Sure, that's a fine idea, but I need to make a quick phone call back to Baltimore. I need to talk to the mayor's chief of staff real quick, and then we can go."

"If you want, you can make the call from my room, I need to freshen up just a bit anyway."

I let him in and show him where the phone is. I step into the bathroom to touch up my lipstick. Outside the door, I can hear Darryl talking in a very official voice to someone.

"Look, Steve, I don't care what the legislators are saying about the program. The mayor wants it, and I don't give a good goddamn how broke they say they are. You need to lean hard on them. Whenever a state crime bill comes down the pike, they're always talking about Baltimore and throwing money at law enforcement. What they need to do is throw some money at special-education programs and get some more damn computers into the city schools. For the same price, the state is willing to give us for automatic pistols, they could buy computers at corporate rate from IBM, so don't give me that shit. Okay, I'm sorry, I don't mean to yell, but we've been fighting for this stuff for a long time, and I think it's time for us to deal with the crime problem at the root and not try to prune back the thorns after they stick the voters in the sides. Yeah, right. I understand. Well, uh, okay well. Do the best you can. I won't be staying here the entire two weeks anyway, so I should see you no later than Friday evening. Will do, see you then."

I come out of the bathroom and into the suite. Darryl is sitting on the edge of the bed.

"Pardon my eavesdropping, but *that* was some phone call."

"Yeah, well, you know how government business can be."

"Hey, tell me about it. I've had a few battles myself working for the federal government. They still haven't decided how they are going to take a woman in a position of authority who knows how to play hardball with the big boys like they've been doing for years."

Darryl stands up, walks toward me, and folds my hands into his. "Is there ever a time when that woman stops playing hardball and softens up a little bit?"

Uh-oh!

He leans over and starts kissing me on my neck. At first, I let him do it. It feels good, but then I remember I really am not interested in this man, and he certainly is being presumptuous.

"Darryl, uh, wait a minute, I don't think this is something we should be doing. I thought we were going to walk around the Quarter."

He keeps kissing my neck as if he doesn't hear me. I really start feeling repulsed by all this and I'm getting angry. I push away from him. He is still leaning forward with his lips pursed like a goldfish.

He really *is not cute at all.*

"Hey, I didn't mean any harm. I just wanted to loosen you up a bit. I mean no one knows we're here, and I told Bonnie I was interested in you."

"Yeah, you told Bonnie you were interested in me, but *I* didn't tell Bonnie I was interested in *you*. Look, I'm really sorry if I gave you the wrong impression, but maybe it would be better if you left, before one of us gets mad. That one of us will probably be me."

Darryl straightens his suit and walks to the door. "Denise, I'm sorry if I upset you. I didn't mean to. Sometimes men can be real mule headed. Still friends?"

"Yeah, sure. Look no hard feelings, I just don't work that way, okay?"

"Good night, Denise."

"Good night, Darryl."

Darryl steps out, and I shut the door behind him. Oh boy! What a night! I asked for excitement, and this is what I get, a pompous ass with a hard dick.

I don't think you need to mention this to Bonnie. Just let it go.

I might as well save the old boy damage to his ego. Looks as if it's going to be the television and me tonight. God, make tomorrow better. What did Scarlett O'Hara say? Tomorrow is another day. Come on, tomorrow.

Eleven

On Tuesday morning, I stop by Bonnie's room to wake her up. It is just after 8:30, and she has not come by my room to get me up. I figure, all the liquor she drank last night is probably still in her system. When she answers the door, I discover I'm right. She looks like she went to bed with a mini hurricane.

"Bonnie, are you okay?"

"Girl, what time is it? Damn, I feel like an old whore after a weekend of working overtime."

"It's 8:35. Are you going to be able to make it today?"

"Denise, I don't know. Remind me not to go out and do any more heavy drinking while I'm here. Whew! Talk about a serious hangover. What's going on with you this morning? Did you sleep okay?"

"I did okay, I guess. I watched a little TV before nodding off."

"TV? Didn't you and Darryl paint the town red last night?"

"No, no. He had to make a call to Baltimore and then decided to go back to the hotel."

"Oh well, maybe you'll have better luck later this week, huh?"

I am standing here trying to figure out a way to tell Bonnie that Darryl isn't what I have in mind when it comes to men. Although I sometimes wonder what I have in mind when I know Darryl isn't even close to it.

"Bonnie, I really appreciate your trying to have me meet someone nice, but I don't think Darryl is really my type. I mean, there's nothing about him that really turns me on, know what I mean?"

Bonnie just kind of grunts from the bathroom sink, as she washes her face. I stare at her for a while. Without her makeup, the scar on her face stands out clearly, and I wonder how she was able to pull herself together after the rape attempt. It also occurs to me that at one time there might have been something between Darryl and Bonnie.

"Hey, Bonnie, tell me the truth. Did you and Darryl ever have a thing?"

She looks up quickly from the sink. Soap is dripping from her chin.

I look her square in the eyes and lean against the doorframe of the bathroom. "I'm kinda curious. I mean, you said the two of you worked closely when you were doing your street reporting, and you seem to be pretty good friends and all."

"Denise, don't you think that men and women can be friends without having a sexual relationship?"

"Sometimes, I guess it is possible."

"Well, sweetie, in this case, you guessed wrong. The truth of the matter is, after that young guy and I parted ways, I was depressed and quite lonely. Darryl was my friend. He was a shoulder to cry on and—well, once, and I mean *only* once, he was more than that. It just happened. We joke about it sometimes but never more than joke. Darryl apologized after it happened and promised that it would never happen again, and it didn't."

A flash of anger rips through me.

Why would she try to hook you up with some stuff she already had? You can get what you want for yourself when you want it.

All of a sudden, I don't feel like waiting for Bonnie to finish getting ready.

"Look, it's almost nine o'clock, and I really need to get going. Do you want to hook up later?"

"Go ahead, I'll catch up with you at the conference later on, okay?"

"Okay, see you later."

I step out of the room and catch the elevator downstairs. The heat and humidity cramping the lobby are nothing compared to the way I'm feeling. I may not be involved with a man right now, and I may not be looking for Mr. Virginal and Pure, but I'll be damned if I have to go in for used goods. No way, no how!

I get to the conference around 9:15. Like yesterday, many people are milling around drinking coffee and stuff, but some young people are also around, mostly college students buzzing about last semester or next semester or graduation. I look at the agenda for the day and then remember this is supposed to be the job fair and college day at the conference. It is somewhat funny. I'm getting flashbacks to my days at Howard and those all-important college job fairs. Like then, many of the girls are dressed like women or trying to be. Too much makeup, heels half as high as mine are, and they're still walking around like their feet are about to fall off at the ankles. I guess that is what happens when you wear sneakers seven days a week.

The young men are not any better, trying to convert "Friday-night funky" into "corporate Monday morning" just doesn't work. The hairstyles are just a little too wild. It is obvious to me that some of these guys didn't get the allowance check from home in time to visit the barbershop. Maybe I'm just getting old, but I also remember very well those rough, poor days, and I was only a bus ride away from Howard's campus.

I slide through the crowd over to a big coffeepot on the table to get a cup and try to finish waking up. My anger at Bonnie melts away, and I decide not to worry about the whole Darryl thing.

Bonnie is only trying to be nice. You have more things to worry about than whom was screwing whom eons ago.

While I'm stirring my coffee, I can hear a pair of college girls talking about something happening later in the day.

"Yeah, yeah, I can't wait to hear him speak again. Last semester he came up to Tulane and had everybody standing on their feet."

"Girl, I missed that one, but I saw him when I first started school a year ago. He is so-so-so fine. Now that he has graduated, there will be several jobs laying for him. But y'know, I haven't seen him out with anyone when he's around town—not since my first year."

"Well, there was a rumor that he was dating this older chick, you know the one that worked at Texaco."

"Wait a minute, isn't that the one who was killed in the car accident last year, or was it the year before?"

"Yeah, too bad, my poli-sci professor said she probably would have been picked to head up the Mayor's Commission on Urban Violence. What would she know about crime and stuff?"

"I don't know, but I know before she died, she was more than happy to commit a few crimes with Tyriq."

I whirl around, forgetting myself, and look right into the faces of these two girls. They both look at me like a pair of deer caught in a car's headlights.

"Excuse me for eavesdropping, ladies, but who are you talking about?"

The girl who made the crime comment speaks up first, "You're not from here, are you?"

"No, I can't say I am. I'm Denise Younger out of the Federal Office of Procurement in Washington, DC."

They shake my hand. They look so young. I can imagine them with ponytails jumping double Dutch not too long ago.

"There's this guy named Tyriq. He just graduated from Xavier. He's into a whole bunch of stuff, mentoring students, frat man, mayor's blue ribbon panels, and stuff like that. He was a powerful student when he was in school. He still has some pull now, I think. He's connected here in New Orleans like a lot of folks only wish they were. He still speaks all over to students about getting themselves together and ready for the corporate world and stuff."

I am a little surprised, and my curiosity is really piqued. "This young man's last name wouldn't happen to be Austin, would it?"

"Yes, ma'am," the other girl says to me.

I almost tell her not to call me ma'am. I am not that old. But, to these post adolescent girls, I probably am, or at least look it.

"So when is he supposed to speak? It's today, isn't it?" I probe.

"Yes, ma'am. There is a special lunch today for the students, and he is supposed to speak."

"Are both of you going?"

"Yes, ma'am!" they say in an off-key duet.

"Well, ladies, I will probably see you there. Thanks a lot. Nice meeting you."

They say good-bye and turn back to their conversation. I head for the first session, wondering all the time what this Tyriq person is all about and just how young he is.

Twelve

By lunch hour, the conference center's main ballroom is crushed with people, as I expected. White tablecloths, crystal glasses, and sparkling silverware adorn the tables, which never have enough elbowroom. Other than Bonnie, who finally joins me at the reserved seating, there's no one at the table I'm interested in getting to know. The food is your garden-variety chicken breast with vegetables, pretty enough but virtually without flavor. The coffee is very strong and very good. I make sure I take in enough caffeine to make my hair stand on end. Bonnie is over her hangover and appears to be back to normal. We chitchat about generic stuff as we try our best to ignore the super important, super dull introductory speakers.

The room buzzes with corporate fat-cat talk until the conference host fights microphone feedback to announce the keynote speaker.

"Ladies and gentlemen, as you finish your lunch, I want to announce a very special treat. Coming to the podium is a young man some of you know or have heard of; a young man who has done quite a bit in the New Orleans community at such a very young age. A powerful speaker with some very innovative ideas about what his generation is doing and thinking about as they move from college into the professional world. He was named the mayor's Outstanding Young Citizen of the Year. He has been a motivating force for young and old alike in the city. Despite helping to spend taxpayer's money when he led a large but *peaceful* protest for community centers in the lower ninth ward..." The crowd chuckles gently at the mention of this. "He is a voice for now, and we hope a voice for always. Ladies and gentlemen, I give you Xavier University senior Mr. Tyriq Austin!"

The crowd breaks into applause that is more than polite. At least a third of the people stand to give the man walking up to the podium an ovation. It is Tyriq. The same young man I met in the lingerie shop, the same young man who gave me a ride back to my hotel, and the same man who stirred the ashes of my heart in the little French Quarter restaurant. Now he is strolling through the crowd of tables to the microphone.

The master of ceremonies said he was a senior. Just how young is this guy anyway?

Bonnie looks at me and shrugs her shoulders. I am probably looking at her as if I am trying to explain nuclear physics to a caveman.

Tyriq smiles at the broad expanse of the room and holds his hands up to quiet the applause. He is dressed in a jet-black linen suit that looks tailor-made, white shirt with black pinstripes, silver tie, and matching cufflinks. This is a student?

"I'm glad to see all of you here. I know you have better things to do than to sit through a plateful of bad food waiting to hear what a kid like me has to say."

The crowd twitters softly at this remark.

"Well, I have just one correction. I did graduate! I'm no longer a student, thank God. But I still don't mind saying to you what most students say to their parents: please send more money!"

This really breaks the crowd up. I kinda get a kick out of it too.

"And just as you say to your children in college, the check is in the mail."

Again, more laughter from the fat-cat crowd; this *is* the same radio voice that spoke to me in the lingerie shop. It's also the same beautiful face I watched curling smoke from those luscious lips at the French Quarter restaurant just a few days ago. Even from my table forty feet away, I can feel his masculine power fanning out over the crowd. Goose bumps rise on my arms.

"In many ways, college students haven't changed. Many of us are still poor, still like to have fun, still worried about how life will be after graduation, who will get fat, who will get married, who will still be around ten years from now, and what homecoming will be like next year. But there's a new side to the modern college student that will burst onto the job market over the next five years or so. That new college student will be more mature, better prepared, and more aggressive than probably any that has come before. They will need to be. Not only will they have to fight other college students from across the nation for the small pool of jobs available to them, but in many cases, they'll also have to go up against the older workers and professionals for those same jobs. Even during my short lifetime, I've seen the economy crumble and fall, taking with it the best and brightest of factory workers and CEOs."

I nudge Bonnie in the side with a sharp elbow. "He said short lifetime, just how old do you think he is?"

She shushes me with a tightly knit brow. "I don't know, hush now."

"Many of you here are doing well. Others are just holding on to your jobs and businesses, yet you have the ability to hire and influence the future of both public and private industry. The students you see around you now could soon be your coworkers and colleagues...or your bosses. A year from now, some of these students could be talking to you about that big project or contract over a power lunch in a downtown restaurant.

"The new ideas mixed with the wisdom and positions you all now hold can make for a powerful, potentially successful combination. But, this won't happen if you're unable to be more open-minded about the changes and concerns that are at the forefront of the minds of today's youth.

"Yes, money and success are important, but global concern for many of today's young people starts in their own communities. Many of the social ills: crime, poor housing, even a lack of common courtesy come about when opportunities are not made for the people who try to do things the right way.

"As a student, if you are hungry or cold or unclothed, you cannot study. If you cannot study, you cannot graduate. If you cannot graduate, you go back home to your parents, if you have them, and create a burden for them. If there is no hope for the students for jobs and opportunities, those same students could be where your hard-earned tax dollars go—to support them on the public-assistance rolls.

"Give a new graduate a job, and they will rent apartments and buy houses. They will buy groceries and televisions. They will get married and have children that will create a need for more, and better schools, which will in turn make for better communities and hopefully fatter municipal-tax coffers. This isn't a new formula. Many of you are products of this old equation, and still our world is changing faster than many of us can keep up with. We are letting our communities deteriorate, and the people within those communities are also deteriorating.

"The generation gap has become a not-so-grand canyon, and in the hole are the drug addicts, the sick, the poor, the world of the dark and unmentionable. We can turn our backs on the canyon and stay on the high cliffs. But remember, if you're teetering on the edge of the cliff above the abyss, the person behind you can push you off or pull you to safety. The choice is yours to make. Thank you for your time."

The crowd leaps to its feet, and a crush of applause roars through the ballroom. I also find myself on my feet next to Bonnie clapping, cheering until my hands hurt and my throat is raw.

The applause continues for at least a full three minutes as Tyriq shakes hands and gives hugs to people on the dais. It takes me at least five minutes to realize my mouth is hanging open, and I am perspiring despite the extra-cold air-conditioning blowing across the room. The applause finally quiets down, and the conference host asks Tyriq to come back to the head table. After another brief speech, Tyriq is presented with a plaque and settles in for some picture-taking and more hand-shaking. The lunch crowd begins to break up. I work my way over to where the cameras are flashing, and the flesh is pressing. I leave Bonnie behind. I'm set on talking to him. My curiosity is on overload.

I'm just a few feet away when one of the fattest of the fat cats puts his arm around Tyriq's shoulders and begins waltzing him away, talking into his ear. I step up and call out his name.

"Mr. Austin?"

He turns around and flashes that same smile I had only seen a few times but already recognize so well.

"Ms. Younger, it's good to see you again, but what are you doing here?"

"I told you I was here for a conference. Well, here I am. I just wanted to shake your hand and tell you how wonderful I thought your speech was."

"Well, thank you very much, but it wasn't a speech, it was an appeal. Still, I'm glad you enjoyed it, and I hope you take it to heart."

At that moment, Bonnie walks up behind me and taps me on the shoulder. "You remember Bonnie Scott, from the restaurant?"

"Of course, I do. I couldn't forget such an attractive woman. Good to see you again, Ms. Scott."

It's happening again. What's wrong with me? I get that brief but intense flash of jealousy running through me.

Denise, you have to get your thing together.

"It's good to see you too, Mr. Austin," Bonnie says. But this time there is no blushing or flirting in her voice. She is all business. "I am putting together a business apprenticeship program at my television station back in Baltimore. Maybe you could help me find an interested student willing to take the career plunge. It could be great for the right kind of young person with some get-up-and-go."

Tyriq smiles at me, sending those warm shivers dancing across my back. He answers Bonnie without looking at her first.

"Does it pay, or is it one of those experience-is-the-reward situations?"

"No, it *does* pay, not much, but there is a stipend," she says, still all business.

"Well, then, I have just the person in mind, Ms. Scott, how about me?"

Bonnie cocks her head to the side and raises her eyebrows, looking at me. "Hey, why not?" she says. "Listen, could the three of us get together later on this evening to chat about it?"

"I don't see why not. Name the place and the time, and I'll be there."

"Fine with me," I say.

"Great, great, look...call me at the hotel around five, and we can decide where to go from there. Denise, is five o'clock okay with you?"

"Uh, yeah, that's fine, uh, sure, I'm game."

"See you then. Nice seeing you again, Mr. Austin." Bonnie grabs me by the arm and gently snatches me out of my daydream. "Denise, are you sick or just out of it? You were standing there the whole time with your mouth hanging open. Wake up, girl, stop lunching."

"Bonnie, sorry, I just, I, well, I just don't know what it is about that man. It's almost as if meeting him or seeing him like this was a wake-up call or fate or something. I just don't know *what* it is."

"*I* know what it is. Your ass is just getting old and horny. I should know. I'm older than you are and I've been there. Hell, I'm still there. Nothing gets the juices flowing faster than a good-looking man with a brain and a purpose. That's what you have here. He's already on the way to becoming something more than a role model. Who knows, he could run for Congress or Senate some day, and all this will just be a line or two on a resume thicker than the Yellow Pages."

"I can see that, he just seems so young. I wonder what drives him to do what he has done already. Why isn't he out with the boys, playing basketball in the neighborhood or still hanging out on campus chasing after some hot college coed?"

"Denise, how do you know he isn't doing any of those things? Even the most serious men have their playful sides. I wouldn't put it past him. Besides, you've only seen him for a little while. Tonight, at dinner, you'll have all the time in the world to ask him anything you want. I know *I* have a lot of questions. If I am going to try him out for this apprenticeship, I need to make sure there is some real stuff to the fluff I've already seen."

Thirteen

Tyriq suggests that we meet at a little restaurant on Jackson Square, a park in the heart of the French Quarter at six o'clock, but Bonnie suggests we get there fifteen minutes early. Although this is supposed to be a business meeting of sorts, something drives me to put on my man-trapping clothes.

Why?

How the hell am I supposed to know? It is a sheer black stretchy silk dress with a daring plunging cleavage. It's barely enough to cover my braless beauties, but not quite enough to make even a one-eyed man miss the swing of my hips. Bonnie is always wearing a pair of slick fuck-me pumps about four inches high, but tonight I decide, for some sinful reason, I am going to outslick her. I slide into a pair of high-heeled sandals with barely enough of the delicate leather strapping to cover my feet and stick on a pair of long gorgeous teardrop diamond earrings to complete my look. They were a gift from Daddy to Mama. Now they are mine.

Bonnie and I catch a cab to the restaurant and rush in the door to escape the unbearable July heat and humidity. We were almost twenty minutes early, but Tyriq is waiting in the lobby with his legs casually crossed. His smile is as bright as a searchlight. I check out the threads. Gray herringbone double-breasted suit, black dress loafers, the ever-present white shirt with cufflinks, and funky, funky, matching gray-black-and-white tie.

Very nice, very nice!

Then there is that subtle sandalwood scent decorating the lobby.

"Ms. Scott, Ms. Younger, we have to stop meeting like this, it could become habit forming."

Bonnie stretches out her hand, and Tyriq shakes it firmly and then presses his lips against her cheek. He turns to me and does the same. I tingle in spite of myself. Bonnie giggles at me and then turns to Tyriq.

"I bet you can charm the panties off of any woman you want, can't you?"

"Bonnie!" I shriek. "What a thing to say, you don't even know this man!"

Tyriq lets a little smile slide around the left side of his face and raises his eyebrows, but ignores the comment. "Ladies, are you ready to eat? This one is on me, if that's all right?"

I say "Sure" and offer him the space to lead the way. When his back is turned, I give Bonnie a playful and slightly annoyed pinch in the side. She just gives a silly schoolgirl look and follows behind Tyriq.

The maître d' seats us on a balcony overlooking Jackson Square. Each chair is more like a mini sofa wrapping arms around us as we settle in. There is a cool, dry breeze blowing off the river, and it makes the heat and humidity bearable.

"Well, ladies, do you want a cocktail? I can suggest something very special that I think you both will enjoy."

Bonnie looks at me and smiles. "Don't try to get us drunk, at least not before we have a chance to get to know you."

"Don't worry, I won't, but you have to try this," he says. "It's one of my favorites."

We agree, and the waiter comes over to take our orders. Tyriq asks for something called Mississippi Moonlight. We glance over the menu, order seafood, and settle in for a comfortable conversation.

"Tyriq, when I saw you earlier, I told you I wanted to recruit a young person for an apprenticeship program I'm starting in Baltimore. It's business and communications, and would probably last for about a year. The stipend is $20,000 and we pay for housing. In return, you become a public relations trainee. You would go to the functions, type up press releases for the television station, and be the contact between newspapers and other PR flaks. Interested?"

"Very much so, sounds exciting. It's just the kind of thing I was talking about in my little speech at the conference today."

"It was a great speech," I break in. "But I have to ask you, if you don't mind, just how old are you? I mean, you're just getting out of college, but you seem to have an old soul. You can't be any older than twenty-seven."

Tyriq looks at me with a grin warm enough to melt ice cubes. "I'm not older than twenty-seven." There is a pregnant pause. Tyriq sits back in the overstuffed chair, looks up at the full moon, and then looks me dead in my face. "I'm twenty-three years old. I'll be twenty-four next Tuesday."

I look at Bonnie with my mouth hanging open. "Oh my God, you're just a baby!"

Tyriq looks at me; his brow twists in subdued anger. "Ms. Younger, I'll thank you very much not to refer to me as a baby or a child. If I say so myself, *and I do say so*, I've done very well to take care of myself during these past ten years or so, much better than many adults I've seen. I don't think in any way, shape, or form that anyone can or will take from me what I've accomplished during that time. I won't allow my age to be a barrier to what I plan to do with the rest of my life. I hope that I have made myself clear about how I feel about that."

I'm embarrassed. He may be twenty-three, but it's more than obvious to me, there's a whole lot more going on here than his years suggest.

"I didn't mean to insult or offend you. It's just that...well, y'know, I don't come in contact with many young men straight out of college that present as well as you do. I am just shocked that you aren't older."

"Hey, look, that's okay. I shouldn't have let my anger flare like that. There have been too many obstacles once people learn my age. It's been difficult for me to get around them on more than a few occasions. I don't like having to prove myself after my age is known. I don't lie about it, but I try to avoid telling it if I can."

The waiter comes over with our drinks. I am glad. This conversation is starting to go downhill, so the interruption is welcomed. The drinks are in tall glasses, and the liquor has a silvery glittering quality, almost like snow in the little souvenir shaker snow globes you buy at roadside tourist shops. Tyriq's mood brightens as soon as the waiter sets them down.

"Here they are! *Mississippi Moonlight*! Drink them slowly. They pack a punch, I hope you like them."

Bonnie sucks on her straw first and stretches her eyelids wide-open. "Oooohh, this is wonderful, absolutely wonderful, but what are these little silvery things floating around in the glass? I've never seen anything like this before. They melt as soon as they get into your mouth."

"Actually they are confection designs. You know, the kind you see in the grocery store. They go on cakes for decorations, but the way the liquor is mixed, they don't melt right away. For some strange reason, they float around instead of sinking to the bottom. Isn't it great?"

"Yes, it is," I say. "It looks like a cloudy martini."

"You better be careful, it's almost as strong," he says.

"I'm not worried about that, I can handle my liquor. It's Bonnie that you have to worry about. When we first came to town, we went out with a friend, and Bonnie got totally zooted!"

"Denise! I can't believe you called me out like that," Bonnie says with feigned anger.

"Zooted? That's a word I haven't heard in years. Y'know, my mother used to use that term...," his voice trails off. Tyriq turns his head to the side and looks out over the people walking around the square below. Bonnie and I look at each other but don't say anything. Tyriq looks up at the naked space just above the middle of the table. "Well...uh, Bonnie...I hope you didn't have too much of a hangover from that night." The quiet at the table is getting uncomfortable.

Bonnie's eyes slide from me to Tyriq. "No, not *too much* of hangover, but I made the promise we all do—never, never, will I do that again!"

We all laugh out loud at that one. That's when the waiter comes with our food.

By the time we are halfway through dinner, I am feeling pretty good. I'm not sure if it's the company, the spicy food, or my second *Mississippi Moonlight*. We talk about Bonnie's program a lot, what Tyriq wants to do with his life, and such. Bonnie's sharp tongue loses its edge. I don't have to worry too much about being hit from behind by any surprise comments. The longer I talk to Tyriq, the more I like him. I don't want the evening to end. That's when I get the first hint that it might—and sooner than I think. Bonnie's eyelids begin to get heavy; I think she ate too much.

"Girl, I think the food and this liquor is starting to get to me, I can barely keep my eyes open. I think it's time for me to head in."

My heart takes a quick dip.

Damn! I'm not ready to go, and I hope my eyes told Bonnie as much.

"Denise, I think I have all I need from Mr. Tyriq right now. I'm going to slide out and catch a cab back to the hotel, if you don't mind."

Tyriq looks at Bonnie and starts to get up. "Bonnie, let me walk out with you and hail the cab for you. You look a little tired."

"Wow, a gentleman! I didn't think they made those anymore," she cackles. "No, no, I'm good. It's just that the drink and the heat here are making me sweat a little, but I'll be okay."

"Are you sure?" Tyriq asks, still standing.

"Oh yeah, really. I'm sure the maître d' can hail a cab for me. Denise, I'll see you tomorrow, girl." Bonnie steps over to me, gives me a quick sisterly hug, and slips through the balcony doors.

Tyriq sits down again to finish his dinner. I begin feasting my eyes on him. I can feel it again, that feeling...like a man. Despite the warmth of the breeze, I can feel my nipples knocking on the doors of my dress. They keep knocking until they look like crab eyes underneath the sinfully thin material.

Tyriq's lips shine as they wrap around a thick shrimp, slippery with butter. The muscles in his jaws work the shrimp slowly. I can imagine him rolling his tongue over the seasoning, tasting the spices, feeling the texture of the meat, and wishing it were me. I can also feel the texture of my dress stroking the sides of my thighs and the occasional catching of my pubic hairs in the clinging fabric.

You need a good waxing, or at least you need to shave.

The more I watch him eat, the more slippery the space between my thighs becomes. I shift my legs once and shift again, trying to calm the wonderfully uncomfortable feeling dancing around my hips. A full fifteen seconds passes before I realize Tyriq stopped eating and is looking at me. My head is swimming, and it isn't just the alcohol.

"Denise, is something wrong?"

"No, no, not at all. I was thinking about something and kind of got caught up."

"What were you thinking?"

"It was...very personal. I don't think I should ask you about anything like this."

Tyriq drops his head, clears his throat, and looks down at what was left of his food. "Y'know, if there is anything about me you want to know, I'll tell you. I'm really interested in the apprenticeship. I'd appreciate anything you can do to help me get it."

"Well, that's not exactly what I was thinking, Tyriq. Bonnie and I don't work together. We just met each other here in New Orleans. We've been kinda hanging out, but I don't have anything to do with the program she's trying to run. I *am* curious about a few things. Why you are the way you are, who you are, where you come from, that kind of thing."

Tyriq smiles, but doesn't look at me directly. "Those *are* personal things, aren't they?" He asks quietly.

"I'm sorry if I'm prying—"

"No-no-no, it's just kind of surprising that's all. Okay, so where do I begin?"

"Well, why don't you begin at the beginning? That's always a good place to start," I say.

Tyriq's face grows dark, and he looks out over the balcony rail at the statue of Andrew Jackson on a horse. The silence is long and loud. I can hear the gentle laughter of people walking around the park and a blues band faintly playing, somewhere in the French Quarter. A minute passes. He is still quiet.

"Tyriq, maybe we should change the subject. I didn't mean to pry into your—"

"I'm an orphan, you might say. I run my own life and I run it pretty much alone."

I try not to act surprised. Fortunately, he is still turned away from me when he says it.

"My mother is in a mental hospital. She had a nervous breakdown when I was ten years old. She doesn't know who I am now. I used to go to see her, but there's not much use now. I haven't seen her in two years. The last time I went I tried to talk to her, but all she could say was, 'Melvin, where's the money?' so I stopped going. Maybe I'll go back to see her again sometime, I don't know."

My shoulders drop, and I slump a little in the chair trying to soak up what he is saying. There is a lot to absorb. The bad thing about it is that I know this is only the tip of the iceberg.

Be careful what you wish for, girlie. You may not be ready for what you get.

"I guess the next question you have is, who is Melvin... right?"

I offer what I thought is a comforting nod and a shrug of my shoulders. "Well, it had crossed my mind, but I thought I would just let you tell me what you wanted to tell me."

"Melvin was my father . . ."

"*Was* your father?"

"Yes, he's dead, killed by the Mini-Mob. That's what they call themselves here in New Orleans, or at least they used to. They were small-time gangsters during the '70s, but they were still pretty dangerous guys. You wouldn't want to mess around with them. My father did and lost. He used to run numbers for a Creole man who ran the Mini-Mob named David Ribaud. Daddy was good at the job and made a lot money at it, but we lived in the projects on the east side of New Orleans and never moved out. Daddy and Ribaud were good friends until he hit the number for $50,000. Ribaud wanted more than his usual cut of the profits, and Daddy said no. He hid the money. When the Mini-Mob came looking for him, they found him on the front porch arguing with my mother and another woman about getting out of the projects and running away to a safer city. We never got there.

"They shot him so many times. The white concrete steps looked like they were painted red. Mama sat there holding and talking to his bloody corpse for almost an hour before the police came. All she could say was, 'Melvin, what about the money? Melvin, what about the money?' I guess she had her nervous breakdown right there. I did not cry then, at least I don't remember crying. The only time I cry about it is in my sleep."

My stomach is doing flips like a kid on a trampoline. I look around the balcony trying to find something, anything to make me feel a sense of comfort. Tyriq is looking directly at me, seldom blinking. His eyes are still intense, but there is pain riding on his lids. It is only then that I realize that my hands reach out to touch his brow. I stroke as gently as I can, trying to wipe away the pain. His forehead is warm, no, hot, as if he has a fever. I sit back in my chair to give him some space.

"Why didn't they kill you or the other woman there? Who was she?" I ask.

"I don't know. I saw them. They saw me, and they had time to kill us all because the police took their sweet time getting there. Nobody asked me anything, and the case remains unsolved. I wouldn't be surprised if my father's murder went into the New Orleans's Police Department's circular file.

"As far as the other woman is concerned, I don't know who she was. She disappeared, or maybe I should say, faded into the ghetto shadows. I've often wondered who she was and why she was there." He looks at me and cocks his head to the side. "You ask a lot of questions."

"Tyriq, if you like, let's talk about something else. I really didn't mean to pour salt into an old wound, I'm sorry, I really am."

A small smile grows in the corners of his mouth. "Okay, so what will we talk about, you, maybe? Maybe we chat about how long you intended to hold my face before you decide you really want to kiss me."

My heartbeat quickens, sails, I swoon, and my mind dips and dives.

Dang, Denise, that was a quick shift! Weren't ready for that, were you? Oh hell, when was the last time you were kissed? REALLY kissed? If you want it, now is the time to get it started!

I part my lips and draw Tyriq's milk chocolate face to mine. His tongue dances across my lips, tasting me through the small opening I make with my mouth. My head is spinning, and I don't care. Our tongues play with each other; his hands reach my ears and gently strum at my earlobes. I can smell him, sandalwood filling my nostrils like a cocaine high, and I'm immediately addicted, wanting another fix. Tyriq brushes my lips with his spicy lips and then pulls away. He has my lipstick on his lips and around his mouth. I laugh because he almost looks like a clown. I'm still swooning, and in the middle of it, I feel a twinge of guilt hit me.

Is this wrong? Are you Eve taking a bite out of the forbidden fruit? You shouldn't be doing this, but damn! That was good.

"Tyriq, that was truly wonderful, but I think we better stop. As a matter of fact, I think it would be best if I go back to the hotel."

Tyriq squints at me and then raises an eyebrow. "Denise, I hope I haven't offended you. I'm sorry if I did. Can I at least drive you instead of having you take a cab? It would make me feel better knowing you got back safely."

This man is too nice, a gentleman to the last.

God, I feel so hot inside—if only he were older, not so soon out of college, and not so damn nice. Men aren't supposed to be so nice. They are supposed to be royal pains in the ass, thorns in the side, ball and chains, pointless penises without a considerate thought in their heads.

God, help you! You need time to think.

"Thank you, Tyriq, for being so kind, yes...I'll take that ride."

He drops four twenty-dollar bills on the table, takes me by the hand, and we walk out of the restaurant. His touch is soft and strong. Damn, I already have that horny man feeling again.

Fourteen

I have a real nice buzz by the time we get to his old Mercedes. Tyriq turns on the cassette deck and pulls out the parking space. The car turns into a time machine as Harold Melvin and the Blue Notes sing *You Know How to Make Me Feel So Good*. I was in high school when that song was sending sexy, forbidden suggestions over the radio. I loved it then, and the memories flood my mind of sitting on the sofa in my parents' old house hugging a pillow and wishing it was a chocolate Prince Charming.

The space between my thighs begins to simmer and burn. The alcoholic buzz is powerful, and my body continues to stir. The hotel is less than five blocks away, but the ride seems to take forever through the hot, steamy French Quarter. One block away, we stop at a streetlight to let people cross.

Tyriq's car needs a tune-up. The idle of the Benz is heavy. I can feel it through the seat. It ripples and vibrates through me. I press my lips together and clench my teeth.

Stop it!

I can feel "honey" running out of me.

Stop it!

I am getting really wet, and the vibration feels wonderful.

Stop it!

Tyriq's scent fills the car, dark and sweet. He is everywhere. *God, help you!*

I close my eyes and try to tell my mind to run away. As soon as I do, my head begins to spin, so I open my eyes again, and my vision doubles.

You need, you want, got to have, horny, damn! Stop it. STOP IT!

He parks the car just a few steps from the front of the hotel. I rub my eyes, and my vision clears, but my head is still swimming.

"Here we are, Denise. I'll come around and help you out."

I keep quiet as I watch him get out of the car. There is no way I can step out of the car without him noticing the dark spot on my dress. If he sees it, he doesn't mention it. We walk through the double doors and through the lobby.

"Would you mind terribly walking me to my room?" I ask.

"I wouldn't have it any other way. I just want to make sure you get in safely, and then I'll be on my way. I'm sure you have a lot of things to do tomorrow."

"Thank you, I appreciate it, Tyriq."

The elevator opens. We step in, and it carries us silently to my floor. The quiet between us seems loud enough to wake the dead.

We walk down the hallway to my suite. I pull out my key at the door but can't find the lock.

Tyriq takes the key from my hand and opens the door. "Denise, I want to thank you for a very, very nice time. Please thank Bonnie for inviting me. I'm sure I'll be talking to her again before she leaves. I'll talk to you soon too. Good night."

I look at him, through him, and sigh. "Tyriq, come in for a moment. I've had a bit much to drink, and although you were able to drive me safely back, I don't think it'll be safe for you to drive all the way to the Garden District until you are at least partially sober."

He squints at me out of the corner of his eye but doesn't move. I step through the threshold of the door.

"C'mon, I won't bite you. Just for a little while . . ."

Until you're satisfied.

"Until your head is clear, okay?"

He nods his head at me gently and steps in. He picks the overstuffed antique chair in the corner of the suite and sits down heavily. I need to wash the heat and humidity of the French Quarter from my face, so I step into the bathroom. Before I close the door, I look back into the room at Tyriq sitting in the corner. He's so beautiful. I can see his shirt dotted with perspiration and clinging to his ample chest.

All of a sudden, I just don't care anymore. It's been a while, too long a while. I'm going to take him. It's just been...I need this for me. Tyriq is going to be mine, even if just for tonight.

Fifteen

I look at my thirty-five-year-old face in the mirror.
*Not too bad, girl, you could pass for thirty on a good day.
So far, this was a very good day. Think sexy. Have you forgotten
how? Maybe not. That feeling crawling around your hips is
enough to remind you.*

I drop one of my straps from my shoulder.

*Yeah, the cleavage is there and working! Let's leave the heels
on. Men love high heels.*

When I step back into the room, Tyriq isn't sitting in the
chair. He stands by the open window looking outside. The air-
conditioning is off, and the heat and humidity sit in the room like
guests that have long overstayed their welcome. I lean against
the wall in what I hope is my most seductive pose—head cocked
to the side, with my right hand across my shoulder.

He speaks to me without turning around. "The natives are
restless tonight in the Quarter."

I smile at him from across the room; I can still smell his scent
blowing at me from the open window.

"When the natives are restless, how does it feel?" I ask, my
voice is just above a whisper, but he hears me.

"I don't know exactly. It kind of feels like the street is vibrating with energy. It almost has the smell of the air right before a beautifully violent rainstorm. It's a fresh but slightly dangerous smell, almost like something special is going to happen. It's very hard to explain."

I walk over to him, brush my hands across the broad plain of his chest, and whisper in his right ear. "If you can tell when the natives are restless, can you also tell when the tourists are restless?"

His heart is a strong rhythm against my outstretched palms. My head is still buzzing from the Mississippi Moonlight. I don't care and don't want to care. He turns around and looks at me. I don't drop my eyes when his meet mine.

"Tourists," he says, "are a different matter."

"Oh?"

"Yes, tourists have a different feel. They're not like the natives. The natives are relaxed and comfortable, even when they're excited by the thick night air of the Quarter. Tourists, especially tourists from the North, are more excited and excitable. The breezes blowing from the Gulf of Mexico and the Mississippi River warm them. The beautiful and hidden history of this city runs through them. Sometimes, it makes them do things they wouldn't ordinarily do. It covers them, makes them tremble, especially if they are in the hands of a native. That is, if they have the chance to get that close."

I pull his face closer to mine, our lips only inches apart. I can taste the hot air between us. It is spicy like sweet curry and ginger.

God! I feel so good. He feels so good.

"I'm trembling. Please, make me stop. I want you to stay—for the rest of the night."

His lips dive into mine, and he presses his body against me. I can feel his "resolve" stiffen against my thighs. The heat makes my silk dress stick to me. His tongue strolls across mine, searches, and then tastes me. My nails lightly scratch at his back, and I hear his breathing quicken. His tongue leaves my mouth and skips to my left ear.

"Why are you doing this? I thought you said I was still a baby," he says with a smile.

I chuckle and pull his ear whisper-close. "You're a gentleman. I can also feel your need for closeness. You're hurting. I'll take it away, if you'll let me."

"Denise, you make me nervous. I'm not supposed to be."

I step back from him and smile into his eyes. I brush away the other strap of my dress and let gravity peel it from my sweating body.

"I'm glad I make you nervous. Nervousness is a form of excitement. Excitement is always so much better than being bored."

I take his hand, lead him out of the sitting area to the king-sized bed, and gently sit him down on the edge. He starts taking off his shirt, but I stop him and stroke his face with a painted nail.

"Mmmm, I'll do everything. There are some things I want to show you about me. So I'm going to need your complete and undivided attention. We've already had dinner. It's time for a rich, creamy dessert, okay?"

He nods at me and braces his hands against the bed. I slowly unbutton his shirt all the way down to his belt line. I can feel him watching me as I taste his stomach and the salty and slightly bitter sandalwood scent there. I race my lips up to his chest. My tongue is electric fire, and he responds to my touch. I strip him of his shirt. My tongue quickens. I could hear him moaning as he kicks his shoes off. I am in control, no longer feeling as if I am robbing the cradle. I can see colors in my mind—purple, red, yellow and green—blending.

Damn, girl, this is gonna be really good!

Perspiration runs down my face and ribs. My palms are sweating as I unbuckle his belt. His pants are spotted and wet around his zipper. I take off his pants and try to find his underwear without looking.

Whoa!

He isn't wearing any—only his muscular brown hips that framed his massive erect...*Wonderful-wonderful.*

I coo in spite of myself. I crawl my naked body across him. I back him up to the head of the bed. My fingers play jazz piano over his face. I dip below his neck, moisten, and then blow air on each nipple, flick my long eyelashes around his belly button, and then saxophone his instrument. I blow and suckle the reed first and then create imaginary keys along his dark shaft, pressing with my fingers and playing a lustful slow tune in my head. He calls my name with a whisper and runs his fingers slowly through my short curly hair. I continue to play my melody below his waist, slowly, gently, almost lovingly. My mouth fills with creamy notes, which I gladly take in my throat, then stretch to cover his body with mine.

"Denise, I want you here. I want to feel the inside of you. Come here."

I want to finish what I started, but I also want to take the plunge. I

want to ride him, cover him, and give him all of me.

"Denise, we have a problem."

My dream of him breaks open, and I fall back into reality. "What?"

"I did not come prepared. I don't have any protection."

Damn! What were you thinking? Why didn't you prepare for this? Saundra told you about having a fling, and you ignored her. Well, here it is! Your ass is buck naked, horny, and ready to do the do, and you ain't got your shit together! You lunched! Double-damn!

Tyriq looks at me and has an apologetic look on his brow.

"I'm sorry. I wasn't expecting anything like this, so I didn't plan for anything, y' know? But I have something else that might work for you."

I raise my eyebrows and shake my head slightly. Tyriq sits up, faces me, putting his hands behind my ass and gently pulls me across his pelvis, stomach, and chest with surprising strength. My sex left a trail of moisture across his body as he opens me over his face. I can feel his mustache tickling me. His tongue begins blazing an adventurous trail through the jungle of my curly hairs and into the swampy, humid walls at the center of my pleasure. His hands—

His wonderful hands!

Hold me balanced and then rotate the palms over the brown snowcapped peaks of my chest. I reach back to snatch my heels from my feet and throw them from the bed. I shudder and flex like a cat waking from a long sleep. One flick of his mouth muscle follows another and another. My pleasures are first a part of me, then distant, then part of me again. He is tireless and wise, talking to my very essence with quiet carnal poetry, soothing me. My body quakes again. I am reaching the edge, the colors are mixing, and swirling, spinning, and...I fall over the cliff. Tyriq quickens his tongue movements to an electric-fan flutter. A melting shock slams through me, my head whiplashes back and forth. My hips rotate fast over him. I scream as if someone stabs me in the stomach. I can feel my thighs become more slick and slippery as I roll off onto the bed next to him. He slowly slides off the bed and walks to the bathroom. I can hear the water running in the sink. My head feels dizzy, my sex is wonderfully aching and swollen, and my body drowns in perspiration. I am tired, and I want him even more.

"How are you feeling? Are you okay?"

I can sense him standing over me, but I don't open my eyes to see how close he is., "Yes, yes, yes. God, I feel good. Come here, I want you to hold me."

I can feel his hands on me again, and then he stretches out on the bed next to me. I roll on top of him, kissing him on his neck and face. I feel empty and not quite satisfied. His sex throbs gently against my thigh. I don't care anymore.

What is wrong with you? This isn't good!

I don't stop because I don't care. I can see myself lifting my body over him. I mount him.

"Denise, no, no. I told you, I'm not protected. You know better than this. Don't do this now, stop!"

I shut him up with a kiss. I can't listen. I don't want to hear him. I squeeze my muscles around him and rotate my hips. He falls silent, stops resisting, and joins me in the dance.

Sixteen

The first thing I feel is the heat of the morning and my own perspiration soaking me.

The air-conditioning must be broken. You'll have to call the front desk about changing your suite or at least fix the damn thing.

The next thing I realize is that the window is open. I can hear the sounds of the French Quarter already wide-awake. Tourists and romantic types clip-clopping on the cobblestone streets in horse-drawn carriages. The acrid smell of the Mississippi floats in from the west side of the city. Cajun and Southern accents mix and mingle with the hot and heavy air. I can also feel my head somewhere in the room, on the floor, on the wall, on the ceiling, maybe even in the bathroom. Anywhere but on my shoulders where it is supposed to be. My vision doubles, triples when I try to lift my head. God! What did I drink last night?

God! What did you do *last night?*

Then it all comes back to me when I feel a hand gently rubbing my stomach. My eyes search to the right. I can almost feel them squeak as if they need oil. Tyriq's cinnamon-colored face is looking at me, watching mine for signs of familiarity, memories of last night. His skin glistens with a faint gloss of perspiration.

"Good morning. How are you?"

I look at him, and a laugh tries to escape from my chest but dies before it gets half way out. "I'm living, I guess. How are you?"

"Oh, fair to middlin'. I slept well at least."

His eyes quickly search the suite. He leans over, kisses me on the forehead, and begins to get out of the bed.

"I'm going to have to leave. I have to open the store in about two hours. I hope you don't mind if I leave in a hurry."

"Two hours! What time is it? I'm going to have to get up and go to the conference."

"Ohhhhh . . ." He looks at the clock on the nightstand next to the bed on his side.

His side?

"It's almost eight o'clock."

"Damn! Tyriq, I gotta get out of here!"

My head is reeling as I carry my rusty-feeling body to the bathroom. I miss walking into the door jam by inches.

Y'all didn't use a condom last night. Shit-shit-dang! What were you thinking?

I can feel semen sliding down my leg, and my sex feels weak and raw. I feel like kicking myself.

This isn't college, and it's not the '70s. What are you doing?

I can hear Tyriq moving around in the room mixed with the sound of the bathroom fan buzzing above my head. I sit down on the toilet seat cover and peer around at the mirror. I almost don't recognize the woman staring back at me. I have three Samsonites hanging under both eyes. My skin looks like cheap grade-school clay and my hair . . .

Damn...never mind!

"Denise? Are you okay in there?"

Even in the morning, Tyriq's voice has a masculine but gentle quality that isn't unpleasant, although it does echo and bounce with the remnants of liquor still churning my brain.

"I'm fine, I'm just trying to put my stuff back where it's supposed to be. Right now, it feels like you knocked it up somewhere around my throat."

I don't hear him say anything. That's supposed to be a joke. I peek out of the bathroom door and squint at the now-sunlit room. He is already completely dressed except for his shoes. He still looks very, very good although now he appears to be on the winning side of a drunken brawl.

"I need to get home, clean up, and then get to work. I wanted to find out if you are available later tonight. I get off at six. Maybe you'd want to have dinner or something?"

I'm feeling strange, really out of sorts, as if I've committed some kind of crime. Tyriq is standing there like a puppy that just brought in the master's slippers and newspaper.

"Tyriq, let me call you at work, or maybe I'll stop by later."

I can feel my forehead knitting and twisting. I can see that he wants to ask me what is wrong. He doesn't. Instead, he takes a couple of steps back and eases into his loafers. I button myself into my white satin robe and sit on the bed. Tyriq leans over, kissing me on my wrinkled and twisted forehead.

"*Will* I see you later tonight?"

I nod at him short and quick, trying to force a smile without much success. His eyes squint at mine from their corners as he quietly steps out the door. I stare at the closed door for what seems like forever. I don't realize I've put my bathrobe on inside out until after I am ready to step into the shower.

Seventeen

AIDS, syphilis, herpes, gonorrhea, and any other nameless kill-your-pussy diseases. What else is out there that I probably have right now or will have by this afternoon? What am I thinking? Could I have been *that* horny and *that* dumb? Was I? I probably caught some kind of weird strain of French Quarter coochie critter disease. Maybe I have something so rare it will probably make AIDS look like the sniffles. My stuff will probably explode the next time I go to the bathroom.

Speaking of my stuff, I am really sore. Tender like collard greens in a day-long slow cooker. Has it been that long since I've had sex? Saundra told me to take condoms with me. But what would I need them for anyway?

No, Denise, you weren't going to have any of it and certainly not with some young college-age kid. Your life is probably cut short now, anyway. Might as well put in an order for a double dose of AIDS cocktail at the local pharmacy. You'll probably use it for the next four or five years until you dry up like a starving Holocaust victim.

There's a knock at the door. I look down at myself. I'm half-dressed and half–made up. I don't move, not immediately. The knock comes again, and Bonnie's familiar voice follows.

"Denise? Are you in there? If you are, girl, let's get those thick hips moving! Denise!"

"Just a minute, Bonnie, I'm still trying to get my stuff together after all that liquor last night!"

My head has cleared considerably since Tyriq left forty minutes ago. My hands shake a little as I wrap my fingers around the door handle and let Bonnie's long legs through the door.

"Ooohhhh, girlfriend! What the hell happened to you? I don't mean any harm, but you look like you aged five years overnight! What happened?"

I roll my eyes at Bonnie's bluntness. "Listen to who's talking! You look like the last rose of summer. I know the liquor took its toll on you too, and you had as much as I did."

Bonnie kinda laughs at that and sits down in one of the antique-styled chairs, crossing her model-beautiful long legs as she does. She is staring at me the way my mother used to when she knew I did something wrong but wanted me to tell on myself.

"Denise, since it looks like you're not going to be ready for the first session this morning, why don't we go and get some breakfast or at least coffee—strong, hot, and black? I know I could use it, and you definitely need to get something on your stomach. My treat, bet?"

You had something strong and black last night!

My jaws are rusty hinges, but I let a small slow smile walk across my face. "Y'know, Bonnie, in so many ways you remind me of my best friend Saundra. You have an uncanny knack for cutting through the bullshit without ever having to get the stink on you."

"I get you. Now come on, put on your clothes and the rest of your face, and let's get down to the hotel lobby. I'm sure we can catch a quick something to eat then get in on the second session. There are some things I need to pick up from it. I definitely don't want to miss it."

Bonnie's sisterly support is all I need to get me moving. I have to, just to keep her curious mother's gaze off my back and out of my face. I don't get the feeling that she's going to ask about last night. But, by the time I am dressed and out the door, I am bursting at the seams to tell her.

We walk across the street to a little café that is serving breakfast. My hangover quickly fades after a few minutes as I eat my fluffy Belgian waffles, thick peppered bacon, and strong coffee. It's only then that I finally drop the bomb on Bonnie about last night. Men aren't the only ones who kiss and tell or screw and blab or whatever you want to call it.

You did and you're telling it all! Well, not all of it. I think you should leave the condom thing out of it, just like you did last night.

"And, girrrrl, let me tell you. It was some kinda good," I say, licking lust and maple syrup off my lips.

Bonnie leans closer as if to tell me a secret. "There's nothing like a younger man to let you know you still got it after all these years. Shit, with all these pretty, young tricky-thicky girls running around this town, you picked a fine young one like that? You got it going on!"

"True, but, Bonnie, I'm sore as hell."

"Oh?" she says. "Been awhile, or was he huge?"

"Both!" We laugh loud enough to attract more attention than we want inside the café. I drop my voice to just above a whisper. "So what do I do know? He wants to see me tonight."

"Do you want to see him, and get some more?"

"Honestly? Yes, it was sooo delicious, and it has been too long since I had some. But I don't know if my sore stuff can take another ride like that so soon. I just don't want him to get the wrong idea about me."

"And what idea is that?" Bonnie's forehead twists with annoyance. "That an older woman got her rocks off, and that's that? Well, I think that *is* the idea, and he will have to live with it. He got his, and you certainly got yours. It is what it is. I wouldn't worry about it if I were you. I just wish it had been me. Lord knows I need a tune-up!"

She's right. What's done is done. But I'm still unsure of myself. Sleeping around or getting a tune-up, as she calls it, isn't the way I do business.

Yeah, but maybe that's your problem. Maybe it's time for a change, or at least, while you're here, you should be open for business, even for just one customer.

Eighteen

The noon session isn't bad at all. The moderator talks about how best to deal with federal government red tape and how to get the best bang for the buck without the huge overcharges for which private contractors are well known. Many interesting questions float around the packed room.

Darryl, Bonnie's friend from Baltimore, is there too. The three of us sit comfortably together near the front for the two-hour session. Bonnie and I beg off lunch with Darryl. I want to find a fax machine and send some information to my office from the session. It might be something they can use before I get back.

Neither Bonnie nor I are especially hungry after the big breakfast we had, so we decide to hop the trolley to the Garden District where Tyriq's shop is. It's good to get some fresh air although the mid-afternoon sun is melting me. I can feel my dress sticking to my back just a few minutes after we board the trolley.

The trolley cruises and bumps through the downtown area just outside the French Quarter. Bonnie plays tour guide, pointing out the fine stained glass windows of shotgun houses. The huge trees with Spanish moss and magnolia blossoms crowd the sky overhead. They provide a little shady relief from the heat of the sun and the humidity. Still, even in the spotty shade, it feels like one hundred one degrees. I am so taken by the scenery that I suddenly realize the trolley rolls right past the shop. We go on another block before we get off and start to walk back.

As we approach the shop, I begin to get cold feet. I start to slow down right before we get to the walkway. There are several cars parked along the street: Jaguars, Volvos, a Cadillac, and several Mercedes, including Tyriq's. I stop right behind it, remembering the intoxicating ride to my hotel less than a day before.

"I'm really kind of nervous about this whole thing, Bonnie. I'm not sure I know how he's going to take what I'm going to say."

Bonnie looks at me, a little irritated. "Denise, look, did you hear anything I said to you earlier today? Just go in there and be the woman you know you are. Take control the way you did last night. Be firm but also be kind. If you handle it right, everything will be fine. So go ahead, I'll be hanging around for moral support."

"Okay, okay, I'll get this over with."

I straighten my posture and pat my hair as we walk into the shop. The wonderful scent of sandalwood candles burning, hits me immediately. Tyriq doesn't see us come in. His back faces the door, and he is talking to a striking white woman with a mane of salt-and-pepper hair. Her eyes cut to us twice. The second time, she holds her gaze for a few seconds and then turns back to Tyriq. He picks up her diverted attention and turns around. He controls his surprise, but I can feel the vibes across the room— warm, solid, powerful vibes. I melt.

"Ladies, welcome to Nightie-Night. Is there something I can help you find, or are you just looking?"

He is talking to the room, but his eyes devour me. Bonnie slides away without responding. I walk over to him, quietly clearing my throat.

"Actually, I think I know exactly what I'm looking for. Something in a cotton flannel gown maybe?"

His brow stitches quickly, and he turns his head away slightly, stifling a chuckle. He continues to watch me. The woman he's talking to when we came in studies our exchange with great interest. As I look at her closely, I realize she wasn't white at all but very, very fair. Her skin is much lighter than Bonnie's is, and she has very sharp, fine features and the clothes to match.

You remember her. It's Tyriq's boss. The one with the stank attitude. Sniff the air again. It's about to get REALLY foul in here.

"You aren't a regular customer. I can tell immediately. I'm Clara d' Beaux. This is my shop, and if there is anything I can find for you, please, don't hesitate to ask my manager or me. He knows everything there is to know about ladies' intimate apparel, and I hope you find him comfortable to deal with."

She doesn't recognize me from my first visit to the shop. Now I have a chance to get a closer look at her. She is obviously one of those blue-blooded Creole women I've heard and read so much about. She speaks her name with a strange accent, Clara-de-boh, as if it is one word. Her perfect creamy skin and large deep-set electric green eyes make her a real head-turner. She has the cold unfriendly air of the evil queen in *Sleeping Beauty*. I really don't like this woman.

"Thank you very much, but I think I'll manage. Actually, this is my second visit here and I am well aware of the efficiency of your manager. He was more than helpful the last time."

If bad vibes are missiles, this is nighttime in Baghdad during the Gulf War. Her eyelids cut her green flinty eyes in half; they slide off us like butter on a hot ear of corn. Tyriq's face is blank stone as he watches his boss's silk wrap flow with her to the other side of the shop. He turns to me quietly. His face brightens only a little as he gestures to the other side of the shop.

"I didn't think I would see you again so soon. But I'm so glad you came by. What's going on? How has your day gone so far?"

"Fine, Tyriq, just fine. Look, I need to talk to you as soon as possible about last night. But this isn't the time and definitely not the place."

"You'll get no argument from me there. I hope you aren't mad. Things did move rather fast. Maybe even a little too fast for me. Admittedly, I've been *affected* by it somewhat."

There it is, Denise. Take control. Play this older-woman thing up now and let him down real slow and easy.

"Tyriq, I'm more mad at myself. I feel that I may have taken advantage of you last night. I want to apologize."

"That's what I wanted to talk to you about. It's what's been on my mind too, but as you can see, I am tied up. Would it be too much to ask if you could come by my place after 6:30 tonight? I need to tell you a few things if I could."

He looks at me with a very sheepish open stare. I can see all his youth exposed, and for a fleeting moment, I almost feel like a mother instead of a lover.

"Sure, I'll come by, and we can have a nice long private chat. Just so we can get a few things straight."

His face lights up like a Christmas tree. "Great, great, that's wonderful. Here's the address. It's not hard to find. Any cabbie will know the street. Six-thirty, right?"

"I'll be there."

I look around for Bonnie. She's at the cash register talking with Clara d' Beaux. I pick up a nice black silk teddy and walk to the counter. Sister diva bitch Claradeboh looks at the teddy and then looks at me.

"Definitely *not* a flannel gown... How would you like to pay for this, miss? Cash? We don't take out-of-town checks." Her gaze has a definite frigid air about it.

I look at her carefully, trying to keep my long-hidden ghetto attitude from cutting loose. "You do take American Express, don't you?"

I put the card on the counter, snapping it with my thumb. Clara d' Beaux picks it up without taking her eyes off me, then looks at Tyriq across the room.

"Absolutely . . ."

"Thank you very much," I say.

She turns her back to me, sliding the card through the electronic verifier. *This woman is really getting to me.* I don't know why, but I do know this: it is time for me to go. The ghetto in me is ready for rebirth, and I am not quite sure I will be able to pull it back if it got out.

Nineteen

Bonnie and I catch a cab back to the hotel. I ride in silence trying to swallow the anger rising in my throat. Bonnie, seeing that my jaws are very tight, doesn't pry. I guess she decides to ask later or not at all. I am not a jealous person, and yet I can feel the green monster trying to hatch inside me. It's a new experience for me. I'm not used to it and don't find it at all pleasant.

We arrive at the hotel, and Bonnie and I split up. I finally find a fax machine to send some notes and information from the conference back to the office. I also want to call my father to see how his Atlantic City trip went with the lady from church. I have not spoken to him in six days, very unusual for a daddy's girl. It's definitely time for me to touch base with him. Saundra also needs an update from me. I can't bring myself to tell Bonnie everything, good as she has been since we met; I just really need to talk to Saundra. I'm just not ready to tell her how young Tyriq is.

Still, I need to unload some of this emotional baggage.

"Okay, okay, what are you going to tell him tonight, Denise? It doesn't appear that you have a real problem with what you're thinking about."

"I'm still not exactly sure, girl. I mean, he's so nice, so handsome, and so well spoken, it seems everything is in the right place—almost."

Saundra is her usual helpful self, a good listening ear and enough advice to rival King Solomon. It still mystifies me as to where she got all her wisdom. She's only a few years older than I am. I guess if you live long enough in the right or wrong way, you learn things. Saundra has been around the block more than a few times.

"This quick sex thing is *really* bothering you, isn't it?"

"Of course, it is." I say, feeling irritated.

"Yeah, yeah, sure, and if he were like a lot of guys, he would have so many hang ups you would probably think he was a clothesline. I don't do this, I won't do that, you can't do this, and you can't do that. If you want to go braless in a linen dress, he'll complain about other men staring at you. Look, girl, stop tripping. This man is as he is for whatever reason. If you are going to break it off, that's on you, but remember this, how long had it been before last night? How long has it been since someone opened a door for you because they were being a gentleman? When was the last time you were in the passenger seat of a man's car instead of driving by yourself? What did Shakespeare say? Better to have gotten some and lost it than to not have gotten any at all."

"Saundra, I don't think Shakespeare said it quite like that."

"Whatever! Can we talk about this or what? 'Cause you know, I know *you*! I will break it down and keep it real!"

"Saundra, are you mad at me? You sound like it."

"No, I'm not mad, but I do care about your black ass, and sometimes I think you are too smart to be so dumb. I don't want you to make any mistakes, but I want you to enjoy your life while you are still young."

"What about husbands and families and stuff like that? I want children."

"Children? Ha, ha, you can have one of my boys if you want 'em. As far as a husband, I've had two and am not sure I want another one."

"You're not being serious."

"I know. I just don't want you to think I'm mad at you, and I want you to know I care, okay?"

"Sure."

"Have you spoken to your father?"

"No, as a matter of fact, I'm going to call him after I get off the phone with you. It has been six days and that is at least five days too long. Besides, I definitely want to talk to him about this church trip to Atlantic City and Ms. Jackson. You know this is a weekend deal?"

"I knew I should have started going back to church. Maybe I could have taken your superfine daddy to Atlantic City and chased him around the roulette tables a couple of times."

"Saundra, you are such a fool, you better leave my daddy alone. You know I know where you live."

We both scream into the phone, laughing as we did in college. I am already feeling better.

❧

I call Daddy after I got off the phone with Saundra, but there's no answer. I should take a nap but I'm not tired. Telling Tyriq that last night is just water under the bridge is not going to be very easy. Thirteen years is a big generation gap. Trying to build a bridge across all that space, all those years will be difficult enough even if he lived in Washington, and he wasn't so young.

Maybe this whole romance thing is not for me. The love thing? Definitely, but does love have to include romance? I like it, but is it practical or realistic to think romance can be maintained forever? Are the two—love and romance—mutually exclusive? Some cultures marry without love ever being a consideration, the prearranged thing. Why not me? Saundra is talking about enjoying life. Maybe she is in the mood to enjoy her life and not be so serious, but if I went through two husbands, as she did, I guess I would feel the same way. I've never come close to having a husband and never even had a man who *smelled* as if he wanted to propose marriage. All my ex ever wanted to do was give me the high hard one, once or twice a month after he came down off one of his marijuana highs. Tyriq is nice, but he's still a boy and has quite a bit of growing to do. Maybe it is time for me to grow up a little too, and stop messing around with my own emotions. Thanks a lot, Tyriq, sweetheart. But it is time for this little fantasy of mine to come to a quick and quiet end—today.

Twenty

I get a wake-up call from the front desk around five o'clock. I feel a little greasy, so I take a long, almost-cool shower, shave under my arms and my pubic hair until I am smooth as a newborn. Even as I dry myself in front of one of the air-conditioning vents in the bedroom of the suite, I can feel the Louisiana heat from the afternoon sun pressing against the windows.

You need to wear something nice, but not too sexy.

A sleeveless ruffled pirate top with my favorite pair of thigh-length safari shorts are perfect. The matching heels are still this girl's prerequisite.

I think about catching a cab right away and think about it again when the humidity threatens to crush my head from both sides, but I want to walk along Toulouse Street for a little while to get my thoughts together. I look at my watch, it's a quarter to six, I still have forty-five minutes, and I'm sure Tyriq will not mind if I'm a *little* late.

The people are out and about on the street and I head toward Bourbon Street. The air is still, and I can smell the strong scent of spicy food as the restaurants prepare for the dinner crowds. There's also the faint stench in the air of what seems like sewage or even rotting garbage. The horse-drawn carriages wait to give tourists a quick view of the French Quarter. I resist the urge to hop a ride, but it wouldn't be the same without someone to go with. Maybe I can persuade Bonnie to go with me.

I daydream for a block or two and realize I am already on Bourbon Street. The burlesque shops are in full swing although I suspect they never really close down. Three little black boys are dancing on a corner in front of a hat half-full with coins and one-dollar bills. I watch them. They are sweating and raggedy. One of them has very bad teeth; I can see them as he smiles at the onlookers passing by. I walk over and drop a five-dollar-bill in the hat. I've never been one to contribute to the street economy of the homeless, but for some reason, I feel generous today or at least at this particular moment. They stop to see what I put in the hat and then look at me.

"Thanks, lady!" one of them says.

I look down into his dark face, which, despite the perspiration and day dust covering it, will probably become very handsome in about ten years or so.

"You're welcome, fellas. Don't spend it all in one place."

"Oh, we won't, we won't."

They go back to their little street dance, harder than before. Maybe someone else will match the five I gave them and allow for a mini spending spree on whatever little boys buy these days.

I do a little window-shopping at a corner trinket shop. There are all kinds of ornate boxes made with stained glass, wood, even ivory, and brass. Daddy is always losing cufflinks and tie tacks (yes, he still wears tie tacks, very old-school) because he will set them on his dresser. One of these boxes might be good for him to put his things in. Later this week, I will come back and get him one. I think he might like that.

It's 6:15 when I look at my watch again. I have spent enough time in the Quarter today. It's time to get over to Tyriq's place and do the do. A cab stops in the middle of the block and drops off an elderly white couple, obvious tourists. I step up as they get out. The man holds the door open for me and peeps at my cleavage as I lean forward to get out. I think his wife sees him. The corners of her mouth turn down into a nasty scowl, and her lips move silently as the cab moves away from the curb. I chuckle to myself.

"Dirty old man."

I tell the cab driver where I need to go, and he turns the cab around, heading out of the French Quarter, cutting the cab onto Canal Street. The trolley cars snake by. Here the tourist crowd is much thinner. There are more working people. They look worn out because of the heat. The women look slightly soiled from the nine-to-five. The men even more so. The street is bumpy, as the cabbie turns right off Canal and onto Magazine Street. It almost looks residential. The street is wide with lots of shotgun houses left and right. This looks like the starving artists' district for lack of a better term. There are all kinds of antique shops situated in what look like private homes. Pottery shops and art shops dot the street between houses. Spanish moss trees cry shade along the sidewalks. Strong large roots have, over time, lifted and broken the concrete sidewalk poured over them ages ago. The cab slows after passing another block and eases to a halt in front of a small but quaint shotgun house. The old Mercedes I have become so familiar with during the past several days sits on an even older driveway. Stained glass wind chimes twinkle and gently sing out in the early evening sun, casting red, blue, and purple light on potted flowers near the porch. I pay the cab fare and get out. When I turn toward the door, Tyriq is standing there. His hands are in his pockets, and he is looking at me. He is wearing an open white raw-silk shirt and baggy linen pants without shoes. He is even more beautiful than the day I met him. My heart shifts slightly to the right. I try to move it back to the center without much luck.

Damn, Denise! This is going to be harder than you think.

I walk across the broken stone walkway to the porch. He smiles at me with all those wonderful white teeth. I feel as if I am walking in slow motion, but I keep walking. He opens the front door, and I step in.

Twenty-One

I am not quite sure what to expect from this meeting. My guard is up, but weak and already losing strength as I walk through the door of the house. I've never been in a shotgun house before, but it is obvious why they have that name. All the rooms line up straight front to back.

Just beyond the front door and the foyer is a long hallway with a door on the left. The house has Tyriq's personality stamped all over it. Artwork hangs on every wall, large and small. All the pieces are ethnic, mostly West Indian and African.

"It's good to see you, Denise. I was worried that you may not show up. Was I being silly?"

"No, no. I said I was coming. I wanted to talk to you."

I am talking to him, but my eyes soak up the atmosphere of this house. When dealing with men, I have found that no matter how slick or sharp their clothes are, how wonderful they smell, or even what they say, it's their homes that tell a lot about them. Usually the houses, if they have one, are sloppy bachelors' pads with no furniture. They also have that just-cleaned-company's-coming look. Tyriq's place is not what I expected.

He leads me into the living room off the main hallway. I smile a little bit at the small cozy living room. It enthralls me. The early evening sun paints vibrant stained glass pictures through the front windows. The colors dance across a long antique sofa sitting against the widest wall. The sofa, obviously, has just been reupholstered in an earth-tone paisley. The newness of the fabric gives it away.

Above it is a painting of an African queen. She is sitting on a colorful throne painted in painstaking artistic detail. A handful of male subjects bow in adoration at her feet. Their muscular bodies shine and glisten as they worship and kowtow around the throne. She looks down at them with a mix of stern command and love. Her body is slender, muscular, and almost totally nude, except for bright chains of gold and barely there royal robes of deep purple and magenta. Her breasts are beautifully full, perky, and fleshy like ripe summer peaches. Her hips are generous and colored milk chocolate. It is, in a word, hypnotic!

"Do you like that painting?" Tyriq asks.

"Yes, uh, yes, I really, really do. It's gorgeous. I've never seen anything quite like it before. Where did it come from? It looks like it cost a fortune."

It also looks like something I could never afford in a million years, even on my inflated government salary.

"It was a gift from someone I was involved with sometime ago. I guess for reasons other than its esthetic value, it's my most-prized possession. I love art, most kinds, but I love the art of my people most. It expresses where we've been, where we are going, and, in some cases, how far we still have to go. Have a seat. Would you like some wine or something?"

"Nothing for me, thanks. Maybe something else later."

I sit down on a huge leather-upholstered antique rocking chair in the corner next to the sofa. It is so soft and comfortable. I imagine it could have been a man, Tyriq maybe, wrapping his arms around my sides. I can't help it. I start gently rocking on it with my legs crossed. The room is cool and dark, but I don't hear air-conditioning. The scent of him is all over the room and mixes with a clean rainforest aroma. I haven't noticed until now, but the living room and the connected dining room are full of plants. Most of them, I haven't seen before. Tyriq sits down on the sofa beneath the painting.

"So, you said you had something you wanted to talk to me about. I'm listening."

I continue to rock in the chair, looking at him. He lights a cigarette and sits back in what seems to be a well-practiced posture of openness.

That coffin nail he's puffing on is going to kill him someday.

"Tyriq, the other night at my hotel room, we did something we shouldn't have. I took advantage of you. I put you in a compromising situation. I came here to first apologize and to say that I don't think it's in our best interest to continue. I am too old for you. It was just a thing. Understand what I'm saying?"

Tyriq inhales from his cigarette and slowly blows smoke across the room. The colored light from the stained glass turns the smoke red, green, purple, and blue. He speaks to me without looking.

Is that a smile I see, or is it the mischief of sun-cast shadows on his face?

I can't say.

"Denise,"he pauses and inhales from the cigarette again, "Denise, I'm sorry you feel that way although I suspect what you're saying isn't exactly what you mean. Yes, I understand perfectly, but I don't agree. Honestly, I don't think you believe what you're saying either."

"Wait a minute, I know exactly what I'm saying, and I don't think you're in the position to assume anything different from what I'm telling you."

Why are you getting angry? That isn't your style. Chill, Denise.

"Obviously, you are dealing with a lot of turmoil right now," he continues. "And trying to handle a great many things. There are things you want and, at least for a little while, you wanted *me* even if it was just for a night. Don't think, just because I'm younger that I don't have the presence of mind to make my own decisions about what *I* want.

"Suffice it to say, when you came into the shop last Friday, one of the first things I thought about, or fantasized about, was how you tasted. I could feel your eyes on me, on my back when I was picking out a few things for you. Besides, who are *you* to tell *me* you are too old for me? You can say *I* am too young for *you,* but it is up to me to tell *you* that you are too old for *me.*"

The look on his face is very serious, almost stern, but his voice is steady and calm. I shake my head, roll, and then close my eyes.

"Tyriq, I just met you, and we had sex, okay? Even if I lived here, which I don't, I think things just wouldn't work out. It was just something that happened. I wanted it to happen, and I let it. It doesn't mean I don't like you. You're a very nice young man. If I didn't like you, nothing would have happened, no dinner, no sex, no nothing, and I don't think—"

"How long has it been, Denise?" he interrupts. "Six months? A year maybe that you haven't been with a man the way you wanted to be?"

He stands up, puts out the cigarette, pops a mint into his mouth, walks over to a fuzzy plant, and gently fingers the large green leaves.

"You know, you say it was something that just happened, but I believe you desire something else, something special, and this age thing is getting to you. I'm not saying I am *the* one, but the way we talked at dinner, the way you approached me at your hotel room, told me there may be something missing in your life that you want from me, or some man. You appear to have everything else. No one should live the rest of his or her life alone, I truly believe that, and I may fit the mold, or at least I would like to. So what's the big deal?"

"The big deal is," I say. "I am leaving here in about a week, you're just out of college, and I am a working career woman who someday wants to get married and settle down and not have to worry about a relationship with a popular, powerful, handsome hormone-filled young man living a thousand miles away. I don't even know when, if ever, I am going see you again. This is too deep for us to be talking about. Damn, I just met you!"

"So if it's so deep and damn, you just met me, why are we even having this conversation?"

I pause, he is right, I want someone, maybe him, but someone to hold me and tell me I'm beautiful and to bury his head between my legs and wipe my tears and hold my hand and take me to church and—

Damn, Denise, get your shit together and stop playing games. Maybe Bonnie and Saundra are right. This may not be a long-lasting relationship. You may just have a fling with a young guy. But here, in New Orleans, who knows you? You can do whatever you want. Let your hair down, what little hair there is, and live a little. Who's gonna know? When it's over, it's over.

"Tyriq, I like you. I couldn't hide that from you if I tried. I just met you, but I like what I see. Maybe we can tone this down just a little bit while I'm here and, y'know, kind of hang out a little while I get my work done at the conference. Would that be okay with you?"

Tyriq turns around and looks down at me from across the room. There is a stifled grin on his lips. He raises an eyebrow.

"I have a counterproposal for this friendship, so quickly formed . . ." I look at him, want to say something, but a gentle stirring start in my stomach. I look down and away from his face as if I expect to see something. Of course, I didn't. When I look up, Tyriq is standing directly over me. He kneels at my feet, and we are almost eye-to-eye as he continues. "How about this? You're running from your emotions, and me. You can try if you want, but I'm coming after your ass, Denise. I know what I like. I know what I want, and I am going to pursue you. I am going to be inside your head and inside your heart. I am about to attack your needs and desires. I am going to drive forward until you tell me to leave you alone or until you give in to me."

I guess the pussy is pretty good, huh?

I feel two beads of perspiration escape from my armpits and slide down my sides as he closes in on my lips. He presses his body against me. His chest is hot, and I can taste minty smoke on his lips. I don't mind. His tongue licks my lips, and I wrap my arms around his neck.

God! You feel so good, so strong! You feel like a man should feel.

His lips cruise my neck and then past my ear. I can hear my breath catching in my throat. He whispers in my ear, "I have something for you, come here, I want to show you something."

I look at his eyes and nod my head like a sleepy five-year-old about to be put to bed. He takes me by the hand and leads me out of the living room and down the long dark hallway. I know we are going to the bedroom, to make love or screw or whatever, and I want to.

Denise is gonna get some! Denise is gonna get some! Nanny-boo-boo!

What I don't know and what I am not prepared for is the big bag o' tricks Tyriq is about to pull out on me. It is just the kind of thing to shut me up about "the older woman" thing from here on out.

Twenty-Two

Tyriq leads me down a long, narrow hallway. Candles guard every inch of our steps. We walk through a clean small kitchen and then through a door that leads to a bathroom. Compared to what I am used to at home, this house is small, quaint, but really tiny. However, I can also see that a lot of love was in the hands that renovated it. The bathroom is as large as a child's bedroom, and it glows warmly with more white candles crying large tears of wax down their sides. A curved claw-foot white porcelain bathtub filled with clouds of bubbles rests against the black-and-white-tiled wall.

"Is this for me?" I ask.

"No, actually it's for me," Tyriq says quietly from behind my left ear. "I want to bathe you. You'll enjoy it, but I promise you, I'm going to enjoy it more."

I can smell eucalyptus and magnolia scents in the dim room. Bright brass fixtures and an antique vanity mirror reflect the flicker of the candle flames. I peel out of my clothes and watch Tyriq watch me from a short wooden stool at the foot of the tub. He doesn't say anything, but his eyes laugh, smile, and lust over me as I step into the almost-too-hot water.

"Damn, boy, this water is hot!"

"Hush, woman! I got your boy right here. Don't spoil the moment." His brow creases briefly, and I offer an apologetic shrug, which he appears to accept.

I bet you won't call him boy again.

My brow beads with perspiration; my tightly curled hair relaxes as the steam and water tease it. Tyriq tears wax paper from a large bar of soap, wraps his fingers around it, and dips his hands in the water. Yet another scent wafts from the thick suds—sweet, almost recognizable—but I am too relaxed and comfortable to think hard about anything.

"Aren't you going to use a washcloth on me?"

Mischief covers his face, but he does not answer my question. Instead, he pulls me to a sitting position and paints my back and shoulders with the suds that covers his hands like shaving cream. I close my eyes and listen to the slurping sound of the soap as his fingers press through the skin of my neck and bless the tightness out of my muscles.

"Sit back," he says, "I want to rinse this soap off of you."

He dunks a small plastic watering can in the water between my legs, fills it, and pours it over my neck, shoulders, and back. I tingle and splash water against the sides of the tub.

"Why are you doing this to me? I bet you do this to all the girls you date, don't you?"

He soaps his hands again.

"Do you want me to answer that question, or do you want to enjoy the moment?"

I lean back with a smile and flick a puff of suds from my pointed toe onto the end of Tyriq's nose. It sits for a moment and then floats back into the tub.

"Oh, okay, I'll leave that alone."

"I think that's a great idea," he says with a smile.

He lifts each of my legs out of the water and covers them with more rich suds. His hands penetrate my calf muscles, my thighs, and the tension of my Achilles tendon.

"I love the soap. What is it?"

"It's an almond-and-palm-oil soap. It's supposed to be good for your skin. Clara sells it at the shop. She let's me take a few bars every now and then."

"Humph, Clara!" I spit. "I can't say I'm too crazy about your boss."

Tyriq chuckles a bit, "Yes, I noticed."

"Y'know something? I think she's kinda diggin' on you with a dirty-old-lady kind of lust."

"Y'think so, huh?"

"I do, I do-do-do." I lean forward and press my forehead against his.

Damn, he's a good-looking man!

"I think she wants to fuck you old-school style."

"Oh? Nawww! I think she looks at me like more of a son, even a grandson."

"Hah! I bet she wants to snatch you up in your collar, throw you down on one of those lingerie display tables, and ride you like a horse on a merry-go-round. Nice...and...slow."

I stretch my puckered lips toward Tyriq's and kiss him. He suckles my top lip gently, cocks his head to one side, and looks at me with piercing eyes.

"That's not going to happen. Besides, this merry-go-round only has one seat and one ticket. Wanna ride?"

I laugh in spite of myself.

Oh yes, I do!

I stand up in the tub, and Tyriq wraps me in a large soft terrycloth towel and dries me from head to toe. I am cleaner than I was when I left the hotel and a damn sight hornier than the night before. He steps through another door next to the sink. I can see the edge of a bed in the room. I pad across the hardwood floor and sit on the edge of the bed. The room, like the rest of the house, is filled with antiques. Tyriq leans against a heavy bureau with a swivel plate glass mirror atop it. He has removed his pants, and his dick is so erect, almost pointing to the ceiling.

Is that the same dick from the other night? It's bigger, much bigger than I remember the last time, but I was drunk then too. Wow!

Tyriq stares into my face and opens the towel around my breasts like a velvet curtain opening on a Broadway stage play. My nipples rise to greet his mouth, which blows cool air as he kneels before me. His lips don't touch them though. Instead, his strong hands part my knees, and he quickly buries his face between my thighs—noisily, hungrily—licking and sucking over the hood of my clit in a swift, unfamiliar, and wonderfully pleasant way. I look at the top of his head twisting between the hams of my legs. The sound is loud and decadent.

Go 'head, baby! Do that. Do that, 'cause you know I love it! This is how a man treats you when he loves you, girl! He kisses your pussy like a man kisses the lips of a woman he loves, with his whole being, with passion.

I lift my heels and place them on the supporting bed frame so that he can get a better angle on my sex. He reaches lower and farther into me. I place my hands behind his neck and guide him across the wetness of my love. I jerk, and he utters a deep sigh every time his tongue paints the tip of my sweet little hill. My mind soars and fantasizes.

This is good luvin'! This is what I want. This is what I need. Just treasure me.

Each time his tongue flickers across my hood, I feel the room spin and my climax creeps a step closer. Then he backs off, comes in with his tongue again, and then backs off again. He moves into my clitoris again with a sweet uppercut flick of the tip.

Damn, it's so hot in here. Why...is...it...so...hot?

I come—hard!

"Omigod! Babylove!" I shout.

I slap the broad muscles of his back with the splayed fingers of my hands. My eyes fly open just in time to see my legs and painted toes point straight out in a perfect strained V just past his narrow waist. I can only jerk my hips to within inches of dropping off the edge of the bed, but he holds me fast. I can feel his hot breath warming me as my lips pulsate. Tyriq stands up and pushes me back on the bed and then presses his face against mine. I can taste me on his lips, and I suck his talented tongue into my mouth. He brushes against my left thigh, hard and ready. I gently wrap my fingers around it and pull him inside my love-worn lips.

"Hold me like you love me, baby!" I whisper in his ear.

He pushes into me for what seems like forever. I think I can feel his fullness in my chest. I try to wrap my legs around his back, but he moves, strokes me up and to the left. I plant my right foot on the bed for balance as I see my left knee move toward my face.

Damn, Denise, he's going to kill you something good!

"*Uhmm-fk!*" I grunt from somewhere deep in my stomach. I can only watch my left knee rock back and forth, absorbing the indescribable pleasure-pressure inside me. He pulls almost all the way out, does it again, but this time up and swings to the right.

"*Uhmm-fk!*" I grunt again, louder this time. I lift my right leg, and I am full of him again, full of long thickness, up to my chest, and lifting my ass almost off the bed. I come again with a shudder and a melting like the wax of the candles burning around us. He reaches into me again with a constant rhythm. His breath is like a slow locomotive in my ear. My head is turning, and I hold on to him. I feel like a little girl spinning on a wonderful merry-go-round. I can see me, that little girl, in my mind, my braids flying in the wind. Tyriq lifts my shoulders off the bed and drives deeper still into me. My head rolls back, and my climax rolls over me like a wave. I'm drowning, welcome and welcome. The little girl on the merry-go-round laughs out loud, and so do I. Tyriq's loins stretch inside me with a sweet strain. He collapses over me, our breathing labored and happy.

How did I get here? Don't worry about it now, just be glad that you are here.

I look into Tyriq's eyes with the same question. The answer is the same. My hips and legs are loose, limp, and tingling. Sleep presses against me like a heavy grandmother's quilt. The last thing I remember before the morning is the Seth Thomas clock rounding eight-thirty, and the ticklish but not-unpleasant feeling of his juices sliding out of me and across the skin of my throbbing thighs.

Twenty-Three

My head is in the clouds for the entire cab ride back to the hotel. The message light on the phone next to my bed is flashing, but I don't care to check. I am high like a drug addict with a new supply. While I am taking a shower, my euphoria continues. I go back to the conference. Even as I walk through the exhibit hall, I feel heady and wonderfully foolish. I'm not hungry because my stomach is filled with butterflies. I'm out of control and don't care until I see Bonnie standing by the door of one of the conference rooms. She wears a pinstriped power suit and folds her arms angrily across her chest. She stares at me as my mother did when I was a teenager, out well past my parental-imposed curfew. I feel a familiar guilt, like a spanking is only moments away.

"Where the hell have you been?" Bonnie hisses at me.

"And a very good morning to you," I say, almost ignoring her anger. "Good morning, my ass! Come here."

Bonnie grips my arm and quietly escorts me to a corner of the huge exhibition hall where no one can see us. Her hold on my arm is eerie, almost the way my mother would grab me after I misbehaved in church as a little girl. We settle in an alcove near the restrooms.

"What's going on with you? I looked all over for you. I left messages for you at the front desk and your room. I was worried! What happened?"

"Calm down, girl. Let me tell you! I decided to go visit Tyriq yesterday, to tell him that our little thang was just that...a *thang* and nothing more. Well, it didn't quite work out that way."

"Whoa, whoa! Back up. What do you mean *thang?* What happened? You mean to tell me you slept with the boy again?"

"Yeah, and let me tell you, there ain't nothing boyish about him. Bonnie, I know it seems crazy, but he is so passionate, responsive, and he listens. It is as if he can feel my words. He's not just sitting there pretending to hear. He really is into what I have to say. And his...oh-ma god, girl!

"Yes, yes, I know. The dick! That young boy turned you out like a new hoe. How long has it been, Denise, three months, four months?"

I sigh.

"Longer, almost eight months. I can't remember anymore, just too damn long. If it weren't for BOB, there would be nothing for me."

"Bob? Who is Bob?"

"BOB is my battery-operated boyfriend. B-O-B."

Bonnie twists a look at me with her head cocked to the side. She nods halfway between sympathy and pity with a chuckle stuck somewhere in the middle.

"I can dig the B-O-B bit. Sometimes it's just easier to do it yourself, but, Denise . . ."—she hesitated, stopped, sighed, and then started again—"I think you need to slow your roll a bit. I'm not trying to get into your business. When I met Tyriq, I was impressed with him...."

"Humph, not as impressed as *I* was," I laugh.

"Girl, get your head on straight and stop trippin'. This is serious. If you did your *thang* as you call it, more power to you.

But now it's time to focus on this conference, get what you need, and then roll out of here next week."

Bonnie is so right. What am I doing with Tyriq other than the horizontal hoedown? Has it been that long since I've had a man? Have I lost control of myself? I've been here for less than a week, and I'm acting like a college coed during spring break. I need to tighten up.

"Bonnie," I say, not looking at her. "Thanks for thinking about me. I know we just met, but I appreciate the sister love. I have gotten quite carried away with this Tyriq thing. I haven't taken the time to think. I guess being out of town where no one knows me puts me in a horny frame of mind."

"Girl, you were horny before coming to New Orleans. You just unleashed the freak when you stepped off the plane, and Tyriq could smell it on you. The steam was radiating from your hips like shimmering heat from the street in the summertime. You might as well have been walking around with a sign on your back that says, 'Fuck me, please.'"

"Damn, okay, okay, I got it!"

"Sorry, girl, I'm just saying. So what are you going to do now?"

"I don't know. I really like him, and despite what you're telling me, he does seem genuinely interested in me, or at least genuinely interested in knowing me better."

"Don't forget about the business apprenticeship at my TV station in

Baltimore. I still am very interested in bringing him on. He is a very good candidate for management training. If he's really interested in you, this would be a perfect opportunity to be near you. Baltimore is just forty miles from DC."

"That may be perfect, but even for him, moving and being near me may be a bit much for him so soon. We just met, you know, and we're having...fun, hanging out."

"Yeah, and backin' that thang up," Bonnie says with a sly laugh. "Either way, all I can do is ask. Trust me, his answer will show what that young brother is really made of."

"Tell you what. I'll call him at the lingerie shop and tell him you want to meet with him, then the three of us can get together, and we can go from there."

"Perfect, but for now, don't you have a few seminars to sit in on?"

I rub the top of my thighs through my pantsuit and look at Bonnie with a bit of mischief.

"Yes, I do, but I think I will just stand in the back of the room."

"Why?" Bonnie asks.

"Tyriq lit my little ass up last night. It's better if I just stand right now, trust me."

Twenty-Four

It is well after three o'clock when Bonnie and I leave the conference for the day. The Louisiana sun seems to kick off its shoes and lean back on the French Quarter as if it was a comfortable old leather chair. We walk without speaking with our blazers off.

Our silk blouses cling to the sweat-soaked skin on our backs. The down-home spicy smell of gumbo drifts past our noses with the drone of air-conditioning units running at full tilt from restaurants with open doors. We resist the temptation calling from our stomachs. Instead, we continue toward the hotel, a cool shower, and fresh clothes.

Inside the lobby of the hotel, the blast of cold air-conditioning is a welcome change from the clutches of the heat and humidity outside. Bonnie and I step toward the elevators when the clerk calls from the front desk.

"Ms. Younger, you have a delivery, ma'am."

"Who? For me?"

"Yes, ma'am."

I look at Bonnie, and she gives me the old "beats me" expression. The clerk disappears behind a wall and returns with a huge plant of fragrant white blossoms.

"What on earth is this?"

"These are magnolia blossoms, and they're in full bloom. Someone is sweetie-sweet on you, ma'am. This came with it."

The clerk hands me a square beige envelope with a melted red wax seal on the back.

"Wow, would you look at that!" Bonnie says. "A wax seal. I've only seen stuff like that in the old swashbuckler movies. I bet I can guess who that's from."

"Mind your business, girl," I say with a smirk. But I do not open the envelope. I just look at the wax seal. It is blood red, like the color of life's liquid when you first prick you finger with a needle. The seal glistens as if its wet, and I can smell Tyriq on the paper, the rich woodsy warmth of his scent stirs and hypnotizes me.

"Open it, Denise."

I can feel Bonnie's excitement mix with mine, but the hotel lobby is not the place for this.

"C'mon, let's go up to my room," I say.

Bonnie grabs the magnolia plant and hops on the elevator with me. The letter weighs heavily in my hands.

What is it, a love letter, a Dear Jane letter; maybe it is a "thanks for lettin' me spank dat azz" letter?

The elevator doors open, and we walk to my room. Bonnie sits the fragrant plant on the table in the open area of the suite and sits in one of the overstuffed occasional chairs next to the table. I cradle the letter in the palms of my hands, still not ready to open it.

"Do you want me to leave and give you a chance to do this alone?" Bonnie asks kindly.

"No, I want you to be here."

"Okay, okay, well, open the damn thing! You're killing me!"

I fold the letter at the wax seal and break it, then slide my painted thumbnail under the corner, and rip the paper along the edge. More of Tyriq's scent seeps out. The paper is beautiful. The edges are irregular like torn tissue paper and framed with a bronze-colored foil. In the middle is a message in a deliberate flowing hand script, rich in lust and emotion. My heart races as I read it to myself and then aloud so Bonnie can hear it.

My Dearest Denise,

Come with me, my dear, with your eyes closed and heart open. Feel my breath on your soul, and force your skin to listen to the words from the richest, deepest corners of me..

Where have you been? Even in this short time, I have felt you. I have felt us, wanting us when we looked at each other for the very first time. I want to taste you again at least once—no, twice, thrice, thrice, thrice, and again. I want to feel all the woman you are. My resolve for you stiffens at the very thought of you, and I am alive at the sight of you. I've tingled at the warmth and wetness of you. We have been together only for a sweet moment, and I bathe myself in each hour. I wrap myself in each minute. My spirit tastes each second. I want my hands to excite you with a journey round and through your body, in a dark public place. I want my lips to speak the sonnets of my affections. Let my arms warm you from the cold, pull you close to me, and let us shut out world.

Tyriq

I look up from the letter and blow a breath of air through my puffed cheeks. Bonnie looks at me and utters a very breathy, "Wow!"

"Oh shit! What did you do to him, girl? Did you steal his virginity or something?"

I look off to the side, shake my head slightly.

"I just don't know what happened, or what's happening here."

"Sounds to me like he's in love or at least in lust. I have never heard anything like that before. That's a love letter, for real. It's just beautiful, powerful, and raw. Do you think he wrote it or copied it from somewhere?"

"Bonnie, I don't know." I am incredulous. "All I know is, I've got to get a handle on this. I'm caught between swooning and just confused. Can someone really have feelings for someone like this in just a few days?"

Bonnie shrugs. "I don't know. The thing about it is, he's not stalking you or anything. He's just tapping you with a little bit of this and a little bit of that, then waits for you to respond. As we used to say back in the day, 'whatcha gonna do now, homegirl?'"

"I think I'll sit down and talk to him in a place that's kind of neutral."

"Oh, you mean in a place where you don't have to worry about being on your back with your knees up around your ears."

I laugh and then give Bonnie a friendly snarl. "Yes, that's exactly what I mean."

Twenty-Five

By the time Bonnie and I get into the back of a cab and cruise through the Southern elegance of the Garden District toward Tyriq's job, it is well past six o'clock. The summer sun is getting low in the sky, but the ninety-plus heat is still hanging around. The cab pauses briefly in traffic. We glance out of the window and watch as an old white man sprays three or four children with a garden-hose water pistol. The children are dressed in bathing suits; the oldest probably has not seen eleven years. The youngest looks about three months this side of six. They dance and jump back and forth in the grass. The man has on a beige straw hat and khaki pants but is shirtless. He is as wrinkled as a red raisin. His aim of water spray gently swings back and forth over the children. He laughs at them with the love of a grandfather. The cab moves forward, and I let out a quiet laugh as a prelude to a daydream.

"What's so funny? " Bonnie asks.

"Oh, I don't know," I begin without taking my gaze from the window. "I was thinking about my daddy. Y'know, DC summers can be like this New Orleans summer, hot as hell. The heat can

137

weigh on you like an anvil. When I was a little girl, Daddy would hook up the sprinkler on our little postage-stamp–sized lawn. The little kids from the neighborhood would run and jump through the cool spray for what seemed like hours. Daddy would sit on the front porch with Mama, and they would talk in the comfortable, easy way lovers talk. I was just wondering how he's doing. "

"Have you called him? " Bonnie asks.

"I did but he wasn't home. He was supposed to be going on a bus trip to Atlantic City with some fast woman from church. My daddy is still fine, and the ladies at church are always trying to get at him. "

"I take it, your mother's not around? "

"No, she died in a car accident about two years ago...," my voice trails off, dragged by the weight of a heavy heart. I am surprised at how quickly I feel tears begin to well up in my eyes.

Damn, I miss Mama.

"I'm sorry to hear that." Bonnie puts her hand on mine and gives it a supportive squeeze. I look at her and give her a hesitant, pained smile.

"Enough of those old memories, I'll just make sure I call Daddy tonight. I'm sure he went on that bus trip. I just hope he had a good time and wasn't uncomfortable with Ms. Sadie Jackson."

The cab pulls up to the front of Nightie-Night. Bonnie pays the driver, and we step out into the hot, thick late-afternoon soup.

"Damn!" Bonnie cries. "How does anyone get used to this rainforest heat?" I laugh as we move toward the tall, thin wooden double doors of Tyriq's shop. I can see a thin sheen of perspiration on Bonnie's cheeks and brow. I can feel it on mine. The toasted yellow spotlight of the sun shows brilliantly on Bonnie's face.

Despite the thin never-to-fade scar of violence on her jaw, I am reminded of just how truly gorgeous she is. For a moment, she reminds me of the kind of melt-in-your-mouth beauty of a young Lena Horne. It is the kind of beauty that makes men accidentally walk into walls or rear-end cars on the street as they turn to look. She is a sweetie pie too. You don't find that in many sisters these days, especially so soon after meeting them.

We open the doors and hit an arctic breath of air-conditioning and potpourri. The store isn't crowded, but business is still brisk. New Orleans has always had a reputation for being a sexy city. Bonnie scans the room looking for bargains. I scan the room looking for Tyriq. By the time I see him in the middle of the store, he is already beaming his spotlight smile at me. He is exquisitely dressed in a black linen suit, plain button-down white shirt, and no tie. As he makes his way across the expanse of the room, I can feel the earth move slightly beneath my feet, or maybe it is between my legs, or both. Bonnie leans a little closer to my ear.

"Girl, I don't mean no harm, but when you're finished with him, can I have some? I just want a little bit, just a corner, just so I can say I had some before I died. I mean, damn!"

"You know what?" I whisper a laugh. "You are just a nasty skeezer."

"I know. It's actually one of my *better* qualities."

"Hush!"

Tyriq steps up, grabs both of my hands warmly, and plants a long moist kiss on my cheeks. It is an exquisite loving gesture of affection. Goose bumps race from my face to my legs in a flash.

"Hey, Denise," he says softly. "Did you get my letter and the magnolia plant? "

"Oh yes! They were wonderful, especially the letter. But I don't know how I'm going to get the plant home to DC."

"Don't worry about it. I can always send you another one." He looks at

Bonnie and winks. "Hey, Ms. Bonnie, with your fine self, how ya doin'?"

"I'm well, actually, and you? You're looking pretty good."

"I am doing *really* good." Tyriq looks at me, then through me. "I'm actually doing better today than I have been in a long time."

"Tyriq!"

A shrill tone bounces from across the room. It is not quite a yell, but it has a stern sharp edge to it, enough to make a few customers jump a little. Ms. Clara *bitch* d' Beaux is standing with her arms crossed next to a large ornate armoire of beautiful barely-there undies. They stand out in stark contrast to the dark cloud of stank-a-dank-dank attitude hanging around her like a bad fart. "May I see you for a moment...please?"

Tyriq gives us an apologetic look and walks over to Nasty Lady Boss. Bonnie looks at me with questions. "What's her problem?"

"That is Ms. Queen Clara 'Already-a-pain-in-my-ass' d' Beaux. I think she has a thing for Tyriq. She probably noticed our little add-water-and-stir attraction to each other."

"Don't you mean add sex and stir?"

I give Bonnie a gentle elbow as we watch Tyriq and his boss go through a quiet, tense exchange.

"I'm not digging this," I say. "I'm going over there."

"No, I don't think that's such a good idea," Bonnie says. "Now that I think about it, coming here to handle your personal business wasn't the best idea either. We *are* at the man's job. See what I mean?"

"Yeah, I do. But we can shop! Since we are paying customers, let's act like it."

"You got that right!" Bonnie says. "Shopping is the cure for what ails you. Hmmm, my stomach is feeling a little queasy. Maybe some new panties or a satin gown is the antidote to make me feel better."

"Bonnie, you are too funny," I laugh.

"I know. It's another one of my better qualities, next to the skeezer thing." We chuckle and snicker as we move to the back of the store. I keep one eye on Tyriq as his issue with the boss continues a bit longer than I thought it would. Sadness and a twist of irritation darken his face, but he stands there and takes whatever Ms. Clara *ain't-never-gonna-be-happy* d' Beaux is dishing out. We try to focus on the exotic, the erotic, the unusual, and the just-plain-comfortable lingerie spread out over the many tables in the store, but the verbal duel between Tyriq and Ms. Clara *why-don't-you-just- get-a-life-a-boyfriend-and-some-dick* d' Beaux finally ends. Tyriq looks at me with helpless eyes and steps through a door behind the counter and out of sight. Ms. Clara *my-ass-is-too-tight-for-me-to-breathe* d' Beaux walks over to us. Bonnie sees her coming and steps to, just like one of your girls who has your back right before a fight after school. It's a good feeling.

"Can I help you, ladies, with something?" she says as she looks at me over the tops of her reading glasses while still appearing to stare down her nose at both of us.

"No, you can't," I say. "Tyriq was actually doing a wonderful job assisting us before you interrupted. Would you mind asking him to return so that we might finish our shopping?"

"Is that all you want, just to finish your shopping?"

I look at Bonnie, roll my eyes and my neck, doing my best to swallow the ghetto tone that is quickly rising in my throat.

"I'm not exactly sure I understand what you're trying to say."

Speak your mind, bitch!

I don't say it but surely wanted to.

"It appears to me that you have taken a special interest in Tyriq. I'm not sure I approve."

"I see," I say as I lean a little closer into her space. She raises an eyebrow but doesn't back up. "And exactly what is it that gives you the right to dictate what a *grown man* does with his time, when he's not working for you?"

"I've known him for many years—"

"But not like I know him!"

"Yes, and that's my point. You hot mamas come to New Orleans with your whorish ways—"

Did she just call you a "ho"?

"And think you can take over. Tourism is one thing. Moral corruption is quite another. Why don't you go and find someone closer to your own age."

I've had enough and I'm ready to go off on her, but Bonnie is much quicker. She unleashes the hounds of her sharp news-anchor tongue.

"Excuse me, but I find it extremely curious that you seem to be so intimidated by two sisters who just blew into town. It seems that someone taking a liking to a member of your staff obviously unnerved you. Perhaps, my friend here has stepped on your toes, or maybe *you* are the one who needs to back off and find a man your own age. Better yet, why not just find anyone. It's obvious from the stress on your face that you need one."

Ms. Clara *snake-in-the-grass* d' Beaux eyes Bonnie with angry eyes. "And just who the hell are you?" she asks under her breath.

"Someone you would want not to fuck with, lady!" Bonnie hisses quietly between clenched teeth.

Just then, Tyriq steps up and is in the middle of it all. "What's going on here?"

We part, and I look at him and found tears of anger welling up in my eyes.

"Tyriq, I am so sorry about this. This is crazy. It shouldn't be happening. I've stepped into something that I shouldn't have.

I'm going to leave and go back to the hotel. Come on, Bonnie, let's go."

"Wait a minute," Tyriq says and puts out an arm to keep me from stepping away. "Ms. Clara, what did you say?"

"Tyriq, this is neither the time nor the place for this," d' Beaux says.

"I know, but I don't like it. Denise, I'm going to stop by tonight, if it's okay with you."

"Yes, that's fine," I sigh and turn to leave. But stop to look at Ms. Clara *not-really-worth-the-time-of-day* d' Beaux. "I don't know what I've done to you or why you seem to have such a problem with me, but I don't bother anyone. Jealousy in any form isn't a good look for anyone."

She just looks back and forth between Tyriq and me, turns on her heels, and walks away in a huff. Tyriq holds my hand briefly and squeezes it warmly. Even as I stand in a stew of anger and sadness, I also feel incredible passion from him. I don't know how, but he calms me.

"Are you ready? " Bonnie asks.

"Yeah, let's roll."

We leave the store with Tyriq standing there, staring after us. The many shoppers continue to pick through the field of bras and panties, completely oblivious to all that just happened.

Twenty-Six

"*Jacob Younger.*"

"Hi, Daddy, it's me."

"Hey, baby girl! How you doin'? It's good to hear from you. Are you back in town yet?

"No, no. I'm still down here in New Orleans. It's hot down here. I'm just trying to keep cool."

"Hey, hey, I know it's hot. I've been there. Deodorant doesn't have much of a fightin' chance in that heat and humidity."

"So, Daddy, did you go on the Atlantic City trip?"

"I sure did."

"How was it?"

"It was great, but things have changed since your mama and I went years ago. The boardwalk isn't the big thing now. It's all the gambling and things. It's a fast, fast town now. Didn't do much gambling, though, I did try some of the slot machines. I think the name one-armed bandit is right. Those things will rob you blind if you don't get up and take a breather."

Daddy sounds so happy and alive, even more than usual.

"Daddy, you didn't mention Ms. Sadie Jackson. Did you go with her?" There is a pause on the phone before he answers.

"Mmmm, yes, I did."

144

"And...?"

"Y'know, it was actually fine. She's a nice lady. We talked about a lot of things, she being a widow too and all."

"Were there any sparks?"

"Sparks? Oh, I don't know about all that. Like I said, she's a nice lady and good company. Honestly, even if there was more to the story, a gentleman never tells."

Daddy, always a gentleman. I wish I can talk to him about my drama.

"Denise, is everything okay? You sound a little distracted, baby girl."

Dang, is he reading my mind?

"Daddy, I'm fine really, I guess it's just the heat getting to me a little. I've been going and going since getting here. There's so much to do at these conferences, you know. I just haven't taken the time to really absorb and enjoy the city."

And even in the hour or so since leaving the lingerie shop, I'm feeling horrible pangs of longing for Tyriq. Stop lying and tell your daddy what's going on.

"I understand, baby girl. Don't work too hard. Take a break when you get a moment—"

There is a knock on the door. "Denise, it's me, Tyriq."

"Daddy, I have to run, there's someone at the door." "Okay, okay...um, one more thing."

"Yes, Daddy?"

"When you're ready to talk, you know where to find me." He knows something is troubling me.

"Yes, Daddy, I know. I gotta go. I love you."

"I love you too, baby doll."

"Denise, are you there?"

"Just a moment, Tyriq."

I get up and find myself almost running to the door. I slow down, stop, take a deep breath, and open the door. Tyriq is standing there with a mystified look on his face. It's replaced with loving relief as soon as he sees me.

"Come in honey," I say.

"Denise, I have to apologize for what happened earlier. I'm so sorry and embarrassed. I don't know why Ms. Clara—"

I press my body and lips against him so fast that his back hit the door with a dull thump. I couldn't help myself. My hands cradle his face, and my thumbs frame his lips. I paint across his tongue like an artist creating a masterpiece. I feel really vulnerable and desirous of him. My head is swimming with longing, and my heart is beating like a bass drum in my chest. I can feel him begin to fill and thicken against my leg.

Denise, that's a dick, a for-real one! Make no mistake about it!

"Tyriq, I missed you just today," I whisper with overheated lust from the bottom of my lungs. "Tell me you missed me, tell me you want me, Honey."

"I want you. Denise!" he says between hungry kisses. "You're all I want."

I open my eyes wide with a smile and look into his but continue to press his back to the door and grind my body against his. I can feel the volume of my horniness increase, and the lips between my legs squeak with moisture.

"Denise, I want to make love to you, now," Tyriq whispers in my ear as he grapples at my erect and wonderfully sore nipples.

"No!" I say and tease his earlobe with my teeth. "I want you to fuck me hard, like you just want to get yours. Don't worry, I'll get mine!"

Tyriq leans his head back, looks me in the eyes, and lifts the summer strolling dress I am wearing above my waist. His hands caress around my hips, searching.

"What, no panties?"

"I don't wear them, unless I have to, just a few days a month."

A mischievous smile appears in the corner of his mouth, and I kiss it. "C'mon, baby," I say. "Come get yours."

He smack-grabs the roundness of my ass and lifts me off the floor. I wrap my legs around him, and he walks me across the suite to the window. "What are you doing?" I ask.

"Getting mine," he says. "Get down."

I unwrap my legs from around his waist and stand on the floor. Tyriq spins me around to face the undressed window. He bends me over, and I press my hands against the window frame to keep my face from pressing against the glass. I hear him unzip his pants as I watch tourists in the Quarter walk back and forth beneath a darkening sky, two stories below. He reaches around my waist with a thick-muscled arm and lifts my hips.

Tyriq enters me from behind gently, slowly, deliberately, and begins to move all the way in, all the way out, and then in again.

Condom, Denise, con-dom! Have you just completely lost your mind?

I don't care. It is just the way I want it, a fuck. I suck air through my wide-open mouth and continue to watch the people walk below us. It is titillating. I can hear and feel the suction of air as Tyriq dips and raises his hips to empty me and then fill me. My chin bounces gently on my chest to his rhythm.

Sweet-sweet good!

That is all I could think until I raise my head to look across the street at the open window of another hotel. At first, I am startled and then even more turned on to see a young white couple standing in the window staring at us. They are embraced in a prom pose and watching. I give them a smirk of confidence, and the woman blows me a kiss.

I close my eyes, shriek, and then shudder. The force of a gigantic climax implodes between my legs, up my chest, and around my thighs, three or four contractions, or maybe five or six.

How the hell do I know?

Tyriq grunts and thrusts against my ass, now drenched with my lustful sweat, and then he comes. I am wet, throbbing, and sore, and it feels sooo deliciously good. We both fall back into the seat of one of the overstuffed occasional chairs. He is still in me. His suit and shirt are still on. His pants are at his ankles. My dress is twisted and wrinkled above my thighs and partially soaked with sweat.

I lean back against his chest, which is rising and falling as he tries to catch his breath. I crane my neck to look at his beautiful face. He is so fine, and I am about to tell him so when a laugh escapes from me. He frowns at first and then looks down at our clothes and starts laughing himself. We laugh and giggle, stop, and then launch into yet another fit of uncontrollable cackling. We just lost it. We laugh as hard as we loved. I look out the window and across the street. My young couple is no longer there, but their curtains are closed.

Twenty-Seven

We wake up from a catnap and shower together. I order room service dinner for both of us. We say little while we eat. We are both famished from the day and from our jumping up and down all over each other. It is almost ten o'clock when we finish eating. Now it is time for me to figure out what is going on. Now, it is time to talk. "Tyriq, honey, we need to talk."

"Yes, we do." His face is open and calm. "I think that's a good idea. You know a lot about me, but honestly I don't know much about you. Other than you're beautiful, sexy, and great in bed, warm, sensitive, and caring—"

"Enough with the compliments already, I'm serious." I am chest deep in his charm again and treading water.

"I'm serious too, Denise, but what did you want to talk about?"

"I want to talk about what we're doing and what happened today with Clara."

"I figure you would. I'm really sorry about that."

"You don't have to be sorry about that. It's not your fault. It's just that this is new and so fast for me. It's exciting, yes! But what is it? What is this? It's a bit of a whirlwind for me.

I've wrestled with the difficult fact that you are only twenty-three years old. Yes, dear, I remember your birthday is Tuesday, but honestly, the extra year doesn't offer me much comfort. My head is spinning, and the reality is, I'm going to be gone by next Thursday. That's one week from today."

Tyriq listens with that same sad face I saw earlier today at the lingerie shop. I stand up and begin to pace back and forth across the living room of the suite.

"And what's up with Clara anyway?"

He sighs, drops face into his hands, and speaks without looking up, "Y'know, I could say simply 'it is what it is' and leave it at that. I could put another hash mark on my belt or above my bed and tell the fellas 'I hit that' when I talk about you, or could just say I knocked the bottom out of it—"

And you wouldn't be lying, baby. You did knock the bottom out of this.

"But the truth of the matter is, that's not who I am. Am I looking for a wife? I don't know, but I am looking for an opportunity for loving—real, authentic loving. I'm looking for passionate compatibility, a good fit. We have no history, no common geography, and no nothing really, except this: our souls have met and brought us together, even if it was against our better judgments."

He stands up, looks me in the eyes, and embraces me. I put my head on his shoulder and close my eyes.

What are you doing? What are you going to do with this young man?

"That's what I want, Denise. What do you want?"

Good question.

"I don't know, baby!" I sit in one of the chairs and look up at him standing over me. "I really don't. I came here to work, not to play. I don't have anyone at home or even a prospect. Maybe that's because I wasn't looking. Maybe it's because I was so absorbed with work and mourning the death of my mother that I didn't think about it anymore after I dumped the last guy. I took care of my own physical needs because I did not want the brother-hassle that comes with relationships or even relating closely. But this is so...so different, and so good. But it can't go anywhere. I don't plan to come back to New Orleans for something that just feels like a fling."

"Is that what it really feels like to you?" he says with sadness.

"Yes...and no. I don't just hop in the sheets with anyone. That's not my thing."

"How would I know that?" he asks quietly.

"Because I'm telling you that's the way it is. That's not who I am."

"Let me say this about that. If I didn't believe you and didn't care, then, yes, it's just a fling and a notch on my belt. But I believe you because you said so. That's all I need, and that's the first step toward trust."

Damn! That's deep. Has any man you've ever dated accepted your word as gospel before? Never! Do you know anyone like that? Did Daddy accept Mama's word just because she said so?

"Honey, listen, what you're saying makes a lot of sense, but I don't know what I want, and we live so far apart. I don't like long-distance relationships. I don't think they work. Let's just say, for the sake of argument that we pursue this *loving friendship,* how would that work?"

"Funny you should ask. I've been seriously considering the apprenticeship offer Bonnie made earlier this week. Honestly, Denise, it has very little to do with you. It's just that I have to get away from New Orleans and move on with my life. I've been a student, a community activist, and a whole lot of other things, but I need to grow, and I can't do it here. Bonnie's offer is right up my alley. I can do the TV thing, learn from her, and if you want, we could see each other on the weekends or whenever.

Isn't Washington, DC only about one hundred miles from Baltimore?"

"Actually, it's only about forty miles away."

"Really? That close, huh? Wow! That's right up the street." Tyriq's eyes brighten. "Well, I'll tell you this. I'm not going to get very far pursuing a career as a lingerie store manager."

A worried laugh makes my chest jump. "What about money? Most internships, apprenticeships, or programs like Bonnie's don't pay at all. Twenty thousand dollars isn't enough money to scrape out a living for a year in Baltimore."

"I'll sell my house. If I leave here, I won't come back to live. Besides, I have a few extra quarters stashed away for emergencies. If I do well, and I plan on it, I could get a career starter gig in Baltimore or even DC. I do have some well-connected friends in the federal government."

He looks at me and flashes an eyebrow raise at me. *That* really makes me whisper a short laugh.

"You think you're pretty smart, don't you?"

"No, I'm just a planner. I know I'm young, but I've had to do a lot on my own. If we work out, I'm sure we could be a great team. If we don't work out, remember this: I will *always* be your friend. That's how we started. That's one of the things Clara has stressed to me for a long-time friendship and planning."

What else has that woman stressed to you? That's another thing you need to get straight..

"Tyriq, I need you to tell me something, and I need the truth. What's the deal with you and Clara? Remember, just as I felt something between us when we first met, I also know you two have something going on. I can feel it, and it's not making me comfortable."

He sighs and turns his back to me.

I don't like this.

"You're right. I do have something to tell you about Clara, a lot in fact."

Uh-oh, here it comes! He's sleeping with that old bitch. I knew it!

I stand up and walk around to face him with my hands on my hips. I have already put oil on the hinges of my neck, and my right index finger is ready to do the back-and-forth pissed-off waggle.

"Denise, I've known Clara for a very long time. We are very close, closer than you might imagine."

I knew it! Here it comes. Dirty old woman!

"She is more to me than a boss, more than a mentor, and we are absolutely more than friends. She is my mother."

Oh shit!

Twenty-Eight

"Tyriq, what are you saying? *That* woman is your mother!?" He tightens his lower lip against his upper lip and nods his head but doesn't say a word. "But that's not what you told me. You told me that your mother is in a mental institution. Is that a lie too? Didn't you just give me one of your 'keys to the city' lectures about the first steps to trust?"

"Wait a minute, Denise, sit down, and let me explain. This is very important."

I am not in the mood to sit down, nor am I truly about the business of listening to what he has to say. All of a sudden, I am afraid. Not only do I want to slow this down, I want to stop it altogether.

"Denise, please . . ." His voice is soft, apologetic, almost pleading. I sigh and plop down in the chair. I am not happy, but I am going to listen, even if it all ends right here as fast as it started.

"This is very complicated and also very serious. I need you to listen very carefully. I have two mothers, sort of. The woman in the mental institution *is* the woman who raised me until the day my daddy was murdered. For the first twelve years of my life, that is the woman I called Mama. Ms. Clara is the woman who gave birth to me."

Huh?

"I know this is puzzling . . ."

"Ya think?"

"Ms. Clara was, among other things, my father's mistress when he was running numbers in New Orleans. Very few people knew about that. It was a big secret. She could and did keep secrets of her own, including the location of the money my father took from the mob. She got pregnant and had me. Somehow, my father convinced his wife that I would be better off, safer even, if I stayed with them instead of Ms. Clara. There are no papers or court documents identifying me as the child of anyone other than Ms. Clara. I guess you could call it a long-term babysitting arrangement."

This is crazy!

"As I said, there were other things Ms. Clara was. One of them was very smart. I also said very few people knew she was my father's mistress. Very few, but there were some, and they were very dangerous people. My father entrusted her with the location of the money so that if anything happened to him or Ms. Clara, there would be enough money to take care of me and Mama."

"Wait a minute," I said. "Why didn't he tell your mother about the money? Or did he trust his whore more than he trusted the woman he loved?"

Tyriq doesn't like my mean-spirited question. I can see the disgust on his face, but he keeps talking.

"Actually, he loved them both from what Ms. Clara tells me, but he also saw that my mother was having a slow mental breakdown. She said it was like a leaking faucet in a bathtub. Not enough to bother you about fixing at first, but you noticed the dripping. It was one tiny drop of mental decline every so often. My father noticed it. Ms. Clara says he didn't tell my mother because of that, and then he was gone, and she went over the edge."

"You said Ms. Clara was smart. What did she do?"

"She told me that she had documentation outlining the illegal activities of the Mini-Mob in New Orleans and the entire state of Louisiana. My father gave it to her. I'm talking about everything from prostitution to illegal gambling, murder for hire, drugs, all that stuff. If anything 'unpleasant' like death should happen to her or me, her attorney would turn her will over to the state and federal authorities. It was our insurance policy. The Mini-Mob knew this, but that didn't prevent them from killing my father. I guess they wanted to make sure she understood that they were serious."

"Why didn't you tell me this in the beginning?"

"Oh yeah, right. I can see myself now, dropping that kind of stuff on you, when we started talking to each other. Don't forget, you were and still are skeptical about how we interact because of our age difference. I didn't want to scare you away."

He makes a good point, again.

"Are you in any danger? Hell, am I?"

He laughs and strokes my face with his hand.

"No, baby, we are safe, very safe. The Mini-Mob is long gone, killed off by rivals or by their own greed and even old age. We used the money to help set ourselves up. Ms. Clara bought the mansion that houses the lingerie store. I bought the little house I live in now and paid for my college tuition."

"Did you spend it all?"

"Oh no, I have almost $40,000 in cash left. There is more that's invested in stock and stuff. That's why I told you I can go to Baltimore, and I'll be fine."

"Damn! How much money did your father take from the mob?"

"Honestly, I don't know, but he ran numbers for them for more than fifteen years, I'm told. I saw a news report on the Mini-Mob once that said they were worth more than $50,000,000 by the time their reign of the streets ended. Daddy wasn't a street thug. He was a boss of bosses. I guess he was kind of a like a corporate senior vice president for the numbers racket. But he got fired, and in the underworld, getting fired means murder."

Wow! This was a lot to absorb. Drama and more!

Whatcha gonna do now, homegirl?

"Is there anything else you haven't told me, Tyriq?"

"Actually, there's quite a bit, but only because we haven't been together long enough to discover each other the way we should. There are no more secrets, just things that I will tell you, eventually."

Slow it on down, Denise. He doesn't know everything about you either. Just take it slow. Don't let your Afro grow!

"So when are you going to tell Ms. Clara about your decision?"

"I'll tell her after my birthday get-together on Tuesday. That'll give me enough time to talk to Bonnie about the details of the Baltimore job."

"You know she's going to hit the ceiling when you tell her."

"Yes, I know, but this is my life, and it's something I would do even if I never met you."

"Oh, honey, but I'm so glad you did meet me."

"Yes, Denise. So am I."

Twenty-Nine

Tyriq spent the night in my room, but there was no lovemaking, no sex, no nothing, just sleep. Even the catnap we took earlier wasn't enough to rest us. We slept like babies. He left early Friday morning to go home and change his clothes. He had to go back to work and, of course, to handle his business. I had my own agenda for the day. I was not interested in much at the conference, and it ended at noon and give the attendees a three-day weekend before hitting the last few days, starting on Monday. Today, I needed to check in with Bruce at the office and with Saundra.

The hotel suite felt strangely empty and almost cool. I walk to the window where the young voyeurs watched our shameless display of lust only a day before. Their curtains are closed, and the street below is only beginning to come alive with people, cars, and the energy that makes the French Quarter's heart beat.

I wonder what Tyriq is going to tell his boss-mother-pain-in-my-ass. I also wonder how I got into this in the first place. I didn't see it coming. Am I working so hard that I stop trying to have time for men or just a man? Do I look that vulnerable, that desperate, and that horny that I am a target for an easy lay?

Yes, you were, girl, but you also wanted to get laid—no, fucked, and fucked good. You've been messing around with BOB, the good old dependable battery-operated boyfriend for so long, you forgot that an upgrade wasn't a plug-in but a man, a real man, young or not. You wanted the kind of man who could knock the bottom out of it, fuck the perm out of your hair if you had one. That's exactly what you got. Yeah, it's been awhile, so it took you awhile to remember what a good dick is. After Tyriq took you to his place and lit your ass up with those orgasmic acrobatics, there is no question about it. And what is an easy lay anyway? Mama used to talk about fast girls when you were young, but now you're a grown woman, a grown-ass woman. If you want to abstain from sex, be celibate or even sell-a-bit, sleep with one man or twelve, that's your grown-ass business, so stop trippin'!

I sigh because I know my thoughts are right. It is my life, my body. Why shouldn't I do what I want and get what I want?

But what else do you want, Denise? It's your heart too. Go home next week and just see what happens. If he comes to Baltimore, see him and see what's up. If it works out, it works out. If it doesn't...next! You'll get something out of it, or you'll get some. That will be enough to smooth those stress wrinkles out of your forehead and clean out those vines that were growing between your legs.

Nothing is growing between my legs at the moment. I am a little sore from last night—no, very sore. Damn! Ouch! What did he put in me, anyway? Now I know what they mean when they say it hurts so good. I need to soak in the tub. I run water in the tub that's almost the size of a queen-size mattress and pour in some foaming bubble bath. Thick, puffy clouds of bubbles form, and a fog of steam fills the bathroom. Then the phone rings. It's Bruce from the office.

"Good morning," I say.

"Good morning, Ms. Younger. How are you?" Bruce asks with a level of cheer in his voice that surprises me.

"I'm fine, Bruce. I was actually planning to call you today, just to check on things."

"See there, great minds think alike. I just beat you to the punch. We miss you around here. Before you ask, things are going very well. The Fellows cell phone deal is done, and we should take delivery around the time you get back. They sent your package yesterday as a gesture of good faith. I'm working on another contract right now to provide more office space near the new federal building in Prince George's county. This could be a sweet deal and well under our initial cost projections."

"Wow, Bruce, you really are on the ball. Do I *need* to come back?" I joke. "Absolutely," he laughs. "This place wouldn't be the same without you.

As I said, we really miss you around here. There's been a lot of work, but certainly not a lot of life in the office."

That's so sweet of him to say, and he hasn't called me ma'am yet. *He listens!*

"Bruce, I appreciate that. Tell the staff not to get too comfortable with my absence. I will be back in the office on Friday. My flight leaves on Thursday morning."

"Why don't you just take Friday off? It's just one more day in the workweek."

"I thought about it, but I really need to come in and see how things are going. I will have been gone for two weeks, after all."

"Either way, it will be good to see you. If you have time and aren't too tired, maybe we can sit down after work for a quick bite so that I can tell you about some of the long-range plans I've been thinking about."

"I'll have to let you know when I get back. I don't know what my schedule is, but pencil me in, and I'll see if I can work it out."

"Will do, by the way, I didn't ask you about the conference. How is it? Are you learning a lot?"

"Bruce, you have no idea what I've learned! It's been a true experience so far."

"Is it hot there? I know heat. I'm from north Florida, but I'm sure

New Orleans can be unbearable at times."

"Oh yes! It's hot down here, like you wouldn't believe. I don't think

I'll ever get used to it, but I do like it here."

Bruce, if you knew just how hot it's been for me, you would wonder if your boss had lost her mind.

"Well, Ms. Younger, is there anything else? Do you need a pick up from the airport?"

"No, I'm fine, that's all. I'll see you next week. Thanks for calling."

"No problem, hon. See you when you get back."

Hon?

I pause, squint, and twist my face. I am about to say something when I hear a soft click on the other end, and Bruce is gone. That was strange. Maybe it was just a slip into comfortable conversation.

Oh, never mind, Denise. You have better things to do than to worry about Bruce.

Thirty

Before stepping outside, I put on an ivory-colored cotton gauze dress and a pair of high-heeled wedge espadrilles. My nakedness just under the material is comfortable and almost cool, even as the thick heat of the French Quarter leans on me from all sides. By the time I leave the hotel, it is almost noon. I have been in New Orleans for one week and feel as if

I had spent a mini lifetime here.

I walk along the streets sightseeing and relishing the time alone. I make my way slowly through the streets, alternately nodding and ignoring the glances and comments of the few men who walk by. I imagine a few of them think they can see through my dress or want to. I window-shop at the antique stores and galleries squeezed next to the narrow sidewalks. I soak up the strong, cool breezes of air-conditioning blowing through open doorways.

This is freedom, Denise. This is freedom from work pressure, freedom from man pressure, freedom from your own self-induced pressure. Free your mind, and your ass will follow. Free to be alone with your thoughts, just for a moment!

I step off the curb that opens to the entrance of an alley, and without watching my step, my heel twists on the end of an unbroken soda bottle.

RIIIIIPPPP! The left heel of my espadrille shreds like an old wicker basket, and down I go, hard! My arms pinwheels and catch nothing until my ass breaks my fall on the cobblestones. I sit there for a moment, embarrassed and alone. No one saw me fall into the alley. If they did, they weren't stopping to help.

"Where is Prince Charming when you need him?" I say aloud. "Will I do?"

I look up and into the crusty, sun-worn red face of man who looks as if he worked outside all his life. He is standing inside the shallow alcove of a closed door just a few feet down the alley. He offers me his hand and peers down at me with reddish brown eyes that look as if they had seen one hundred years. On he his bare forearm there's an old fading tattoo. A pair of twin humps facing each. I'm instantly uncomfortable, but I don't know why. His hands are thick and a little dusty, but after my tumble, I am a little dusty too.

"Oh, thank you so much!"

He lifts me to my feet and pulls me toward the alcove a little farther from the street. I take off my ripped shoe and then the other, and put them in my hand with my purse. I look at the dirt that redesigned my dress.

"I don't think anybody saw me fall. That was so kind of you."

"Ya probably won't dink so after dis here, missy," he says through gritted teeth.

I look up with a question on my face and find the answer at the business end of a very large, and wickedly sharp knife.

SHIT, DENISE! You're being mugged!

"Try to scream, and I'll shush you with dis here blade. Gimme da purse, and I'll let ya go."

I am pissed and scared. I want to kick him in the balls, but the knife is close enough to my face to be out of focus. I lift my arm and don't say anything.

He snatches the purse from my trembling fingers, runs off down the alley, and disappears. I stand there staring after him in the dark shadows of the alley, barefoot, dusty, and once again alone with my thoughts. That's how my day started. I should have kept my ass at the hotel. I'm ready to go home.

Thirty-One

I probably should call the police, but I don't. I limp back to the hotel with a bruised butt and ego. I probably look like a woman on the front end of homelessness: dirty from the tumble off the curb and the shoes in my hand that started as great fashion-statements are now candidates for the nearest trashcan. I hold on to them until I get to the hotel lobby and then toss them at a trash bin being pushed by one of the hotel staff. My defeated walk past the front desk does not go unnoticed by the clerk.

"Ma'am, you okay? What happened?"

I try to sound bright and almost cheery, but I don't think I quite pull it off.

"Oh, I'm okay, I just took a little tumble in the Quarter and tore my shoes, but I'm fine. I'm going up to my room, thanks."

I can see the clerk's gaze mixed with concern and disbelief out of the corner of my eyes, but I am not in the mood to chat about my terrifying midday adventure. I press a hand against the cool metal of the elevator frame and push the "up" button.

"Ma'am, if you need anything, anything at all, please call me at the front desk. That's what we're here for."

"Thank you, I'll let you know!" I say through clenched teeth, more at the soreness of my ass than impatience. The clerk takes

165

a step back from me for a last look and then quickly walks back to the front desk. Another clerk is handling a growing line of people checking in and checking out. The elevator doors open, and it is empty...almost. I step in with my head down and bump right into Bonnie. *Damn! Sistah can't catch a break.*

"What the hell happened to you?"

"Girl, you don't even want to know," I sigh.

"Denise, you are a mess...," Bonnie says and gives me a supportive shoulder hug. "I was going to grab a bite, but I need to sit with you for a moment. C'mon, let's get you to your room. And where are your shoes? Dayum! What happened?"

I give up and give in, feeling more vulnerable now that Bonnie is here like a big sis. We step off the elevator and walk down the hall toward my room.

"I got mugged!"

"Oh shit!" Bonnie says. "Are you okay? Did you get hurt? Did you call the police? Were you by yourself?"

"Yes, no, no, and yes, I was by myself. If I weren't, this probably wouldn't have happened."

I don't have my key to the hotel room. My purse is gone

"This is not my day," I grunt. "I've got to go back down to the front desk and get another key." At this point, I can feel warm tears begin wetting my face. I am really starting to lose it. I've never been robbed before. I slowly realize how close I had come to getting my throat cut.

"I'll go and get your key for you. Just stay here. I'll use the courtesy phone and run down the steps. It will be faster. I'll only be gone a minute, sit tight!"

Bonnie picks up the wall phone and calls the front desk. She tells them what she needs without spilling what few details she knows about my ordeal. She hangs up the phone, gallops down the hall to the emergency stairway exit, and disappears through the door. I stand in the middle of the empty hallway, feeling very alone. I start thinking about what Bonnie told me about her ordeal years ago that left her with an Al Capone scar in the middle of the beauty of her face. I can't imagine what that did to her emotionally back then. Maybe caring for me is an instinctive reaction to the fear she felt when she was attacked years ago. *Been there, done that, got the T-shirt.* The elevator doors open, and Bonnie steps out, but she isn't alone. There is very tall and ruggedly handsome brother in a light blue shirt and dark pants. It takes me a moment to realize Bonnie has a police officer in tow. I really don't want to talk to anyone about this. I just want to let it go. I lean back against the wall next to my room door and then hop off. Yup, my already-plump ass is wake-you-up sore and probably swollen from the alley fall.

"Here she is, Officer," Bonnie says as she walks up. "I have your key, let's go inside."

"Bonnie, I really didn't want to file a report. I'm okay. I just want to go in the room and try to forget about it."

"Miss, I'm Officer Marshall Jackson. You may not want to file a report, but we might find the guy or your belongings, and we want to be able to return them to you or even get you to ID him."

Bonnie slides the key into the lock and lets us all into my room. I step into the bathroom and look my face. I look old with worry and sadness. I think they call it rode hard and hung up wet. I feel like it. Tears mixed with sweat walk mascara streaks down my face. I look as dusty as I felt. My dress is a mess, and I am sad and pissed at the day.

"Officer, I don't mean to be rude, but do you actually think the New Orleans Police Department is going to start a dragnet to find some raggedy-ass country white man who stole my purse? I don't think so. Besides, the purse was worth more than what was in it. He can keep the fifty or so dollars that were in it. I locked my wallet in my room safe. It was more frightening for me than profitable for him. I'm safe, so I'd feel better if you would leave and let me clean up and calm down."

Officer Jackson seems unfazed by my insistence that he find crime to fight elsewhere. But he decides not to fight me. He pulls a business card out of his left breast pocket and hands it Bonnie.

"Miss, I'm leaving my card with your friend here. If you change your mind, please call us. New Orleans isn't perfect, but we still try to protect the tourists and the people that live here. We want you to come back to visit. Are you sure you're okay?"

"I'm fine!" I say without looking away from the mirror.

Mr. Tall and Ruggedly Handsome Policeman says something to Bonnie and then leaves the room. I put my hands on the sink, hang my head, and exhale. Bonnie steps into the bathroom doorway and rubs my back between my shoulder blades. I look at her over my shoulder.

"Bonnie, thanks for coming to my rescue. I thought I could deal with this on my own, but I guess I really needed a friend."

"Hey, hey, sis, that's what friends are for. Do you want to talk about what happened?"

"Not really, but I could use an extra favor."

"Name it."

I walk past Bonnie to the desk and scribble a phone number on a sheet of paper. I hand it to her.

"Could you please call Tyriq for me? Just tell him to stop by when he gets off this afternoon. I wanted a bit of a break from him, just to breathe. After this, though, I really could use a man's support, even if it's a young man."

Bonnie looks at me, smiles a worried smile with the corner of her mouth, and picks up the phone on the desk. I take off my clothes and jump in the shower. When I get out of the shower and dry off, Bonnie is gone. There is a note on the desk from her. It says Tyriq will come by after six o'clock and she will call later to check on me. I grab one of the gowns I bought from Tyriq's store and put it on. I am not feeling sexy, just vulnerable...still. I collapse backward on the bed and immediately howl at the persistent soreness of my butt cheeks. I gently roll over onto my stomach and fall asleep, waiting for Tyriq to come.

Thirty-Two

I am awakened from my nap by Tyriq's knock at my door.
My ass is still sore from the spill I took in the French
Quarter. My mind is still troubled by the double mountain tattoo
on the mugger's arm.

*Yeah girl, you were jacked ol' school style. Vulnerable,
violated and fresh meat for the slaughter. You need to watch
where you're walking, where you're going and be aware of your
surroundings. The next time, you could loose more than your
purse and fifty dollars.*

Tyriq embraces me at the door and immediately he senses
something's wrong.

"Denise, are you okay?"

"I'm fine, fine. It's just been a difficult day. That's all. Have a
seat so we can talk."

"Difficult? How so what happened?"

"Don't worry about it Sweetie. Sit down. Let's talk."

He sits on the plush sofa in the living room of the suite. I
stand at the window looking out on the street below and let out
a long sigh.

"Tyriq, honey...what do you *really* know about me?"

"What do you mean?"

"I mean exactly what I asked," I say gently. "What do you *really* know about me?"

He pauses, and I can feel him thinking, but I don't turn from the window. The sun is fading, and the street below is thickening with people. "I know that you're a wonderful, caring, and sensitive person. You've shown me that you're open to friendships and loving relationships. You're kind and a great listener . . ."

"I'm a good fuck and an easy one too, wouldn't you say?" The bolt of anger that runs through me surprises both of us. Tyriq stands up with his hands open at his sides.

"Whoa, whoa, what's going on? Where did *that* come from? What did I do?"

"What do you know about me, Tyriq?" I turn on my heels from the window. My anger and voice rise. "What's my favorite color?"

"I don't know."

"Well, um, what do I do for a living?"

"You didn't tell me, other than you work for the federal government." His eyes and mouth are wide-open with confusion.

"You didn't ask me what I did for a living!"

"No, I didn't. It wasn't really important."

"Not important, huh? But you know enough about me to get the pussy, don't you? I know all about the drama with your mother and your father and the Mini-Mob. Do you know about *my parents*? What's *my* father's name or my mother's? Are they living? Who is my best friend? Who is yours? Do you have a girlfriend? A good-looking thick-dick young brother like you *has* to have a ton of them! You didn't learn those little sex tricks at Xavier's University's library!"

Tears begin streaming down my face.

Denise, you are losing control. Why are you so pissed off? Loosen up, girl! Get it together. Calm down.

Tyriq walks toward me. His face darkens with confusion and mystery.

"Denise, what's going on? What did I do?"

"Tyriq, look...this thing with you this past week was just that, *a thing*! We've had a couple of rolls in the hay. You got your freak on, and so did I, so let's just call it what it is. I'm going to go back to DC in a few days, and I'll have some great memories about a great time, but that's it. We will go on with our lives."

"Wow, I didn't know you felt that way about me, about this. I know things happened fast, but if my memory serves me correctly, *you* were the one who came on to me after our first dinner together. I liked you when I first met you. I am wonderfully attracted to you, but I was more interested in feeling your spirit than feeling you up! If all you wanted to do was hit the sheets, I would have left you alone!"

"How could you possibly know what you wanted from me? You just met me. You didn't know me, and you don't know me now!"

"But I know what I felt, Denise. I felt that I wanted to know you. The first time I saw you, my heart was beating so hard in my chest. I thought I was getting sick, that maybe I was having a heart attack. It wasn't just your face, your body, your voice. It was your *you*, all of you! I wanted *you*. Do you believe in love at first sight? I never did before, never thought about it until you walked into the shop a week ago.

"Every day since seeing you that night, the feeling stuck with me. I can't explain it. It's in the air around you. It fills me up, rushes over me at night, and disturbs my sleep. Even standing here near you now, and I can't make it go away!"

I put my hands over my face still wet with tears. My anger drains away, replaced with a longing and a strange sadness. I sit on the bed and look at up at him. His sadness matches mine.

"Tyriq, I'm sorry. I shouldn't have shouted at you like that, but honestly, what am I going to do with you, really? You're so young . . ."

"My birthday is Tuesday. I'll be a year older," he says with a smile.

"Don't joke. I'm serious, baby. You want to do this thing at Bonnie's TV station, but I think you're doing it for the wrong reason. I'm a grown woman in the middle of my career. You want to just pull up stakes and move halfway across the country, hoping that we might develop more than lust and infatuation for each other. Honey, let me tell you, reality ain't like that."

"Hold on a minute. I'm young. I know that—and maybe even inexperienced in the ways of the world—but I'm not dumb. I'm done with school. Do you really think I want to sit on my hands and be the manager of a woman's lingerie shop for the rest of my life? There's a world out there I haven't seen and know nothing about. Here's my chance to see it, to be a part of it, to do something with it.

"Don't misunderstand me. If I never met you and this opportunity presented itself, I would still take it. Meeting you just made the decision easier. "Oh, about the girlfriend thing? I don't have one, haven't had one in a while. The ones I meet are too young for me, not in body, but in mind. But if you have a problem with me moving near you and cramping *your* style, I can stay in Baltimore and find my own way. It won't change the way I feel about you now or ever, but no one can ever accuse me of staying where I'm not wanted!"

"That's not what I meant, honey." I really begin to feel the full weight of his emotions.

Duh! He really digs you, girl. Your pussy must be the bomb! Stop it, Denise! He says it's not about that. Well, what is it?

"I just don't want you to make a mistake or have regrets. There's an eleven-year age difference between us. You are just starting out in life, and I wouldn't want to cramp *your* style. There are quite a few cuties and plenty of hoochies in Baltimore."

Tyriq sits on the edge of the bed next to me. His warm, handsome smile slips into the corner of his mouth.

"I'm not the only one in the room who doesn't *know* someone. There's still quite a bit about me you don't know, or at least you underestimate me. I'm already with a cutie, and she has a little bit of hooch in her."

I look at him with a twisted mouth and my neck rocking back and forth. "Who are you calling a 'hoochie'?"

"I'm just saying. My mother has imparted *some* wisdom to me over the years. One of them was a bit about women. She says every refined woman still needs a little bit of hoochie in her to keep her interesting, even if it's just a pinky toe's or a foot's worth, but not the whole body."

I fall back on the bed and laugh in spite of myself.

"Oh my," I sigh. "What am I going to do with this man?"

"Don't think about it. Just let it happen, just like everything this week has happened. I'm not crazy. I don't bite. I think we can learn from each other. If it works, it works. If it doesn't, it's not as if I can't take care of myself. I never said I was moving in. I have the money to take care of myself, and I made a promise to myself a long time ago, not to fail, no matter where I might be living. I can't afford to fail. I have too many things I want to do with my life.

"What *do* you want to do with your life, Tyriq?"

"Great question. Is it safe to say this is part of the learning process?"

"It's safe to say that, yes," I say.

"Well, I would like to own a chain of women's lingerie stores. But I want to make fine lingerie affordable for every woman."

"Doesn't Victoria's Secret kinda have the market cornered there?"

"No, not at all. It would be different. There would be men and women working there. Who knows best what looks good on a woman but a man? Customer service would be top-notch, and like Nightie-Night, it would be the kind of place you would want to spend time in browsing, with a tea and coffee room in the back. There would be a pedicure and manicure room with soft lighting and soft, smooth jazz playing. It would be a shopping and relaxing destination. Eventually, I would start a nonprofit division to help get decent quality clothes to the poor."

"What kind of clothes? Lingerie?" I laugh at my joke, but think better of it.

You should never laugh at someone's dreams, Denise.

Tyriq ignores my joke and gives my question a serious answer. "Actually, sweetie, think about this. You're a struggling single mother of two, and I give you and your children two or three nice, clean outfits each. Well, I would also give the mother a long satin nightgown as a gift, courtesy of my company. Nothing super fancy, but it would be an elegant finish to the donation and a way to make her feel just a little bit better about herself."

Wow! That is an idea. If a store like that existed, I'd go. Coffee, pedicures, and new panties, I am totally sold!

"For now, it's just a dream. The TV station internship would help me learn the ropes of business and meet some of the right people. This isn't just about being near you. This could change my life!"

"I had no idea about any of this."

"You didn't ask me," he smirks again. "You've made your point, touché."

A church bell tolls somewhere in the dark distance of the Quarter. I look at the digital clock next to the bed. The 12:00 glows bright red. An emotionally draining Saturday has come and gone. Tyriq sits up on the bed.

"Denise, I think I better go. It's been a long day and night for both of us."

"No, please stay. I want you to stay."

"I'm not going to stay if you meant some of the harsh things you said. It's not about the sex with me, it's about the *you, with me.*"

"I know, and I'm truly sorry about what I said. I'm just a little afraid of the rest of my life sometimes." I sit up and rub my hands across his shoulders. "Please stay?" I say with a sheepish smile. "I want you here with me tonight."

Tyriq releases a long, deep sigh and nods his head without speaking. I take him by the hand and lead him to the bathroom. We shower together, washing, holding, and kissing each other in the warm steaming streams of water. I can feel his long thickness come alive against my hips, and I turn around to face him.

"All week I've just had sex with you," I whisper to his chest. "I want to make love to you now."

"Denise, that's all I know how to do."

He palms my cheeks with his hands; I grip his neck and climb on him like a tree. My legs wrap around his trunk, but he pushes my legs down and kisses me, slowly, gently, all the while massaging knots in my neck. It's as if his fingers brought them to the surface of my skin, and the water washes them away. The kissing turns into tongue caresses underneath my chin and then between my breasts. I am starving for this as if it's the first time in a long time. Tyriq draws his hands from my neck and allows the heels of his hands to drag across my nipples as he squats below my belly button to my shaved-bare mound of Venus. He speaks in long, slow, wet whispers to my hooded bud. I want to laugh because the extra water from the shower and his lips make a surreal loud slurping sound. Like a kid drinking from a water fountain. Waves of pleasure wash over me, and I grunt, happy and almost satisfied. I push him off the balls of his feet. Tyriq lands on his ass with a wet splat. His face is drenched with me and shower water. Now it is my turn to squat over him. I lower my hips, and he enters me with a slow brilliance. The painful goodness forces my lips into an open O, and my breathing comes in syncopated starts and stops.

The water from the shower challenges my balance, and I hold on to the wall of the shower. The muscles in my thighs are burning, but I don't care. Tyriq's grip carries me with the rhythm of a lazy summer's swing, back and forth from the head to the base of his dick.

"Oh...my...gawd! This...is...so . . ." Good! I can't finish. I'm dizzy and my breathless words were wonderfully interrupted by a climax that stacks on top of another before the last is finished. I can only whimper with pleasure as my insides jump and pulsate. My vision doubles, blurs and doubles again. My skin tingles and the shower walls tilt. I can feel Tyriq's own rising tide of pleasure blending with the massage of the shower against my back.

Then...sweet, sweet darkness.

Thirty-Three

S unday opens with bliss. I wake up late in the morning
to a wonderful breakfast from room service: apple
cinnamon–stuffed French toast, glistening spicy sausage, and
coffee that embraced my tongue with caffeinated love. Tyriq had
ordered and paid for it without putting it on the room tab. I am
still feeling the aftereffects of our love *(love?)* in the shower.
Tyriq told me I passed out, but came to after he pulled me out
of the shower. I don't remember a bit of it. My body feels light
and relaxed after hours of heavy, motionless sleep. I can't ever
remember sleeping like that. Maybe that's how babies sleep,
just a few clicks above unconsciousness. It is wonderful. Tyriq
sips on coffee and watches the national news talk shows while
I gorge myself on the morning feast. We say little, and that's
okay. We're content to feel each other's company in silence.
We eventually get out of the hotel well after noon and walk the
Quarter arm in arm like comfortable old lovers. It is hot as usual,
but I've learned to ignore it. We walk for a while, and after some
prodding, Tyriq convinces me to show him where the mugging
happened the day before. I don't mention the strange tattoo on
the muggers' forearm. It's not important.

Are you sure?

We head to the alley; the cobblestones where I landed and the soda bottle I stepped on are still there. Tyriq studies the area and looks around as if to find the mugger standing nearby.

"Denise, I know you aren't going to be in town much longer, and I don't want to sound like a broken record, but please, please, please, when you are alone, be careful." His warning is stern, but his voice is gentle and comforting. I can't help but feel a rising tide of affection for him. I look into his face and press my lips to his. My tongue flickers slowly and playfully in his mouth. I feel a chill of mountainous goose bumps in spite of the heat. He pulls his mouth away but holds me in a firm embrace.

"You know something," he says. "Some people would call a public display of affection like that on a busy street, poor taste."

"Reeeally?" I chuckle mischievously. "Okay, so what do you say?"

Tyriq's eyes narrow and focus on mine. "I say, do it again."

I do as he says and give his crotch a firm, discreet squeeze. I feel a growing stiffness there. "Whatcha got working here, baby?"

"Woman, you are crazy! Let's move on before I take you somewhere and do something really nasty to you!"

"Oh? You mean you haven't already?"

"I guess, but I don't want to dump my entire bag of tricks on you at once."

"Dang, baby, sounds like I have more to look forward to."

"Of course you do, and not just in the bedroom. I told you how I feel about you, and how I'm learning to feel about you, moment by moment. I think our getting to know each other is really going to be interesting." I drop my head, thinking about what to say. "Babe, remember you've only known me for a week. I'm not perfect, not by a long shot, and I'm still wondering how far our compatibility goes beyond New Orleans. I just hope you're not disappointed with the all-of-me you get to know."

"I'm not perfect either, and I know you have a lot of concerns about us. But I say, just let things happen and see where they go. That's how I'm looking at things. One day at a time."

Tyriq's last line reminds me of a popular song Mama used to sing when I was a little girl. "*One day at a time, sweet Jesus, is all I'm asking of you.*" I wonder if Mama would approve of what her only little girl is doing with this man, or with her life.

She only wanted you to be happy. Is this what happiness is—just living in the moment until it's gone? Do you love this man for this long minute of life and wait for it to end or stretch, perhaps into an hour or two? Take it now, Denise, because you have nothing else, and it's good. Let it be good until it shows you signs of being bad. Just don't let fear get in the way of your happiness, for however long it lasts. But what about Ms. Clarabitch? Stop it, Denise. We are talking about the boy's mama. Boy? Man? Sigh! Whatever!

"Haveyoudecidedhowtotellyourmotheryoumightbeleaving?"

"You let me handle my mother, and there's no 'might' to it. I am leaving."

I tingle at the thought of seeing Tyriq on the reg. More goose bumps quack over my skin when I imagine his massive manly thickness fitting inside me again. If this is what "turned out" meant, I am completely there, inside out.

"So when are you going to tell her? I'm not really comfortable with my first interaction with her last week. We didn't get off on the right foot, and that was just a chance meeting. I'm really worried that she is going to make things hard for you."

"Denise, I want you to remember one thing. As possessive as my mother is, she loves me. I pay my own bills although she signs the check. Once I've made my decision, this one, and others, it's a done deal. She knows that and always has. I was my own man long before I became a man."

"I'll trust your judgment on this. You know her much better than I do."

"That's my girl. Hey, are you hungry?"

"I am a little, even after that huge breakfast."

"Fine, you haven't had any real Louisiana gumbo since you've been here, have you?"

"No, babe, I haven't."

"That's a sin, a crime, and shame. Let's go get some down-home, down-home."

"I'm game. Lead the way."

We walk arm and arm through the Quarter and finally stop at the Gumbo Shop. The place is old, but quaint and clean. It's packed, but the maître d' finds a table for us amid the first-timers and the long-timers. The spicy smells of gumbo that have been cooking all day make my stomach call out with a hungry growl. Tyriq hears it and laughs at me as we sit down. He orders gumbo and a couple of bottles of something called Dixie Beer.

While we are waiting, I talk about Mama, Daddy, and my life. He asks me why I am not married, and I tell him about my job and the few loves in my life. There have been men, lovers outside of the few loves, but they were like cold butter on hard toast, they just scraped or tore at my insides. Most of them just never seemed to stick. Other times, I never seemed to want to wait around until things warmed up enough for them to stick. I cut them loose before things got any more unpleasant.

Tyriq talks about his life and his focus on the next chapter of it. I ask him about his past, friends, girlfriends, and women friends, whatever! He talks about them and saves me the greasy details, giving me just enough to understand that he is no rookie when it comes to women. But something or someone is missing, and I am dying to ask him about her.

"Tyriq, aren't you forgetting someone?"

"What do you mean?" he asks, but he knows what I am talking about. "Didn't you date a woman who worked for Texaco?"

He looks away from me. His eyes squints, and his lips purse against the memory of something familiar and painful.

"How did you know about her?" He does not look at me, and I begin to feel uncomfortable. I am not going to be dishonest about what little I knew.

"A couple of students were talking about it right before your speech last week. They said she was killed in a car accident. Is that what happened?

"Yes . . ."

"If you don't want to talk about it, you don't have to. It sounds very personal and very serious. I don't want to get in your business."

He turns and looks into me with a pointed intensity I can feel as well as see.

"Denise, you *are* in my business. You are in it, under it, all over it. You have been for more than a week. Yes, it is very personal, very serious. She is the reason I'm with you now.

Me? What the hell did that mean? I had to hear this.

Thirty-Four

The Dixie Beer and the gumbo come just as Tyriq is about to tell me an intimate tale of love and death. I give him a breather while we eat and sip quietly. The beer is smooth and rich without the bite that most American beers have. I am not a beer fan, but I can drink this often if it were not so fattening.

The gumbo is better than the beer. It's better than just about anything I had ever tasted! It *is* spicy, but it does not light up my tongue. Every mouthful is a guilty pleasure and a heavenly indulgence of full flavor. It is just plain damn good! I want another beer and a bowl of gumbo.

Tyriq orders another round of both for me and gives me an "I told you so" smile. I think about what he's about to tell me. As curious as I am, this is too personal a thing to discuss in public.

Maybe it's just a too-personal or a too-painful period.

"Y'know, Tyriq, you *really don't* need to tell me about this part of your life, at least not right now. I understand. Really, I do, honey."

He looks at me with a humorless smile curled around the corners of his mouth.

"Yeah, but you really want to know, don't you?"

"Yes, I have to admit to my curiosity. I mean, what little I heard about it is intriguing. Your omitting her from our earlier conversation was a little—shall I say, suspect."

"Yes, I guess it was. I didn't mean to be deceptive. This isn't an easy thing to talk about. But if I didn't talk about her, all I've said to you about you and the way I feel would be... disingenuous."

Damn, Denise, there's a big fat twenty-dollar word for your ass!

"Did this *she* have a name?"

"Yes, she did. Her name was Viquetoria Love. That's spelled v-i-q-u-e-t-o-r-i-a, but pronounced with a long 'vee' sound at the beginning. Strange isn't it?"

Strange? Yes, but beautiful too! I'm already jealous! Tyriq sighs and continues.

"I was nineteen and a brand-new college student when I met Viq. She was young too, but ten years older than I was. She came to Xavier to lecture my class about corporate America. She was a bit of a token for Texaco. You see, Viq didn't just work for the company. She was their youngest executive. She was vice president of public relations for the Southern district at twenty-eight years old. Viq had clout, power, and of course, she was paid. "As a matter of fact, the first thing most of us thought when we saw her walk into the lecture hall was that she looked like success and smelled like money. On top of it all, she was drop-dead, freakin' gorgeous. She was graceful and sexy, a lot like you, Denise."

"Thanks for stroking my ego, babe!" I smirk a little.

He probably added that to turn down your simmering jealously. Smart man!

"Soooo, what did she look like? Was she pretty?"

"Oh yeah she was! She was tall, slender, and just beautiful. Her skin was the color of the perfect creamy Coppertone tan. Her hair was like a lion's mane of copper fire."

Tyriq faces me as he spoke but looks through me at some imaginary vision, hypnotized by his memories.

"Was she white?"

I knew you were going there! I just knew it!

"No, just a light-skinned sister, but she wasn't pale. I'll tell you, though, all that was suspect, and during the question-and-answer period after her speech, I said so. I mean, I knew she was smart, and I saw that she was good-looking, but my naiveté and all-around big-sexist, skeptical mouth basically said that she may have done *other* things to get where she was so fast."

"Wow!" I say. "You really said that?"

"Well, yeah, I did, in so many words. Back then, that's how I thought too," Tyriq says sheepishly. "She set me straight, though, just enough to embarrass me in front of my fellow students and friends. It was also just enough to prompt a sincere apology after it was all over."

"Obviously, she accepted the apology."

"Yup, she did, but there was more. She decided to teach me a real lesson about life. Maybe I should call it a foundational life lesson. Ignorance is a dangerous thing at any age. If you educate someone early in life, it can really open their eyes. That's what Viq did for me. She talked to me about education, office politics, social graces, and y'know, stuff like which fork to use, what wine went with what kind of meat, how to buy suit.

"It was all the stuff my mother tried to teach me, but I wasn't hearing it. I guess because it was coming from my mother. Not to mention the fact that I was lusting after her and didn't know it."

"How could you not have known that you wanted her?" I ask.

"I didn't know. It wasn't her body. It was her mind that I really desired. Everything she shared was interesting. It wasn't just what she said, but how she said it. She was never inappropriate, and no one saw it as being wrong. It was a mentor-mentee relationship. For two whole years, there was never more than a peck on the forehead or a kiss on the cheek from her. I met dozens of important people and ran in circles I could not have imagined. All the while, she would introduce me as her 'special project.'"

"Did you find that even a little insulting?"

"Maybe I should have, but you have to understand. Prior to this, all I knew was the drama of my personal history and the protection of my mother. This was someone who took a real interest in me outside of what little family I had. I discovered later that Viq wasn't grooming me for the world after college. She was grooming me for herself. She was making me into the man she wanted, and I went with it. I didn't know any better."

"Didn't she have boyfriends or lovers?"

"I think she did, but I never really knew. A woman as good-looking as she was had to be getting hers from somewhere. She wasn't getting it from me, at least not at the time. If there were other men around, she kept that part of her life away from me. It wasn't hard to do. During the first two years, I never went to her place. We always met at her office or on campus or at my little place.

"For a long time, I never knew where she lived. I asked her about it, but she would always say something like it wouldn't be appropriate or not today, maybe another time. But by the time we became involved, we were so close and spent so much time together, I'm pretty sure I was the only man in her life."

"How did things move from this so-called mentoring relationship to you being her lover? I mean, it had to be a heady thing for you, dating this corporate big shot and all."

I'm not jealous of this woman anymore, but I am salivating at the intrigue of the relationship Tyriq had with her. He sighs and continues with the story.

"Like I said, we had been friends for about two years when things changed. I started becoming politically active at school during my junior year. People outside of school began to take notice of things I was doing. Viq encouraged me to stand up for my fellow students, lead protests, speak out at city council meetings, testify at the state capital in Baton Rouge, stuff like that. I guess she figured I could use the big mouth that brought us together for something good."

I give him one of those "get to the good part" looks.

Okay, okay! Land the plane baby, land the plane!

"So anyway. The night of my birthday, when I turned twenty-one, she took me out. She was going to buy me my first legal drink. I guess she wanted to make sure I didn't get too drunk. That was a laugh. I wasn't much of a drinker back then, a little wine but not much more. I got smashed, plastered, lit up, too right, twisted, whatever you want to call it, I was there. We were at a bar in the warehouse district. I had two double rum and Cokes, and that's all she wrote."

"She wasn't drinking with you?"

"Oh, hell yeah! I don't remember what she drank, but I do remember the conversation. She started talking about how much she liked me and how socially and politically dangerous it was for her to do anything more than mentor me. I asked her what she was talking about, and she said, and I quote, 'If you weren't such a young tender, I'd take you home and do you right now.'"

Tyriq's brow and lips twists with an old rusty anger. It's making sense. Earlier, I challenged his image of himself as a man, just as she had. He didn't like it then or now.

You're not going to do that again, Denise.

"When she said that, what did you do?"

"I got pissed off, stood up, fell down, and climbed back in my chair, but I told her that I was young but was more than enough man for her, with her Ivy League bullshit refinement. I guess I kind of surprised her. All this time, I was just going along like a good little guy, but she struck a nerve. I also realized that I had fallen in love with her and wanted to be treated like her equal and not some *project.*"

"So what happened?" I ask.

This is getting good!

"Well . . ." Tyriq winces a bit. "She called the waiter over, paid the check, got up, went outside to catch a cab. She didn't say a word. When the cab came, she got in and left the door open, then looked at me, and said, 'Are you coming, Mr. Man?' I got in, and she took me to her place. It was a tall condo building overlooking the waterfront. It was crazy-slick! It was nice, only one bedroom but expensive. It was very modern, not my type of setup. I thought it was cold looking, but still very, very nice."

"Sooooo what happened?"

"You sure you want to hear this?" he asks.

"Tyriq, after all this, I can't believe you're punkin' out on me with the juicy part."

He rolls his eyes and smirks.

"You're just X-rated, that's all. She showed me the place. The truth is, she took me to a huge bedroom with a double king-size bed in middle of it. She pushed me down on the bed, and we went for it. That's how it happened, that was the beginning of us. Drunk as I was, I still tried to knock the bottom out of it, break her back. Y'know, all that stupid young macho stuff. Viq wasn't having any of it. She slowed me down and took me into her heart. I could feel it. It was the most beautiful thing I had ever experienced. She cried and told me she loved me. I told her too. I thought it was the liquor talking, but the next morning, as we nursed our hangovers, we talked about it, and she told me she loved me, again. She talked about being afraid to love me but couldn't help but give into her feelings. She was so vulnerable at that moment, but for me it couldn't have been better. I was in love with her too, pure, simple, raw, and new."

Tyriq has that far-off look in his eyes again. I reach out across the table and place his hands in mine.

"How did she die?"

He drops his chin to his chest and blows a gentle burst of air from the corner of his mouth.

"Viq was funny, y'know. With all the money she was making and all her style, she kept the car she had when she was in college. It was a convertible burgundy Volkswagen Beetle. She used to tell me that it almost fell apart on her around the time she started making enough money to restore it.

"But she had a car accident. It was all over the news. She was driving just a little too fast, and a big delivery truck ran a stop sign. The convertible top was down, and the car ran under the truck broadside, between the front and rear tires. The frame of the windshield ripped off. She wasn't wearing her seatbelt. That's it."

Tyriq's eyes float in tears, and his bottom lip trembles. I can feel a lump in my throat, and a tear on my cheek surprises me.

"Honey, I really didn't mean to take you back through that. I'm so sorry. I didn't know."

"It's okay," he says, dabbing at his eyes and clearing his throat. "I guess I surprised myself. I thought a year was long enough to move on. Sometimes, it takes a little longer. Sometimes, there's always a part of someone you love with you. Maybe I have a little of both still going on with me."

Did he say a year?

"When did all this happen? Did you say a year ago?"

"Yep, a year ago this week. It happened the day after my twenty-third birthday."

Damn!

Thirty-Five

I get over the sadness of Tyriq's personal tragedy quickly enough to offer him the support of a friend. I am amazed at his strength and his ability to share the loss of a first true love. By the time we left the Gumbo Shop, it's dark. Sunday night in the French Quarter, and the weather has cooled enough to be comfortable, even with the humidity. We walk back to my hotel, silent and thoughtful. We have become a couple in just a day or at least more absorbed, intertwined, and involved. I have become a confidant, a sponge, soaking up everything Tyriq pours into me.

"I hope I haven't dumped too much on you to scare you away. I have to admit, for a young'un, I've had a lot going on."

"That's true, but I did ask, so I kinda got what I asked for."

"But did I scare you?"

"No, honey, you didn't." I smile at him. "Really. I'm cool. It's your life, and you seem to be handling it."

"Yeah, I don't have a choice."

We approach the hotel doors, and Tyriq pauses. "Aren't you coming up?"

"No, I need to go home tonight, babe. Besides, I need to talk to my mother about leaving New Orleans."

190

"I'm sure that's going to be a lot of fun," I say with bitter sarcasm. "I'm sure she's going to think this has something to do with me. I'm sorry for making your life hard."

Tyriq gently lifts my chin with his hands.

" Hey, hey, what's going on here? Just let it flow, babe. I'll handle my mother. As a woman, I'm sure you know how she feels."

"No, not really. Remember, I don't have any children. I've always wanted one or two, but a husband, children, white picket fence, and a goldfish don't appear in the cards for me."

"Like I said, I'll handle my mother."

Tyriq tenderly kisses me on my forehead, then embraces me with his powerful arms, and really lets me have it on the lips. I want to melt right there.

Wow, this is so good!

He lets me go and holds my hands in his.

"I'm going to run, but I'll call you tomorrow and give you the details of my little birthday party."

"Okay!" I sigh a smile and let him go. He winks at me and trots off to his car. I watch him go and turn to go to my room.

Denise, you are smitten, taken, cloud-nined, sprung, dick-whipped, whatever. "You got that right," I say to myself as the elevator doors open, "like never before." I lean on the wall of the elevator and close my eyes. That little girl inside giggles at me, out loud.

Thirty-Six

"He's *how* old?!"

"I know it sounds crazy, Saundra, but it just kind of happened."

I have not spoken to Saundra since shortly after I arrived in New Orleans. She is kind of pissed about that, but when I tell her about Tyriq's age, she really starts trippin'.

"Are you out of your fuckin' mind, Denise? No, wait, that's it. You don't have any more fuckin' mind 'cause you've been letting this boy fuck your brains out! Why didn't you mention his age??"

"Why are you so pissed at me?" She cuts her volume in half.

"I'm not reeeeally pissed at you. Maybe I'm jealous. Hee-hee-hee. I'm mad 'cause you are getting turned out down there. And I'm trying to play house with David."

"What's wrong with him?"

"Nothing I can't fix with these hips. He's just taking things slow. That's cool. I'll deal with it. He's a nice brother. But don't change the subject! What on earth are you doing with that boy? He's got to be slingin' some monster dick!"

"Can you say Godzilla?"

"Daaaaaamn, so it's like that? Can you hook a sistah up?"

"Don't try it, girlfriend. I have plenty for him. But I *do* have to pull my pussy back down out of my chest when we're done. Whew! Girl, you just don't know."

"But I sure would like to!"

We fall out laughing on the phone, and I roll around on the bed with joy. "Enough of that, Denise. So you say he's going to take a job in Baltimore in about two months. Let's keep it real. What's up with that? Are you trying to hook up with this kid like *that* or what?"

"I'm just taking this one day at a time. Who knows what the future holds?"

"Who knows what the future holds? What are you talking about?" Saundra is getting excited again. "Sis, I'm not trying to cock block. It's a little late for that, but for real...how do you know this kid ain't some kind of junior pimp in training? He could be after your little nest egg. You are easy pickin's!"

Me? Easy pickin's? She's got some nerve.

"What are you talking about, easy pickin's? You need to explain that!" I can feel my teeth clenching as I wait for an answer.

"Denise, we've known each other too long for me to lie to you. It wouldn't be love, if I didn't tell you the truth, even if it's my truth. Fine as you are, any man is going to look at you. When you walk by, he's going to see the steam coming from the crack of your hot ass. You're a beautiful person, and I love you, but you've been horny, lonely, and needing more than just a high hard one from a man. Don't think that any man with half a brain and some insight can smell it on you? That's all I'm saying. I don't know the young brother, ain't seen him. But I do know this: I'm going to let you do your thing. I'm going to be there to share your happiness or catch you if you fall. You're my ace girl, and I just want you to be careful. There ain't no bigger trap than a fine young man with Godzilla swinging at you."

Saundra is right. I have to be careful. Eddie Murphy said a long time ago, give a starving man an old stale cracker, and he would say it's the best cracker he ever tasted. Am I really desperate?

I don't know, Denise, ask BOB. You remember BOB, don't you? Your battery-operated boyfriend. Even Godzilla gets tired of tearing through your bush and wonderfully ripping your coochie. But BOB saw a lot of tireless use before you took this New Orleans trip. There's nothing wrong with BOB, but you can't talk to BOB, BOB won't take you to dinner, and BOB sucks at giving hugs.

"Girl, your honesty gets on my nerves, but I know it's all about love. You wouldn't be a friend if you didn't tell me what you were feeling. Like I said, I'll just take it one day at a time. Tyriq and I could end up just being friends, lovers, whatever. I do like him, *a lot*. I'm not going to lie about that, and I admit I got my nose wide-open—"

"Yeah, legs too!" Saundra quips with a laugh.

"Okay, okay, I got it, I got it, but you have to understand. He listens, he is patient, he talks, and he makes me feel like he would defend and support me like a real friend, just like you."

"Yeah, just like me," Saundra chuckles. "You're cute and all, and I love you, but you ain't my type."

"Saundra, they don't come any crazier than you."

"I know that's right! Speaking of cumming, let's get to the kiss and tell. On a scale of 1 to 10, how is the stuff?"

"Whew! Girl, please, 1 to 10? He's at least a 25! It's almost like his dick is made of crack, and I'm strung out. Rehab can't help me. I've never felt anything like it. When we're together in the sheets, it's like an out-of-body experience. I don't know how to explain it. And that's *after* he spends a lifetime munching on the groceries below. Shoot, yesterday I kinda passed out when we were doin' it in the shower. He just does it for me."

"Damn, Denise, I'm just mad you!" Saundra says with a smile. "Does he have a brother, a friend, even a forgetful moment when he can think I'm you? He-he-he-he-he-he-he. I'm cracking myself up. Looks like I'm going to have to just keep working on David, like I said, and keep your daddy as some spare change."

"Oh my goodness! I have to call Daddy. I've not spoken to him in days either."

"You are slippin'. Do you want me to check on him for you?"

"Girl, you know Daddy loves you. You are always welcome at his house, but I think he might have a little piece of a girlfriend. If you do check on him, you should call first instead of dropping by like we usually do. I'm going to call him and let him know I'm okay."

"Will do. You're coming home Thursday night, right?"

"No, Wednesday early afternoon, can you pick me up?"

"Dang, no, I can't. I'm sorry. I have to work. I have an important meeting in the afternoon."

"No problem, I'll get Bruce from my office to pick me up. He offered to last week. It will give me a chance to catch up on what's going on."

"Cool. Call me when you get back. I'll see you after I get off, if you're not too tired from traveling."

"That's fine. See ya."

I leave Bruce a message on his voice mail at the office. I'm sure he'll be able to rearrange his schedule to pick me up.

Wait a minute. What are you saying, Denise? You're the freaking boss. Of course, he's going to pick you up if you say so. Don't start slippin' and trippin'. And don't get soft. You run a tight ship, and your happy staff works hard. Expect them to do what they're told.

I pick up the phone and call Daddy. The answering machine picks up. I look at the clock. Hmmm, almost 10:30. Why isn't he home? He's usually in bed at this hour. I left a message of love and hung up.

A few more days of the conference before going home, nearly two weeks of working down here. I will be glad to see DC. I take off my clothes, catch a shower, and collapse on the bed. I turn the TV on to see the local news. By the time the first commercials ended, the newscasters were watching me sleep.

Thirty-Seven

The conference is winding down. Even for long ones like this, you can tell when people and the events are running out of gas. The usual crowds are thinning. Exhibitors are packing up the displays. Tired, convention-worn bodies are pulling suitcases on wheels and hailing cabs to the airport.

I still have energy for the last sessions, and plenty of people are still there. Bonnie stops in, and we sit together in the back. The information about taking your office and staff "to the next level" is pretty good actually. Most of the managers have a briefcase full of complaints about their staffs. The more I listen, the more blessed I feel. I do have to step up my game on rewards and appreciations for my staff. They are happy now, but you just never know when they will bolt on you for a few thousand dollars more.

The session ends at one. Bonnie and I decide to grab a bite back in the French Quarter. It just occurs to me that I have not seen or heard from her since Saturday.

"Hey!" I say to her as we sit at a little corner bistro. "Where you been, girl? I've not seen or heard from you in two days."

"I know, I know. I feel bad about that too. I've been really busy trying to get stuff done back in Baltimore. Especially trying to get Tyriq's application pushed through. I think it's a done deal. Usually there's a bit of a selection process for the intern, but...I have clout. Those folks will pretty much give me what I ask for. How are you feeling?"

"Everything is cool. I wanted to tell you that I really appreciate you hanging in there with me."

"Whoa! You don't need to thank me for anything! Sisters have to stick together. Too many of us spend too much time trying to tear each other down. That's why I'm getting Tyriq the hookup. I mean, I know you like him, but he will really benefit from the program. He's sharp, and if I didn't think he would be good for the program, I wouldn't help bring him along. That's one of the other things that took awhile. Several of the news anchors have nice rental properties near the station. Tyriq doesn't know it yet, but there will be several places he can choose from. He won't have any problem finding a place to live."

"Wow, you have been busy!" I say. "That's wonderful. Are you going to be around tomorrow, or are you going back to Baltimore."

"Why? What's going on? I leave tomorrow night. I still have to get the final approval for all the interns in the program. There are actually about five others, but he's the only one from out of town. If everything goes right, Tyriq can come up at the end of September. That's when the program starts. What's going on tomorrow night?"

"Well, tomorrow is his birthday. There's a little get-together. I don't even know where it's going to be. I'm sure I'll hear from him at some point today about the details. I thought you might want to go."

"Humph! I don't know about that."

"Why not? What's wrong?"

"I'm sure his boss is going to be there. I don't think she's a big fan of mine. I'd love to go with you, but after I bit her head off in the store last week, I don't think that would be the best place for me to be."

"Hmmm, yeah. Good point!" I say. "I'm not so sure I'd want my mother around the woman who cussed her out in her own place of business."

Bonnie's eyebrows shoot up, and a lot of confusion and surprise color her face.

"Did you say 'mother'?"

Damn, Denise, did you just let the cat out of the bag? I slap my hand over my mouth.

Bonnie's eyes get really big. "I guess that was supposed to be a secret?" I put my forehead on the table. Both hands are covering my mouth. *Well, Denise, looks like that big mouth of yours works for things other than sucking Tyriq's dick.*

"So much makes sense now," Bonnie says with an "aha" tone. "She's not the lusty older woman. She's the mama bear protecting her only cub."

"Yeah," I say with a moan. "That's the deal. I feel awful. It was a big secret, and Tyriq told me during a real moment of personal revelation." Bonnie reaches out and pats my hand. "Don't worry about it. The secret's safe with me. I couldn't care less actually. I don't care who his mama is. But if that's something he doesn't want to get out, I suggest you tighten *your* tongue."

"You are so right." I am still feeling pretty bad about the slip when the waitress brings water to the table, takes our orders, and speeds off to the kitchen.

"Next topic," Bonnie says. "What are you going to do when you get back home?"

"What do you mean?"

"Well, you have two months before Tyriq moves to town. Do you have any drama to clean up? Y'know what I mean, any fine bald-headed chocolate—stripper-bodied men hiding under your bed?"

"I wish!" I say, and we both laugh aloud. "No-no, nothing like that at all. I guess that's how Tyriq was able to pick me, the horny one, out of the crowd. At least that's what my best girlfriend says. He saw me coming."

"Ehh, I wouldn't say that. From what I've seen, you picked him. Not that it really matters who picked whom. The only thing that matters is that you look at it for what it is."

Bonnie leans forward with a look of gleeful conspiracy. "Here's the deal. He's young. He'll be what—twenty-four tomorrow? You're about thirty-six, right?"

"I'm thirty-five!" I say with attitude.

"Yeah, whatever! Anyway, that's an eleven-year difference. He's very mature, but let me give this situation the benefit of the doubt. Let's say you two fall in love, and you have one of those wonderful, loving long-term relationships that our parents had but no one has anymore. In ten years you will be forty-five years old, he'll be thirty-four. Your ass will be, at best, pre-menopausal, and his dick will still get hard every morning. He's going to be fit and fine, and you will be working it out in the gym to keep up with the sisters who will be the same age you are right now.

"Keep it real! Is that something you will want to deal with? Will you be able to compete and keep up? I told you, when you first introduced me to him, I thought he was fine on his worst day, and he's just starting out. Wait until he gets a little seasoning under his belt. All I'm saying is just take it slow."

"I know. I got the same speech from my girl at home. I am being careful. I mean, this could just be a fling. I don't think it is though. He's so intense. I think he's serious about a lot of things including me."

"I'm just saying. I don't want you to dive too deep into this water with your nose open so wide that you drown."

"No, I'm cool, really Bonnie. But thanks for your concern."

I patted her on the arm. The waitress walks over to our table with our lunch skillfully balanced on a tray. We eat and talk about Bonnie's life and more about me. We finish and walk back to the hotel in the midday heat. By the time we get to the front doors, we are both drench with sweat. I go to my room and find an envelope on the floor behind the door. It is an invitation to Tyriq's party. I open it and I am impressed. It's not "y'all come." It's a "your presence is requested, please attend."

> *Miss Clara d' Beaux requests the pleasure of your company*
> *at the twenty-fourth birthday celebration in honor of*
> *Mr. Tyriq Austin*
> *Tuesday, the twentieth of July seven o'clock in the evening*
> *Love's Gallerie*
> *300 Chartres Street*
> *New Orleans, Louisiana*
> *Attire: Warm-Weather Elegant*
> *Dancing shoes and warm wishes strictly required!*
> *Regrets Only*
> *504-555-6969*

Wow! That's some invitation and at an art gallery too. This is going to be a real to-do. I look at the invitation again and notice writing at the fold. I open the fold all the way and read a message in woman's handwriting.

We need to talk, tomorrow!
Clara d' Beaux

Oh, shit! Now what?

Thirty-Eight

"Let me repeat that back to you. That's flight 569 arriving at Washington National at five thirty in the afternoon. Is that right?"

"Yes, Bruce, that's it exactly. Where should I meet you—at the taxi stand area?"

"Are you kidding? I'll pick you up at the baggage claim when you come in. I'm sure it's been a long trip, and I know you don't want to lug your bags all the way down to the taxi stand pickup."

He really IS a sweetie. That's so considerate! I wish he came in chocolate instead of vanilla.

"Bruce, you don't have to do that. I can manage."
"I wouldn't have it any other way."

"I give in. What's going on anyway? Did you guys blow up the office or something?"

"No, not at all. It's just good to have the boss home. I'll see you tomorrow afternoon."

"Thanks again, hear? I really appreciate it."

I hang up the phone and look at the birthday invitation on the nightstand. *Sigh!* I hope this woman doesn't want to get ugly with me. This *has* been a long trip. I'm not trying to mix it up with her.

But you know what? If she wants to tighten up, I have two words for her, "no bullshit!"

What I really need to do is pick up something to wear and buy Tyriq a gift, something he will really remember.

And remember you too!

I look around the hotel room. I can't remember where I put *it*. I walk to the closet, pull out my suitcase, and open one of the side pockets.

"Here it is."

The letter he wrote me last week still has the scent of his cologne on it. I hold it up to the light, and I can see the wide irregular lines of his writing.

"Oh yeah, my sweetheart, I have just the thing for you." I laugh quietly to myself. "I'm going to get something I know you're *really* going to like."

The phone rings. *Who's calling now?* "Hello, baby girl."

"Daddy! Where have you been?" My heart melts. It is so good to hear my daddy's voice. "I called you last night, and it was late. Where were you? I was a little worried."

Daddy chuckles his usual secure, comfortable laugh. "Now, girl, I told you not to worry about me. I'm fine. I was...out, that's all. You aren't the only one who has a social life. Yes, I'm what you might call a 'gently used Negro,' but sometimes, gently used is better than brand-new."

"Daddy, you are silly. Have you been out with Mrs. Johnson from church?"

"Would that be a problem if I said yes?"

"No, I said before, it's okay. I would like to meet her, formally, if you are getting serious."

"Ain't nobody said nothin' about gettin' serious!"

Whoops, I know that tone and his Southern drawl. It only comes out when he's irritated. Just take it easy, Denise. Remember, Daddy still loves Mama.

"All we're doing is keepin' company."

"I know, Daddy, and that's all right with me. I just would like to meet the lady who has my daddy's attention more than I do."

He calms down right away and assures me, "Denise, you know you're my number one love, after your mama. You always will be. Don't ever forget it."

"I won't. I promise."

"When you come home, you can meet Sadie. She would love to meet you. She has actually asked me about it."

Sadie?

"So how has your trip been?"

"Hot, hot, hot. New Orleans has the kind of heat that just sits on you and won't let you up. Just when I call myself getting used it, I go inside and get used to the air-conditioning."

"Did you learn anything down there or meet any interesting people?"

Daddy, Sadie ain't got nothin' on what I met down here!

"Oh yes, the people here have been great, and I've learned quite a bit. But look, I'm not going to stay on the phone. I have some more running around to do. I'll be home tomorrow night. I'll come see you Thursday, if you're not too busy with Ms. Sadie."

"Ha-ha, you're funny girl. I'll be here waiting on you to come home. Love you!"

"I love you too, Daddy. Bye."

I hang up the phone, grab my purse and the party invitation, and dash out the door to Bonnie's floor. I hope she's still here. I need her to go shopping with me for a snazzy dress and Tyriq's gift. When I get to her floor and bang on the door, she opens it right away.

"Hey, what's up with the banging? Are you okay?"

"Yeah, girlfriend, I'm fine. Look, when does your flight leave?"

"Not until eight o'clock. I won't get into Baltimore until late. I'm going to pay for the extra hours here at the hotel. I'm not sitting in the airport for six or seven hours after a noon checkout."

"Cool, come shopping with me. I need something slick for the party tonight."

"Shopping? Now? What's the big deal? I'm down for shopping, but it's just a little get-together, isn't it?"

I hand her the invitation. When she looks it over, her eyes get really big. "Daaaaayum! I like this. This is all right! Shooo, this makes me want to change my flight and go myself."

"It's something, isn't it? Come on, Bonnie, help me pick out something sexy, but not too over the top. I want something glamorous, but I can't look like I'm trying too hard."

"I think we can find something at one of the boutiques in the Garden District. But we need to hurry up. I still have to pack my stuff to go home." We grab a cab outside of the hotel and get to the Garden District in no time. There are lots of bridal shops mixed in with the mansions. I've never seen so many beautiful gowns. Unfortunately, that's *not* what I am in the market for. The cabbie keeps driving until we spot a cutesy little dress boutique not too far from Tyriq's shop. Time is beginning to tick away, so we decide to take a chance. We pay the cabbie and step up the flagstone walkway. There is a little sign in the window of the store.

"Heart's Desire. That's cute," I say.

"I guess," Bonnie says. " But let's give it a try."

We walk in, and I immediately fall in love with the place. Dozens of shoes, styles cute to sexy, hide the long narrow walls of the shop. Several racks of party clothes and cocktail dresses stand in the middle of the store.

A sweet voice comes from the back of the store. "I'll be with you ladies in just a moment! Feel free to look around!"

"First things first," Bonnie says. "What's the attire?" I hand her the invitation, and she reads it again.

"Hmmm, 'warm-weather elegant.' I guess that means hot-hot."

"Hot-hot?" I ask. "I don't get it."

"It means—"

The voice came from behind one of the dress racks, "Hot weather and hot, fierce looks! You are right on target, Miss."

We crane our necks as the owner of the voice walks out in plain view. The voice is sweet, and so is he.

"It's so nice to have you both here at Heart's Desire. I'm Billy, and this is my shop. What can I help you find?"

How about some masculinity? Stop it, Denise! Three girls are better than one.

"I'm looking for a nice cocktail dress. Like my friend said, it should be hot-hot."

Billy is extremely thin for a man, but he is well groomed, and his makeup—

Did I say makeup? Yuck!

It's very well done.

Dang, his eyebrows are arched nicer than yours.

Billy looks me up and down. He has one hand on his hip and the other tapping the side of his face.

"Sweetie, you have a wonderful shape, and I think you're barely a size 6, right?"

"That's right," I say.

"But tell me this, what do you think is your best asset?"

"Besides my face you mean?"

"Honey, with that cute face, you are already halfway to hot-hot, even without the dress."

"Thanks for the compliment. I think my legs are my best asset."

"I think so too," Bonnie chimes in. "I think you also need something to bring out you milk-chocolate skin tone. A nice, warm color would be nice."

Billy purses his lips and sucks his teeth. "You almost don't need me. Girlfriend seems to have it together. But I said, *almost.* I have just the thing. Sit tight."

He slips gracefully away toward the back of the store. We can hear the scrape-scrape sound of metal hangers on metal clothes racks. Bonnie leans her head toward my ear and whispers, "Is that Billy, b-i-l-l-y, or b-i-l-l-i-e?"

"Bonnie, stop!" I giggle. "You're being bad. He-she's trying to help!" We both crack up but straighten our faces when we hear Billy or Billie walking back to the front of the store.

"Heeeere we are," his high-pitched voice sings out. All Bonnie and I can say is, "Woooowwwww!"

Billy holds out a short bronze-colored cocktail dress. It has an understated silky shine and a daring V-neck plunge with spaghetti straps. It is perfect.

"Oh my," I say. "That's really beautiful. I love it. The mini-pleats are elegant, and the high waist is wonderful."

"Actually," Billy interrupts. "It's called accordion pleating, and the high waist is called empire. The word looks like 'empire' as in Empire State Building, but it's pronounced 'ahm-peer.' I wouldn't want you ladies to appear ignorant of the fashions you wear."

Bonnie rolls her eyes and does her own imitation of Billy's voice, "No, we wouldn't want to appear ignorant, now would we?"

Billy rolls his eyes too, but ignores Bonnie. "Would you like to try it on?"

"Yes. I would. How much is it?"

"It's $350, but if you find a pair of shoes you like, it's yours for $300."

"Bonnie, could you please find me something sexy to match this in a size 7 and a half? Remember, heels, heels, heels—the higher, the better."

"You got it, girl!" Bonnie says, still imitating Billy.

When I step out of the dressing room, Bonnie is standing there dangling a pair of four-inch-high, sand-colored Stuart Weitzman C-F-M-Ps from the tips of her fingers. The old, tried, and true come-fuck-me-please sandals never fail. They have crystals around the ankle straps and front vamp. They match the dress perfectly, and they are comfortable. The price isn't as comfortable.

Damn, Denise, are you really *trying to pay $275 dollars for shoes, plus $300 for the dress? Go on, if you're going to look good, you get what you pay for.*

I plunk down the old American Express Card and pay for my goodies. Billy takes $25 off the shoes because Bonnie buys a slick pair of CFMPs too.

We thank Billy and catch a cab back to the hotel. Bonnie is ready to pack and go home. I am ready for tonight.

Thirty-Nine

I help Bonnie pack her things. We exchange home information and promise to get in touch when I get back to town. We hug each other in the lobby as she waits for a cab. She is sad, and I can feel a lump in my throat too. Our little New Orleans adventure is coming to a close. It's been barely two weeks, but we have become instantly tight, like sisters. She's a lot like Saundra, just more refined. I can't wait for them to meet.

The cab comes; she hops in and is gone. I turn to walk back into the hotel to get dressed for Tyriq's party but suddenly remember.

Denise, the gift. You forgot the gift!

I look up and down the street in a mini-panic for an antique store.

You were so busy trying to find an outfit to look cute, you forgot about his birthday gift. Drama, but don't lose it. Just go back to the Quarter and find an antique shop.

I hail a cab and hop in.

"Where you going, miss?" the cabbie asks.

"Need you take me to the area where all the antique stores are. I need to find a gift."

"A gift, at an antique store?"

"Yes," I say, now getting impatient.

"What kind of gift, maybe I can make a suggestion."

"I need a fountain pen, something really nice and rare."

"I've got just the thing, but you need to hang on. We have to go 'cross town to Magazine Street. They may be ready to close 'bout six, but I think we can make it."

"Hit it, let's go!" I say. And he takes off. I look at my watch. It is 5:30, and I am in a panic to make it there, hopefully find what I want and get back in time for the party. It seems as if the traffic gods are on my side. We zip through traffic with relative ease for rush hour. By the time, we hit Magazine Street; it is fifteen minutes to six. The cab pulls in front of a glass-front store called The Write Place. I hop out and ask the cabbie to wait for me. I step in the doorway and am greeted by who I first think is Santa Claus—bearded, balding with wire-rim glasses, and all.

"We are about to close, ma'am. You will have to come back tomorrow."

"I can't." I beg, "I'm looking for a birthday present for my sweetheart, and the party's in just a few hours. I know what I'm looking for. Could you please just give me a few moments?"

I put on my on the puppy-dog-eyes look. He is obviously related to Santa because his kindness gets the best of him.

"Okay, heh-heh. I was in love once, and I know what it looks like. Come on in."

In love? Is that what's going on here? Two weeks, Denise? I don't know about that.

"What are you looking for, dear?"

"I want a *really nice* fountain pen."

"Oh really? How nice is really nice?"

It just occurs to me that I have no idea how much a *really nice* fountain pen costs. With the meter running on the cab, I am not trying to take out a second mortgage for this gift, even if it is for *my sweetheart!*

"I want something special. I am even hoping for something antique, but I don't want you to hurt me."

Santa man laughs again. "I have just the thing. Is $200 dollars hurting you too much?"

I wince at the thought, but shrug my shoulders. "That's my limit." He disappears in the back. He is gone for a minute that seems like five. I look at my watch and then at the cab sitting out front.

"Here we are, dear. It's been reconditioned to work like new, but it's the kind of pen I used when I was a boy in grade school, just a little more fancy." Santa man opens a flat velvet box in front of me. I could not have asked for something better. The pen is large, but not overbearing. It is onyx black with a carved gold cap and nib. There is a scratch in the gold, and I can see that someone, a long time ago, got a lot of use out of it. "This is an Aurora pen. It's Italian and about sixty years old. As I said,

I reconditioned it. It writes wonderfully, but I didn't do anything to the outside. That's where the true value is. They can cost hundreds and, in some cases, thousands of dollars when they're new, but I think today because you can see a little damage, I'll be a saint for the cause of love and let it go for $200. I'll wrap it up with an inkwell. Does your sweetheart know fountain pens?"

"I think he does. If he doesn't, he will after he gets this one. But if you can do it for $150, I'd appreciate it even more. You were in love once, I think you said." Santa Man laughed and nodded his head on the deal. I gave him my American Express card. He rings it up, gives the pen a quick polishing with an old rag, and gift-wraps it with red paper and wide gold ribbon. I grab it and quickly step toward the door.

"Dear? I made one mistake."

I turn around with my hand still on the doorknob. "What's that?" Santa Man walks toward me. "I said the true value is the pen casing. Actually, the true value of the pen is the quality of the love letters he'll write to you, with it."

I look at him with his short, full white beard and receding hairline. I reach up and plant a kiss on his pink cheek.

"Thank you, Santa Man," I say softly and walk out the door to the cab. When I look back from the cab, he waves good-bye with a sweet, puzzled look on his face.

Forty

Getting dressed for the party is pure luxury. The silky dress slides around my body like the caress of cool satin sheets. Despite the four inches of stiletto I am standing on, the shoes are actually very comfortable, enough that I can dance all night if I want. I look down at the bottom of the hem.

Don't do too much spinning, girl. You might give everyone more of a show than you want. Remember, sit like a lady, and all will be right with the world.

It's short but very sassy. I have to admit; the home pedicure I gave myself makes my feet too sexy for my own good.

No wonder men have foot fetishes, even I can see how they would be turned on.

"Settled down, you still have Tyriq's mama-drama to deal with," I say to myself as I touch up my makeup. I mist my chest with a last bit of perfume, brush my shoulders with a little glitter dust, pat my hair, and get ready to put the diva strut in my step.

Damn, girl, you look good!

My watch tells me it is almost 7:30, time to make a fashionably late grand entrance. I pick up the birthday gift and catch the elevator down to the lobby. There are plenty of cabs outside so I don't have to worry about breaking a sweat in the heavy early-evening heat. The cab cruises through the crowded streets of the French Quarter. A temperature sign outside of a bank flashes 92, then 91 claustrophobic degrees.

When Ms. Clara d' Beaux said "warm-weather elegant" on the invitation, she knew what she was talking about.

I hope she doesn't make a scene, especially at a party. What does she want to talk about anyway?

The cabbie turns onto Chartres Street and hits the brakes immediately. "Whoa! What's going on with that?"

"I'm sorry, miss. There's a bit of line here. I didn't know we were going to have to wait."

I crane my neck to see beyond the car in front of me. At least five other cars are inching along. I can only guess this is where the party is.

"This must be some kinda big thing up here. What is it?" he asks me. "Oh, it's just a little birthday party for a dear friend of mine," I say. "Little party? I don't know about that. There's the mayor's limo, and there's the president of the Xavier University walking up. I've given him a ride in my cab before."

As the cab inches up the street, I notice several people strolling and sweating up to a storefront art gallery. In the huge window is a neon script sign that spells out the name "Love's Gallerie." Next to it are tall double doors open like a mouth, devouring a trickle of people walking in. There are two more cars ahead of us. The valets are moving as fast as they can. Their once-crisp uniforms are sweat-stained from perspiration. I feel sorry for them.

"You can let me out here," I say to the cab driver. "This is fine. Here, keep the change."

I open the door just in time to see a hand reach out to me.

"Can I help you out of your cab?" It's a man a little older than Tyriq, but just as chocolate and just as handsome. He is dressed in a beautiful steel gray suit. Two men behind him are watching and are obviously with him. "Well, thank you, sir. I can always appreciate a gentlemanly gesture."

I stretch my legs out of the cab. The two men behind Mr. Gentlemanly Gesture lean over to catch the full view of me. I try to ignore them, but they are obscenely obvious.

"Um-um-umph!" one of them grunts. "I hope there's more of *that* at this party!"

I look at him over my shoulder. "I seriously doubt it."

"Whooooa!" the other one screams. "She just took you down a notch or two, didn't she? Ha-ha, ahh-haaa!"

Gentlemanly Gesture steals an annoyed look at his boys and quick-steps to catch up with me.

"Miss, you sho look fine this eve'nin. Can I escort you in since we're going to the same place?"

"Oh, that's very nice of you, I'm flying solo tonight. But thank you for helping a sistah out of a cab."

"I don't see how someone as fine as you can be flyin' solo. I'm a great copilot."

That was funny and original.

"Well, from the looks of things, I'm sure you will find all kinds of planes to pilot here tonight."

I wink at him and walk on to the door. I can hear him and his buddies in a not-so-quiet conspiracy of admiration behind me.

Get your diva on, Denise!

I lift my chin as I walk through the door. A man in a white linen suit punches a hole in my invitation and lets me in. The gallery is deceptively huge. It's obvious to me that this was a small mansion when it was new. Now, artwork is everywhere—paintings, sculptures, charcoal drawings, oils, and watercolors, almost all of them by black artists.

The large main room connects to several other rooms by high archways. Dozens of people milled around, flowing in and out of the rooms. The mixed-age crowd munch on hors d'oeuvres. The wine and other spirits flow freely. Jazz, laughter, and friendly conversations color the room and get louder as I walk toward the back of the gallery. The crowd thickens and gets younger. I can feel the eyes of several men undress me as I walk past.

I kept Tyriq's gift guarded as I approach a large circular parlor. There he is, in a beige-gray–striped sharkskin suit.

Clean as the board of health and pussy-drippin' fine!

Tyriq is holding court, smiling, laughing, and chatting up with the handful of people that is surrounding him.

"And when I told the mayor I was leaving his Commission on Youth and Young Adults to manage a women's lingerie store, he said, 'I knew there was something strange about that boy!'"

The crowd of about twenty people breaks up in loud laughter. A well-dressed tall man shakes Tyriq's hand, gives him a hug, and leaves with a pair of other men with earpieces dangling.

I guess that's the mayor of New Orleans.

I'd forgotten what a big shot Tyriq is in town. He's so busy greeting and glad-handing, he doesn't see me, but someone does. Standing in the corner, holding a half-full glass of wine is the lady herself, Ms. Clara d' Beaux. Our eyes meet, and for the first time since I met her, the steely coldness is gone. It is replaced by...something else. I don't know, but I'm sure I'm about to find out. Clara gestures with her head and wineglass toward the back of the room. I nod and begin to weave my way through the people. Mercy intervenes.

"Denise! Honey, you made it!"

Tyriq excuses himself and steps lightly over to me. He embraces me and plants a soft, sensuous closed-lip kiss on me. There is a very audible moan from the crowd, peppered with a few "oohs" and "ahhs." I feel a twinge of embarrassment and surge of pride as Tyriq dabs at a smear of my lipstick on his lips.

"Everybody." He raises his voice and gets the attention of the room.

Oh dear, what is he going to say? I'm not ready for this.

All I can do is stand as poised as I possibly can and smile.

"I want to introduce everyone to my new lady-friend. This is Denise Younger. She is an absolutely wonderful woman, and I hope you all have a chance meet her."

Dozens of glasses are raised and a warm group hello murmurs from the crowd. I wave and turn to Tyriq, still smiling, but not 100 percent pleased with the group introduction.

Quietly, I told him, "Tyriq, *honey,* you didn't tell me you were planning to introduce me to the world tonight. Don't you think that's a little much a little soon? And what's the deal with the kiss?"

His brow knots a little bit. "You've never objected to my kissing you in public before. Why now?"

"We weren't in front of people who know you," I say. "I don't know these people, and we haven't known each other that long."

"Oh? Well, we've known each other long enough to have sex nine ways to Sunday. What's the difference?"

He's gotcha there, homegirl. Better quit while you're ahead.

"Denise, let me say this: if I'm into you in private, I'm into you in public. I'm not going to hide how I feel. If others don't like it, too bad. If you don't like it, we have a problem."

I look around the room and relax when I realize no one is paying me or us any attention.

"I'm sorry, Tyriq. You just caught me off guard. I'm fine. You can kiss me anytime, anywhere, in front of anyone you want."

The stress on his forehead quickly fades into a smile that covers his entire face.

"That's my girl!" he says. "Listen, I want to personally introduce you to a few people."

"Honey, I would love to, but I need to talk to your mother."

"I know you do."

"How did you know?"

"I told her to talk to you. If she didn't, *I* was going to stop talking to *her*."

"Wow, don't you think that's a bit much?"

"No, it's important that she talk to you. Besides, she knows I wasn't *totally* serious."

He is looking over my shoulder. When I turn around, Clara is only a few feet behind me. She walks up and hooks an arm inside one of mine.

"Let's you and I have a nice little chat, shall we?"

Clara's voice is still formal, but not the angry, tense tone I first heard at the lingerie shop. I look back at Tyriq for support, and he shoos me away with a smile, then turns to receive a birthday hug from an attractive overweight woman in a wickedly tight loud pink dress.

"Where are we going?"

"There's a terrace out back where we can be alone. It's cooler there." Clara leads me down wide steps and through French doors. She is right.

It's private and cooler. What she doesn't say is that it is also beautiful. The terrace overlooks a sculpture garden of marble nudes and postmodern abstracts. Magnolia trees stand guard over a carpet of deep green grass. The sounds of the party seem miles away. I lean on the smooth marble rail that rings the terrace. I don't look at Clara.

"What do you want to talk about?"

She sighs long and deep. Her eyes scan the sculpture garden as if she were hoping to find the right words there.

"When I first saw you, and the way my son looked at you, I knew he was smitten. I thought you were going to take him away from me."

"Wait a just minute! That was not my intention!" I interrupt. Clara gently raises a graceful hand to quiet me.

"I said, I *thought* you were going to take him away from me. What I didn't know was that he was leaving me, *and* the world he grew up in long before you came to town. You were just the final piece of a puzzle that had been coming together for years."

She steps closer to me and looks me over with a slight smile.

"I'm an old woman with old ways. Yes, there was a time when I felt the kind of passions that have ignited between the two of you. I felt that way about Tyriq's father, but it wasn't to be. Not like my dreams hoped for, so long ago."

I look away from the garden and look at Clara. Even at her age, she is a breathtaking beauty. The warm colors of the setting sun make her look almost angelic.

"Before I knew you were Tyriq's mother, I thought you were a lusty old woman, jealous of his attention for me."

"Oh, I was jealous, but not lusting, just worried. He's all I've had for so long. There were men and such. You can only stay away from them for so long, but Tyriq is my constant. What you saw was a mother's fear, nothing more, nothing less.

"I understand now."

"I'm glad you do, but I want you to accept my apology. I was hoping that you would bring your friend with you. Y'know, the one I had, um, *words* with. I wanted to apologize to her as well."

I reach out and squeeze Clara's hand. "Your apology is accepted, and

I'm sure when I speak with Bonnie, she will understand."

"There is one more thing I have to say. I don't know if this is appropriate, but I have to tell you. I'm old-school and not used to these modern-day shortships?"

"Shortships? I don't understand."

What is she talking about?

"We used to call them *courtships*, but things happen so fast these days, I call them shortships."

I stifle a laugh that jumps to the back of my throat and threatens to spoil the intimate mood of the conversation.

That's pretty funny, but also true. Things happened really fast.

"What I'm saying to you, Denise, is that Tyriq is falling in love with you, fast. I know him. He doesn't see it yet, but it's coming. He likes a lot of people, but only loves a few. When it happens, he falls hard and completely, just as he did with Viquetoria. There is something really special about you because you swept him off his feet."

"Ms. Clara, there was a lot of sweeping on both sides, I think."

"Good, good. Both of you have brooms. That will make it harder to make a mess of things. I don't know where you two are going with this, or even if it's going to last longer than next week. All I ask is that you be careful with my baby's heart while you have it."

"I wouldn't have it any other way. I like him too, a lot. I've even surprised myself. We'll see what happens after tomorrow."

"Yes, we will."

Clara reaches over and gave me a mama's hug. I can feel tears on my shoulder. When she lets go, she pulls out a handkerchief and dabs at her eyes. I take her hand and start walking toward the French doors.

"We should get back to the party before we're missed," I say. Clara dabs at her eyes and then pats her salt-and-pepper mane. "Do I look okay? My eyes aren't red, are they?"

"Clara, you look as beautiful as you did the day I first saw you."

"Great, I must have been a sight. That day I felt as if I had been chewing on lemon peelings all day."

"C'mon, woman," I say with a playful laugh. "Let's go get a dance with your son."

Clara pats my hand as we follow the sound of the music back to the party. We leave our differences sitting on the terrace, waiting for a cool breeze to carry them away.

Forty-One

More people show up at the party even as others are leaving. Tyriq and I dance like old lovers. Clara and I laugh like old friends.

Most of the people at the party are long-time friends of Tyriq's. Others are like his surrogate parents or grandparents, friends of Clara's who knew her from way back when. Still others are crashers who just want to party. Tyriq doesn't care. Tonight, everyone is a good friend, and Clara doesn't want the food to go to waste. I meet many guests and remember few.

From one of the many round tables set up for the occasion, we watch as more than a few couples hand dance and gyrate to Jazz and Zydeco music. I sip on a sweet dessert wine. It is plentiful, and I have my share. I am feeling good, too good, and just a bit mischievous. I pull his head to my lips and wet-whisper in his ear, "I want you, baby, right now."

He looks at me and rolls his eyes with a smile. "You don't want to leave now, do you?"

I look around the room, and then I grab one of his hands from the top of the table. I pull it under the tablecloth draped across my thighs and put his hands under my dress. His hands explore my thighs until he feels the warm and wet of me. He

221

gently caresses the hood of my clitoris once. I stir and moan. His eyes grow big as he nervously scans the room to see if anyone is looking at us. No one notices. I squeeze my thighs around his hand and giggles at him.

"You *did* say you would kiss me anywhere, anytime, any place. Is *this* where you draw the line?"

"Is that a dare?" he asks.

"Call it what you want, but you better do something about it quick. Somebody's going to walk past and wonder why you have your hand up my skirt."

Tyriq looks around the room again. "The bathrooms are upstairs. I'm going to go up the steps. Wait about a minute, and then come up. I have an idea."

He leans over and kisses me on the cheek while he takes his hand from between my thighs. Tyriq gently sucks the tip of his middle finger, winks at me, and walks up a carpeted staircase to the second floor. Clara comes over to the table after kicking up her heels on the dance floor.

"Where's Tyriq? I want to give him a big birthday hug."

She is quite drunk and is having a hard time maintaining her graceful airs.

"I think he went to the bathroom. I'll go check on him."

"You do that. I'll be here or on the dance floor, or wherever."

"Yes, Ms. Clara."

I grab his gift from the table. The gift-wrapping is getting a little worn from my handling it all night. I bop up the staircase and down a long dark hallway with several doors.

Where is he? These old mansions are beautiful in the daytime, but spooky at night.

I feel a quick, strong tug at my wrist. I let out a scream as Tyriq snatches me into one of the rooms.

"Are you crazy?" I cry out. "You scared me!"

"Sorry, babe. Come here." He leads me through the dark room and onto a marble balcony overlooking the terrace where his mother and I buried the hatchet just hours before. I toss his gift on an antique parlor chair, just inside the balcony doors.

From the balcony, I can hear the sounds of romantic giggles and whispers from several couples strolling two stories below. We can only make out their shadows weaving around the sculptures and dim landscape lighting in the garden. It is still warm outside, but it is no longer the offensive heat of midday.

Instead, I can feel my own heat getting the best of me. I drop the spaghetti straps of my dress and expose my breasts to the air and to Tyriq. He leans into me, popping each dark button in his mouth and cleaning it like a cat would clean itself with its tongue.

This is so crazy-good, Denise. What has gotten into you? You need to protect yourself. This is day 12 without your pills, no condoms. Dang, girl! You are off the chain!

I reach my hand down to his waistline and then farther to the wonderful thickness I have become so used to. He presses my back against the cool, smooth marble wall and continues to suckle over the dark peaks of my breasts. I am ravenous, and my desires burn a hole in the common sense the back of my mind is trying to tell me. I peel off his suit jacket, and he drops his pants. Tyriq's hands, once again, palm my ass as I reach back to hold the edge of the balcony's marble rail.

"Get it, baby. Get it, baby, just get it!" I hear myself say.

I part my thighs and allow his love to take me. My head kicks back with a shock of full, deep pleasure, and I am lost in his kisses. We embrace each other in a sweet, awkward rhythm until my body trembles, explodes, and finally melts all over his wonderful-wonderful .

It is just too wonderful-wonderful, Denise. This is truly getting your diva on!

After we recover from our pleasures, I walk back into the room and slip out into the hallway to the bathroom to freshen up. Tyriq does the same and joins me back on the balcony. For a moment, we stand there enjoying the faint sounds of the music downstairs, and we look at each other and fall out with grade-school laughter.

"Oh my goodness," I say to him. "What are we doing?"

"I think we're just doing our thang!"

"You got that right, honey. We *are* just doing our thang, and I've made a decision about *our thang.*"

"Really, what's that?"

I turn to him and look him straight in the eyes.

"I've decided to let *our thang* just take care of itself, tomorrow and the day after tomorrow. I've been wondering if this is just a horny fling and worrying about my feelings, not to mention what others might think. I'm just going to let it go."

"I think that's a good idea."

I hug him and put my head on his chest. I can hear his heart beating and smell his cologne. It's comforting just to be here, in the moment.

"Oh, I almost forgot. I have to give you your birthday gift. I've been carrying it around practically all night."

"I thought you just gave it to me," he says slyly.

"Honey, if *that* was your birthday gift, then you've turned thirty since

I met you."

He laughs as I reach inside the balcony doors, pick up his gift from the parlor chair, and flick on the outside light so he can see it.

"This is for you. I hope you enjoy it and understand the meaning behind it."

He unties the gold ribbon and tears into the crimson paper. Tyriq's eyes light up as he opens the cushioned velvet box and sees the pen.

"Ohhhhh, wooooow," he whispers. "This is—ohhhh, wooow. Do you know what this is? Do you know how rare this is? Ohhhh, wooow. This is too much. This pen is worth hundreds of dollars, at least. You really didn't have to do this, Denise."

"Do you like it?"

"Do I? Ohhhhh, wooow!"

"I heard that much already," I say with a smile.

"This is incredible. I love it!" He looks at the packaging and sees the bottled ink covered with tissue paper. "And it has ink too. That's old-school!"

"Well, enjoy it. I expect to get plenty of letters and poems."

"I promise. I will write those! This is the nicest gift I've ever received. Thank you, honey."

"You're welcome. Now let's get back downstairs before your mother misses us. It's late, and I have to get back to the hotel soon. I haven't packed or anything."

We walk back downstairs and see that the crowd of people is thinning. The musicians are winding up their last set, and the caterers are cleaning up. Tyriq says his thanks and good-byes. I chat with Ms. Clara and then have one of the valets hail her a cab. She is tore-up-from-the-floor-up and is probably seeing double, if not triple, from all the liquor she drank. She kisses me on the cheek and gets in the cab. I go back to Tyriq to tell him she will be all right.

The art gallery owner is a tall dark-skinned, bald woman of striking beauty. She walks over to hug Tyriq and then tells us to go home. She'll make sure all is finished and settled with the band and caterers. I hug her too. We hop in a cab and zip off to my hotel. We hold hands but are quiet during the short ride. Sadness is already creeping its way into my chest.

Forty-Two

I don't remember if I had any dreams when I wake up, but my head hurts from a hangover, and my face is wet with tears. Tyriq is still asleep beside me in bed. His breathing makes a soft hissing sound, like a hospital respirator. I slide out of bed and into the bathroom to clean up. It is after 10:00 am, less than two hours before checkout and less than three before I leave hot-ass New Orleans and what appears to be *the* experience of my life.

I turn the shower on and stand in front of the mirror while the bathroom fills with steam.

All that drinking you did last night really dehydrated you, girl. Pull yourself together. This is it. No regrets, no sob scenes. You need to pack your things and get back to the real world.

Listening to the rational you is never easy. The rational you is always telling *you* the same thing *you* would tell a friend who asks you for some keeping-it-real advice. Now my heart aches, and I'm not trying to hear it, at all. I cool off the shower spray, get in, and try to wash away last night's sex, this morning's hangover, and the tears that now begin to roll down my cheeks.

When I walk out of the bathroom, Tyriq is sitting on the edge of the bed, examining the fountain pen I gave him, rolling it

226

slowly between his fingertips. I sit next to him and plant a long, soft kiss on his cheek.

"I'm glad you showered before doing that," he says with a chuckle. "Oh really," I say. "Well, you're probably pretty ripe and salty yourself. I suggest you jump in the shower and scrub some of the rust off your crusty behind. You know, that old *twenty-four-year-old* crust."

"Oh, so now that I'm a year older, I'm crusty?"

"You're not getting any younger," I say.

Tyriq reaches over, locks me in a bear hug, and starts tickling me I giggle, laugh, scream, stand up, and try to wriggle free. Then I cry, not just tears but a very real mournful, ugly cry.

"Denise, what is it, baby? Calm down!"

"Oh my, God, Tyriq!"

"What, what?"

"I'm going to miss youuuuu!" I wail with a long pause after each word and collapse my weight against him. He holds me and sits me back down on the edge of the bed. The tears and the heartache keep coming and coming. There is nothing I can do to stop it. It hits me all at once. I haven't cried like this since Mama's funeral. Tyriq says nothing. He just holds me, rocks me, and lets me cry until I am empty and exhausted.

"I'm sorry, " I say in a horse voice. "I didn't mean to do that. I couldn't help it."

"Honey, I understand. I'm going to miss you too." He looks at me, and his eyes are red and tired from his own crying. "But we won't be apart for long. I'll be there in a month to sign the lease for my apartment in Baltimore, and in two months, I'll be there for good. Then you won't be able to get rid of me."

"I know. I'm being a big baby. I'm really sorry about this."

"Don't worry. Come on now. Pack your stuff. It's getting late. I'm going to take a shower and get you to the airport."

I wipe my eyes and begin packing my clothes. Tyriq showers and throws on his suit from the party.

"I'm going to pick up my car from the gallery, and I'll be back to get you."

"I'll be downstairs," I say.

He dashes out the door and down the hall. I keep working on my luggage, clearing out the closet and the drawers. I don't want to leave anything behind. I have the bellman pick up everything, and I follow my bags to the lobby. Tyriq is pulling up outside the front doors. The bellman packs the trunk. I turn around and give the hotel one last look, then hop in the car. Tyriq pulls out into the street and holds my hand. We glance at each other during the ride to the airport, but sit in silence. All we want to say had already been said.

I am almost late for my flight Tyriq and I barely have three minutes to say good-bye. It's best, I think. No more tears this time, just a passionate embrace and promises to call when I got to DC. After checking my baggage, I have to run to the gate. I plop down in the last empty seat next to a window. Minutes later, the plane backs up, taxies down the runway, and takes off. I am going home.

Forty-Three

"It's really good to see you, Ms. Younger! You look like you picked up a bit of a tan in New Orleans."

Bruce is especially cheerful as he loads my bags in his car at Washington National's pickup/drop-off area. I am especially tired. The four-and-a-half-hour flight seemed an extra hour longer. The food was bad as airplane food often is, and I slept uneasily off and on. It's good to see Bruce, however. He is another reminder of just how long I have been gone. "Yes, I did get a bit of a tan. The sun was brutal there, and the heat was worse, but I survived. I learned quite a bit at the conference, much of it could help our office run smoother and more efficiently. You'll see when I get back into the office."

"Are you hungry?" he asks.

"I am, actually, but I'm more tired than anything. I really need to get home."

"Suit yourself."

He opens the door of his Honda for me, and I sit down. Within minutes, we are zipping over I-395 toward downtown and then to Northwest DC. We avoid the rush hour traffic clog by sheer luck. The bumper-to-bumper is heading out of the city to the Virginia and Maryland suburbs as we head in. Bruce peppers me with questions and runs down more details about what went on in the office and the government while I was gone. Certainly, nothing is as interesting as my stay in New Orleans, but Bruce has done a great job keeping things afloat. It's another feather in his cap as far as I am concerned.

As he pulls into my driveway, I look at my watch and see that we have made good time. We lug my bags into the house and go around opening the windows because the house has a closed-in, stale smell. I say good-bye to Bruce and promise a debriefing tomorrow at the office.

As soon as he leaves, I pick up the phone and dial Nightie-Night in
New Orleans. Tyriq picks up after a few rings.

"Nightie-Night. Our summer sale is on right now. Save 20 percent on all ladies' bras and panties."

"What do you have for those of us who don't wear panties?" I whisper in my most seductive voice.

"Oh, my dear, we have a very special private trunk show for you because you have a very special trunk."

"You are just bad," I say laughing. "I'm finally home, safe and sound."

"Good, I'm glad, and I miss you already."

"Don't get me started. I was fine all the way home, and now here you go. Look, I just wanted to let you know that I'm home. I still have to call Daddy, Saundra, and Bonnie—and I'm really tired. We'll chat tomorrow after work, okay?"

"Cool, baby. I'll talk to you tomorrow."

"Tyriq?"

"Yeah?"

"Thanks for everything, really, thank you."

"It was your pleasure."

"Get off my phone, you are so bad! Bye!"

"Bye, Denise."

I laugh at myself as I hang up the phone. It's so easy for us to be lovers, but in that short moment, I realize something that I did not really see in New Orleans. It's also becoming easy for us to be friends.

Yeah, you lusted after him from the moment you saw him, Denise, but you were too busy screwing to notice some other stuff. You really *like him. He's fun to be around.*

Yes, and he's not here now, and that's no fun. This is the beginning of a long, lonely, and very difficult two months. I know the first month is going to be rough, but nothing can prepare me for what's going to happen after that. I have no idea how much my world is about to change I'm not ready for it, no way, no how.

Forty-Four

For weeks after coming home from New Orleans, I try to bury my head in my work. I have to. My daydreams are distracting and often tempt me to keep my fingers buried between my legs.

Talking to Tyriq at least once and sometimes twice a day doesn't help either, especially when your man is as fine on a long-distance phone call as he is in person. Let's just keep it real, Denise. Fantasizing is a muthafucka!

I have plenty to keep me occupied and entertained outside of work. As a few weeks turn into a month, Saundra's cat-and-mouse game with David refuses to let up. From listening to her, it is hard to figure out who is the cat and who is the mouse, but she is slowly discovering what is between his ears is even more interesting than what's between his legs.

At work, Bruce and I have actually become rather close. We often go out to lunch to talk about political office strategy. I am not a political appointee, but my boss is. There has been talk that President Clinton and the new Democrats coming into office are going to clean house. Just in case that housecleaning reaches my level, Bruce and I are keeping our resumes polished. I'm his boss, but we've also become buddies and political allies. If I move up or move on, I am going to reward his loyalty.

I finally meet Ms. Sadie Jackson of the second church pew on the left. She is not Mama, but she's not supposed to be. She is supposed to keep Daddy company and keep him happy. She is doing a fine job of that. They look cute together, and that is all I care about.

All this plays out in my mind against the backdrop of my love life. I'm counting down the days until Tyriq will come to visit: one week after his application for the business apprenticeship was approved; Saundra and I find ourselves at the Baltimore-Washington International Airport as Tyriq's plane is about to land.

Next, we go to Baltimore to do some apartment shopping. Bonnie sets everything up. Time has flown by so fast, and I am in a bit of a whirlwind. I've done so much running around trying to prepare for his arrival; I've worn myself out. For the first time in my life, I actually feel as if my energy level is at an all-time low. It's late morning on a Friday. Tyriq is only going to be in town for the weekend, and we have a lot to do.

"I can't believe I'm finally going to meet this young tenderoni of yours. You know he better be fine, or else I'm going to talk about you."

"Saundra, behave. He *is* fine, but that's not the point. He's scrumptious, sweet, and kind. He has a pretty good head on his shoulders too!"

"What about the one between his legs? How's that workin' for yah?"

"You know what? I'm going to change your name to Nasty Girl. It fits you to a T." I grit my teeth at Saundra with feigned anger, and she laughs at me. "But let me be clear, if the LAPD had beaten Rodney King with Tyriq's stuff instead of their nightsticks, he wouldn't have lived to say 'can't we all just get along?'"

"Now who's being the nasty girl?" Saundra screams with delight. "I know. That was bad, wasn't it?"

"Yup and good too!" We laugh loudly and high-five each other. We are so busy laughing and cutting up, neither of us notice when Tyriq walks up behind me and baritones a smiley faced, "Hi, baby! I'm here!"

I jump out of my skin, and my heart is in my throat. "Oh my god! Where did you come from?" I squeal.

"Oh, I wanted to make sure I was the first one off the plane. I figured you would be here waiting, and you were. So do I get some luvin', or do I have to start working to earn that all over again?"

I stand on my tippy-toes and lean on his lips like I am about to fall over. My heart is racing, and all I can hear is the hmmm-mmm-uhmmm of me enjoying every second of his long-overdue kisses. I finally pull back and blow out a long breath.

"Hi, baby," I whisper.

"Hi, yourself. Um, I think we have company." He points his chin at Saundra. "Oh dang, girl! I'm sorry. Saundra Davis, *this* is Tyriq Austin. Tyriq, this is my best friend in the whole wide world."

Tyriq reaches out and gives Saundra a firm bear hug and a peck on the cheek. "I've been looking forward to meeting you. But Denise didn't tell me that you were as pretty as you are."

"All right now," Saundra says. "He's fine, smells good, and most of all, honest! Denise didn't tell you I was hard of hearing, did she?"

Tyriq looks back at me with a puzzled look on his face. I shrug my shoulders, just as confused.

"Yeah, I am a little hard of hearing. Could you repeat that thing you said about me being as pretty as I am?"

Tyriq and I roll our eyes, and Saundra laughs loud enough to turn a few heads.

"Gotcha!" she says.

"Let's get out of here," I say. "We have to meet Bonnie in Baltimore by one o'clock.

Tyriq only has a carry-on, so we leave the airport, pile into Saundra's

Caddy, and cruise up the parkway to Charm City.

Forty-Five

Saundra takes us straight to Television Hill and WTSQ-TV12 in Baltimore. When I ask her how she knows where the TV station is, she mumbles something about dating a reporter "back in the day." I do not press her about the details. I figure I will get the lowdown on that adventure later.

Bonnie greets us in the lobby and gives Tyriq a great big hug. It does not take long for Bonnie and Saundra to hit it off. Bonnie gives us a tour of the TV station. By the time we are done, you would have thought they were separated at birth. It's an instant sisters' circle.

Later when we go apartment hunting, Tyriq says little. We saw two before he settles on a beautiful one-bedroom apartment in a renovated nineteenth-century mansion. One of the news anchors at the TV station owns the building in the historic Mount Washington section of the city. Bonnie said George Washington slept there, slipped there, or spit there during the Revolutionary War. I guess that's enough for the little spot on the map to claim his name. We stand on the wide front lawn of the building checking out the neighborhood.

"So this is it, huh?" I ask Tyriq.

"Yeah, I like it. It kinda reminds me of home in a way. It has a little bit of history and lots of character."

"I think it's spooky. Aren't you worried about the ghosts of slaves creepin' around at night?" Saundra says, almost to herself.

All three of us look at her at the same time. She looks at us and ducks her head sheepishly as if someone threw a wad of paper at her.

"Sorry about that."

We chuckle and shake our heads. "Who's hungry?" Bonnie asks.

"I'm starving," I say. "I'm more than ready for something on my stomach. It's been jumping and twisting all day."

"Lunch is on me, or actually it's on the TV station. We can grab something at one of the cafés near the Inner Harbor. Tyriq, give me a check for the deposit, and I'll handle the lease details for you when the news anchors come in for evening newscasts."

"Thanks, Bonnie, I really appreciate all your help." Tyriq gives her a one-arm hug. "It just makes this transition so much easier."

"No problem," she says. "Just handle your business when you start the program and don't fuck up! Remember, I vouched for you."

He laughs at Bonnie's cussing and shakes his head. "Don't worry. I'll make you proud."

"All right, I don't want no stuff outta you. There are some really sharp folks in the program!"

"You have nothing to worry about," he says and flashes that brilliant smile I've become so used to seeing in New Orleans. I feel a warm tingle as we pile into Saundra's car and cruise toward Baltimore's harbor.

It's a done deal, Denise. Tyriq is as good as here. One more month and he's a forty-minute ride away. You really did it, met a man, and he left his home for you*! Wow, now* that's *some heavy shit.*

I ride quietly, thinking about what's to come next. Tyriq asks questions, and Bonnie plays tour guide as we cruise downtown on I-83. We sit outside at one of the Harbor bistros and order something green, leafy and healthy. Afterward we talk and laugh, poke fun at the tourists and each other. Tyriq holds my hand, and I smile at the light breeze blowing in from the Chesapeake Bay. I am full, but my stomach still hasn't quite settled down. I try to ignore it. Other than that, it is a perfect summer day. I haven't had a day like this in a long, long time. I don't want it to end, but eventually it gets late. Bonnie takes a cab back to the TV station. The three of us hop back on the parkway to DC. Friday is pretty much gone. In less than a day and a half, my lover and friend will be winging his way back to the Crescent City. Tyriq has been here for less than nine hours. Even as he sits next to me in the big backseat of Saundra's Caddy, I am already missing him.

Forty-Six

7/2

We say good-bye to Saundra as she drops us off at my house and promise to see her before Tyriq leaves to go home. The ride back to DC seems to have settled my stomach, but as I unlock the door and let us in the house, my entire body feels unsettled.

Unsettled? That's one way to put it. Or maybe how about this? Your ass is as horny as the nose of a rhinoceros. Yeah, it doesn't get any more accurate than that. What do you think, Denise?

I spin around on Tyriq as he is pushing the door shut with his rump. I grab him by the collar with both hands and pull his face to mine like a schoolyard bully.

"I've been waiting for this for more than a month, baby," I whisper. "It's time for you to handle your business!"

Tyriq does not say a word. He just leans forward and presses his forehead against mine. My grip on his dress shirt tightens. One and then two buttons snap off. He grabs me by the back and thighs, carries me as if he's Prince Charming into my living room, and then stops.

"What's wrong? " I ask him.

"I just remember something. I've never been here before. I don't know where your bedroom is." He looks at me and starts laughing. I laugh too.

"Thebedroomisupthestairs,downthehall,lastroomontheleft."
"That's too far to walk, and I can't wait that long. "

Tyriq drops me on my sofa with a gentle bounce and pulls at his shirt and linen pants until he is naked. I come out of my heels and junk-in-my-trunk shorts. I start on my blouse, but Tyriq is already in it. We're both naked in a flash, and he squats between my legs.

You know that look, girl. That's the licky-licky, sticky-sticky look. Serve it up on a platter, Denise.

"Wait, babe, " I say. "You're a guest in *my* house. That means it's time for me to be a gracious hostess. Stand back up. "

He does as I say, and his thick chocolate, LAPD Rodney King–beat-'em-down is bouncing in front of my face.

"Ohhhh, Tyriq. I miss you, baby! "

I grip him around the base and slowly, gently French-kissed the head of his dick. I speed up and then slow down, massaging him the way I massage my arm when I put lotion on after a hot shower. Tyriq's hands play and rake through my hair. The first drops of him are sweetly salty, and I paint up, down, and across the dark pulsing veins of his thickness. I take a deep breath, stretch my mouth wider, and take all of him. His head is thick, and his skin is hot in my mouth. I am losing myself in the moment, wet, and wanting love, no longer feeling the need to get rid of the horniness. I just want to be close to him, just want to please him, just want him to know that I...we are special.

Tell him, Denise, do it now.

I look up at him, and my eyes smile at him. I add more pressure beneath his head and more friction on top. Seconds later, Tyriq stiffens, squeezes, and massages my shoulders, then fills my mouth with thick, hot, sticky-sticky, and wonderful-wonderful.

I taste it before taking it all down and gently pull and milk more from him until there is nothing left but his heavy breathing. I take him by his hand and sit him on the sofa. I sit astride him and place my head on his neck and shoulder.

"Denise." He licks his lips and swallows. He voice is raspy from breathing so heavily. "That was so damn good. I've never felt anything like that in my life. "

"I know you haven't. That's because there's only one me. Remember this, honey. There's a lot of sex out there, but there ain't a whole lotta luvin'. When you discover the difference between crazy sex and that ole-school, heart-blinding luvin', you'll never want the sex again. "

"So how do I know the difference?" he asks.

"Oh, sweetheart, it's easy, and I think you already know."

"How can *you* tell?"

I shift my weight to one side and look him in the eyes. "I can tell, and you can tell with one simple sign. After the crazy sex, a man gets up, puts his clothes on, and leaves you. But with that ole-school, heart-blinding luvin', a man just...gets...up!"

I reach down and begin stroking him again with my middle and forefinger. He is semi-hard for several minutes, but slowly begins to respond to my touch.

A hard man is good to find, but a young man can always get hard! Hee-hee.

"Now *that* makes a lot of sense to me," he says.

"It should," I say. "And *this* should quiet any other doubts or questions you may have, honey. "

I shift my weight again, pull him up inside me, hip-twist and rock-ride him as slowly and as deliberately as I can. I smile and watch him watch me. I enjoy exploring the perfection of his face with my eyes and while he explores the delicious inside of me. My breathing coos, hiccups, and hitches in my throat until my hips can't take it anymore. I shudder; speed up, and finally lost control. I whimper with joy and drop my head to his shoulder and neck again. After a moment or two of rest, we finally go to the bedroom and collapse into each other's arms. I look at the digital clock next to the bed. It is 10:58 pm. We're asleep before eleven o'clock.

Forty-Seven

Saturday is my day to play tour guide for Tyriq. He wants to see the Washington DC most people who live here take for granted. We walk the National Mall in the hot August sun, see the Hope diamond at the Smithsonian, hold hands at the National Gallery of Art, and marvel at the mixture of classical Greek and Roman architecture of the many monuments.

We get buzzed on honey wine and eat our fill at an Ethiopian restaurant in Georgetown. It is my favorite food, and I love eating with my fingers. Tyriq enjoys wrapping the spicy lamb, cabbage, and collard greens with the flat spongy bread—a sensuous experience. After dinner, we walk, talk, and window-shop until both of us are ready to collapse. I drive us back to my house as the sun begins losing strength. It has been a wonderful day, and nothing could have been more perfect.

When we get home, sticky and sweaty, Tyriq jumps in the shower. I check the messages on my answering machine after noticing that the red message light is flashing for attention.

BEEEP!

"Heyyyyy, Denise, it's Saundra, like you didn't know. Whassup? I hope you're still getting those old cobwebs cleaned out of that coochie of yours. I want to hear all the juicy details.

Don't leave shit out, either. Haa-ha-ha-ha! Call a sistah when you can! Luv ya! Byeee!"

That daggone Saundra is out of control!

I laugh to myself and push the button again. *BEEEP!*

"Denise, this is your father. Saundra told me you have someone with you I should meet. Is that so? Call me."

Does Saundra have to tell everything? Why does she have Daddy all up in my business?

I'm going to tighten her up when I see her. Speaking of tight, Tyriq comes down the steps, drying his tight, lean body off with a towel. He is scrumptious looking. I devour him with my eyes as he wraps the towel around his waist.

"I hope you didn't hear that message from Saundra," I say.

"Yep, I heard it and the one from your father too."

"I'm sorry. I'm so embarrassed."

"What are you embarrassed about? It's not like I expect you to keep me a secret from your best friend. I'm sure Saundra knows where all the scars, bumps, and hairs are on my body," he says with a deep laugh.

"Noooo, not exactly, but I did tell her we had a good time."

Tyriq laughs again. "A good time? Ohhhh-kaaay, I guess I'll have to translate that into 'Denise went down to New Orleans and got some,' but it's cool. Men talk, and I know sisters talk too. No big deal."

"So, Mr. Man, what did you tell your boys about me? I'm sure you told them you got some old stuff, and they got a big laugh out of it."

I start getting a little bit of an attitude. I hope it doesn't show. I'm going to look like a hypocrite if I start getting pissed about him sharing booty stories with his buddies.

"Funny you should mention that."

"Uh-huh!" I grunt.

"Actually, *my boys,* as you call them, know me. They know what I like in women. I didn't give them the juicy details like

Saundra wants, but they know you are worth every minute of my time, in bed and out. That's why I'm here now."

He does it again! Just when I think I am going to get pissed, he cools me right out. I walk over to him from the answering machine and start rubbing my thighs against the terry cloth towel he has around his waist. The towel, or rather what was hiding beneath it, is beginning to respond. But he backs up and gently pushes my hand away. I look at him with a small scowl planted in the middle of my forehead.

No, he isn't trying to keep you away from his wonderful-wonderful.

"What's wrong?" I ask.

"Nothing, babe, wasn't there another message on the answering machine, from your father?"

"Yeah," I sigh. "I forgot you said you heard everything."

"So what's up? Am I going to meet him or what?"

"I don't know," I say and sit on the living room love seat.

"Why don't you know? I met Saundra and Bonnie. You met my mother. What's the big deal?"

"The big deal is I met your mother by accident. Bonnie was with me when I met you, and Saundra is my girl. But my father is different."

Tyriq looks at me, walks to the kitchen, and leans on my breakfast bar. His back is facing away from me, but I can hear the anger in his voice.

"If you don't want me to meet your father, sounds to me like you're not serious about me."

"How serious can I really be, honey?" I said softly. "We've only known each other for a little while."

"Oh, so I'm just someone to play with? Someone to clean the cobwebs out of your rusty coochie?"

Damn, Saundra! I'm going to kick your ass when I see you.

"No, no, no. I'm just kinda unsure about everything. I'm unsure about me, you, about what I'm feeling, what love is, about everything!"

Love? Where did that come from?

Tyriq picks right up on it too.

"Who said anything about love, Denise?"

"You did!" I say, raising my voice and standing up from the love seat. "I listen very well, Tyriq. You said you believed in love at first sight, remember?"

He drops his head but doesn't turn around.

"Yes, I did say that, and I do believe in it. I guess I'm the one who knows where his heart is. You see, Denise, for me, it's about quality time, not quantity. Call me an incurable romantic, but that's where I am. That's *who* I am."

His voice is slow, somber, almost sad.

I don't know what to say or think, so I don't say anything. Tyriq walks upstairs and, a minute later, comes back downstairs. He has a pack of cigarettes in his hand. He taps the box against the back of his hand with a quick popping sound and walks out the front door as the last pinches of dusk are draining from the sky. I follow him after a moment and peer at him through the screen door. He sits on the porch glider, blowing long plumes of smoke toward the quiet city street just beyond my front lawn. It just occurs to me that I had not seen Tyriq smoke since going to his house in New Orleans.

That was at least fifteen orgasms ago. For you, girl, that's a long time.

What do I say to him now? How I feel is how I feel. Am I uncertain or just scared?

How about a little bit of both?

I do not know if he sees me behind the screen, but he isn't looking for me. He's in his own world, a world of looming heartbreak that's about to ruin an otherwise perfect weekend. If I ever introduce Tyriq to Daddy, today is not the day.

It's nerve-racking enough having the new man meet your parents when things are good. You can't introduce a pissed-off black man to your folks, ever! As a matter of fact, you need to make sure his anger has dissipated and a few days have passed before you even think about it again.

I take in a deep breath and reach for the cordless phone. I dial Daddy as I walk up the steps to my bedroom. He picks up the phone on the second ring, and I make up something about being tired and having a tight schedule. I don't give him any details about my weekend visitor, and he doesn't ask. Maybe he can hear the I'm-not-ready-yet in my voice. I hang up the phone and think about calling Saundra to sulk a little bit, but I decide to wait until after I take Tyriq to the airport in the morning. But morning is a long way off. It is just after nine thirty on a hot summer night, time to sip wine, listen to the crickets chirp, and have quiet, thoughtful conversations with your man by candlelight. Instead, I find myself walking upstairs and collapsing heavily on my king-size bed. It feels acres wide and very empty without Tyriq next to me.

Here's a surprise for you, homegirl. See how quickly someone can fill a void in your life you never really knew you had? It doesn't even hit you until a little bit of fussin' lets you know just how deep in it you are.

I close my eyes and fall asleep on top of the bedspread feeling very much like my old self—very much alone.

Forty-Eight

I wake up in a sweat, afraid and confused. The last bits of an unpleasant dream fade away as I look around the bedroom for Tyriq. The bed is just as it was when I fell asleep, empty. The time 5:45 glows bright red from the digital clock. I slept through the night. Coffee and Tyriq are on my mind. I slip quietly downstairs. My heart sinks as I discover Tyriq asleep on the sofa. I turn the coffeepot on and wait for my dose of caffeine. I pour two cups and sit his cup on a coaster on the coffee table in front of the sofa. I ease myself into the love seat, listen to Tyriq breathe, and watch the sun slowly wake up through my living room window. When I look at him after a few minutes, I find his eyes quietly focused on me.

"Good morning," I say.

"Hi."

"I haven't seen you smoke since I was at your house last. What's that about?"

"After that night, my desire to smoke went away. I wasn't a big smoker, but I guess a kind of calm came over me, and I just stopped."

"I see," I say. "Sooo now you've started up again?"

"It kind of hit me yesterday. I guess I wasn't done after all." I pause and look out the window again, thinking.

"Why didn't you come to bed with me last night?" Tyriq reaches for his coffee mug and sips it.

"I didn't think it was a good idea for me to join you. I wanted us to be on the same page about us. If we weren't, it wouldn't be fair to you or me to be there and make love or have sex or whatever."

He sighs and slowly shakes his head.

"So is that the way it's going to be now?" I say, more ticked at myself for allowing things to spiral so far, so fast.

"Denise," he says sitting up. "It doesn't have to be this way. I just want to continue to get to know you. Up until yesterday, I was happy with the way things were going. Just cruising along and seeing where things go."

"Cruising along?" I say as I stand up and feel my stress level jump. "What makes you think I have time to just cruise along? I'm thirty-five years old! *You* have time to just cruise along! *You* can cruise all *you* want. You can cruise for the next five years, and you still will not have seen thirty.

In five years, I will be forty! You hear me, Tyriq, the big four-oh!"

He sits there looking at me with that same look of peace and calm I know so well. There's even a smirk that grows from the corner of his mouth. "What's so funny?" I hiss. He is smiling now, and the sunrise shows

brightly on his straight white teeth.

Dayum, girl, that man is fine.

"You know what's so funny? I'll tell you what's so funny." He puts his coffee mug down and walks over to me.

"You are afraid of your dreams coming true. "

"What do you mean? I've never talked to you about my dreams." I look at him, confused but trying to understand.

"You don't have to. But I've had a chance to see your world. You have a good job, a good life, good friends, a father who loves you, and a wonderful spirit. You just don't have the love of a man to share all those blessings with."

What's he been doing, eavesdropping on my dreams? How does he know these things?

"I don't need a man to be happy," I say and turn my back to him.

"I never said you did, Denise, but you want one. I'm just here with open arms, trying to give you what I believe you want—a full, solid, loving, passionate relationship."

"How do I know you're the one for me?"

My back is still turned. I don't want him to see my tears streaming down my face.

"How do you know I'm *not* the one for you?" he says barely above a whisper.

Tyriq puts his hands on my shoulders and gently turns me around. My face is a mess of tears. He kisses both streams on my cheeks and embraces me.

"Denise, honey, I want to fill myself up with you. I want to drink you like that wine we had yesterday. I want the sweetness of you, the buzz of you. I want all my days to blossom with us."

Preach! C'mon with it! Wellll! Amen!

Tyriq lifts my face to his and looks at me.

"I know what I like when I see it. I just wish you were as certain as I am."

I press my lips together, close my eyes, and shake my head at the battle going on in my head.

He's so young, but give him a chance. Let's see where this goes, really*! Stop fighting and let him into your heart. It was so easy to let him into your body. Unlock the door to a little room in the corner of your heart and let him sit a spell. If he acts right, maybe he can stay a little longer and get a bigger room.*

I pat him on his broad shoulders and look at him in his eyes. I let out a big sigh.

"Listen. I'll make a deal with you. I'll let go and see where this goes. Honestly, I'll do your cruise-along thing, *if* you quit smoking.

"Oh, just like that, huh? You just turn on and off like that?" he says, looking at me with a skeptical eye.

"No, baby, I *don't* just turn off and on like that. I've always been turned on, but the barriers have been guarding my heart. I'm going to let them down. But if I do that, I want you to be around to see what I really have to offer. That means no cigarettes. Okay?"

"Fine, but I will need your help."

"Hey, no problem. You'll be in Baltimore, and we can work on that together. There is one other thing I want to say. You were right about me."

"Oh? How so? "

"I was getting in the way of letting my dreams come true. I think I was dreaming about you long before I met you. "

Tyriq leans over and kisses me like a man in love.

Oh, I certainly hope so.

"C'mon."

I pat him gently on the back as I pull away from kisses that threaten to make my knees give out and give up some quickie coochie.

"You have a plane to catch."

Forty-Nine

I know something is wrong before I open my eyes Monday morning. I'm awake but lie here without lifting my eyelids to greet the workday sun. My mouth is full of spit, and my stomach churns with a sickening slowness. I take a deep breath and try to resist the urge to gag. It has the opposite effect. I sit straight up, toss the bedspread off my body, and run to the bathroom. There are only six steps, but number 6 seems to take forever before I can reach it. I make it to the toilet by slipping on the balls of my feet. My knees come crashing down on the bathroom rug with a thud, but my stomach tightens against my midsection too hard for my knees to care. I lost everything in my stomach to the water-filled bottom of the porcelain god.

The more I try to calm myself down with deep breathing, the more my guts cut loose. I heave and heave until nothing but bitterness tastes on my tongue. My head throbs; my stomach cramps, and the muscles of my midsection are weak and pulsating. I start thinking about the really fattening, really delicious over-breaded seafood from that ghetto fish-and-chips place on U Street.

Mama always said that if you really don't need to eat it, don't. It always promises to make you sick, and now you may have a

252

mild case of food poisoning. You always listened to Mama, so why didn't you listen this time? You didn't have to have any of it. Maybe you're just tired. You've been away from home a long time, girly.

Yeah, I am starting to get scared, and I have lived long enough to know, I have good reason to be. For two months, I've ignored common sense. Then I ignore the signs. I can't ignore them anymore. I have fucked up, royally!

Fifty

"You're what? What do-you-MEAN PREGNANT? How did that happen?"

Saundra is standing my kitchen with a half-empty glass of wine in one hand and all the attitude a black woman can muster, balled up in a fist planted firmly on her hip. "I mean, I know how it happened. You were down in hot-ass New Orleans with your hot ass in the air with honey dripping from it. But for real...how did *THAT* happen?" she shrieks.

I just sit there on my love seat, staring at the carpet. I cannot say a word. I just shake my head.

"Are you absolutely sure?"

"Yes," I say.

"You took a home pregnancy test?"

"Yes."

"You saw your doctor?"

"Yes."

"She did a pregnancy test?"

"Yes!"

"Twice?"

"Yes, yes! Saundra, I'm knocked up and fucked up! Damn!"

"Didn't you think? Neva mind! No, you didn't think, but I'm not going there. I was the one who was booty-loose and freaky-free. That's why I'm playing Big Mama now. You were the one who was always careful. I'm just at a loss. Why did you let this happen?"

"I thought you just said you weren't going there?"

Saundra looks at me and sighs. She goes into the fridge and freshens up her wineglass. She brings me a glass of orange juice and sits on the sofa. "So what are you going to do now?" she asks. The shock is gone from her voice. It's replaced by supportive seriousness.

"I don't know. I'm really scared and worried," I say. "How long have you known?"

"I got the results from my doctor just yesterday. The morning sickness has been hitting me every morning for almost a week. It's a mother! I don't want to eat anything because it will just come back up. Other than my doctor, you're the only person who knows."

"When are you going to tell Tyriq? He *is* the father, isn't he?"

I look at Saundra with the same attitude she gave me earlier. "Of course he is!"

"I'm just asking. I don't want any more surprises." I sniff and her and roll my eyes.

"I don't know when or how I'm going to tell him, but he's going to have to know."

"Sounds to me like you are thinking about having the baby."

"I am thinking about it. But I can't ask him to stop his life and be a father right now. His life is already going through a lot of changes with moving and the job in Baltimore."

"Denise, how long is this job program supposed to last?"

"I think about nine or ten months."

"Hah! Bingo! Whether you want him to stop and be a father or not, it's unavoidable. It's going to happen. What are you going to do, hide your belly until the job is over? You were never been a big person to begin with. "The sooner you make a decision about the pregnancy, the sooner you will be able to tell him what's next, or not." "What do you mean 'or not'?"

"I mean, sis, if you decide not to have the baby, you don't have to tell him anything. You know what? It's one thing to have a Mr. Fine to roll around in the sheets with, but if you have the baby, you have to figure out if this is the man you want as the father of your child. You *will* be connected to him for the rest of your life."

Saundra couldn't be more right. As crazy-acting as she could be, she was more grown-up than you give her credit for sometimes. She had to be a grown-up. She has two boys to raise. Now, Denise, it's time for you to be grown-up. Make a decision and do it fast. Tyriq will move to Baltimore in less than four weeks. But you will talk to him long before that. When you do, you don't want him hearing drama in your voice and asking probing questions.

I sigh deeply, close my eyes and massage my temples with my fingertips. "I got a question for you." I look at Saundra nursing her wineglass. "How do you feel about being called 'Auntie Saundra'?"

Fifty-One

Two weeks have passed since I discovered the pregnancy. I speak to Tyriq almost every day during that time but can't find the courage to tell him. He never suspects that something is wrong. Maybe that's because he is too busy getting his life together for the move to Baltimore. It is the best diversion I could have had, but Saundra is bugging me to tell him *and* Daddy too. There is no way I am going to tell Daddy first, and despite my desire to tell Tyriq face-to-face, by the time he moves to Baltimore, I'll be right in the middle for my first trimester.

This charade has gone on long enough!

Yes, it has. I look at the clock. It is just after seven o'clock. Tyriq will still be at work on a Saturday night. I decide to call him at home and leave a message. He can call me tonight after work, and we can have a long talk. I relax my grip on the phone as the line rings on the other end. I can feel the muscles in my jaws tensing while I wait for the answering machine to pick up.

"Hello?" Tyriq answers.

"Um...hello? Um...Tyriq? You're home?" I say and immediately feel an unpleasant rush of adrenaline.

"Yes, baby, I'm home. This is a pleasant surprise. What's happening?"

It's a surprise all right, but it won't be pleasant for long!

"What are you doing at home? I thought you were supposed to be at the shop on Saturday night."

"I usually am, but I have so much to do, and my mother knows it, so she told me not to come in today. The movers have been here to take away the big stuff and hold it in storage in Baltimore. The rest of the stuff, I have to pack up on my own. I'm almost done, believe it or not. Did you try to call me at the shop?"

"No, no. I didn't. I was calling to leave you a message. I wanted you to call me when you came home."

"Well, I'm here now. Is there something wrong?"

He already knows there is. His question sounds more like a statement. I can feel the hesitation in his voice.

"Well, that depends," I start. "It depends on how you feel about children." There is silence on the other end of the phone. I cannot hear him breathing. He clears his throat but does not say anything. "Tyriq, are you there?"

I hear the flint wheel of his lighter zip and the telltale sound of a smoker blowing out a long exhale.

"I'm here."

His voice is low and frighteningly calm.

"So you're telling me that you might be pregnant?"

"No, I'm telling you that I *am* pregnant."

"Wowwwww, Denise. That's something else. How far along are you? "Almost two months."

"How long have you known about this?"

"Two weeks now."

"Why are you just telling me this now?" His voice is serious, but calm.

"I didn't know how. I was scared, and I didn't know what you would say or how you would feel."

I can feel myself beginning to come apart. He is silent on the other end of the line, and I can hear a steady tapping, like a pencil or pen tapping on a table.

"Aren't you going to ask me if it's yours?"

"Nope," he says.

"Why not?"

"Denise, I know it's mine. In my heart, I know it's mine."

"Are you upset?" I ask.

"Upset? I wouldn't say upset. I'm just—wow, y'know?"

"Yes, I know. So what are we going to do?"

"What do you mean what are *we* going to do?"

"Just what I said. What do you want me to do? Do you want me to keep the baby?"

"I don't see how we have a choice in the matter. But *you* are carrying the baby, so you need to tell me how you feel."

"Tyriq, I don't think that's fair for you to put this all on me. We did this together, and we need to make this decision together."

"Denise, I'm not putting this all on you at all. I have my thoughts, but at this moment how you feel is more important."

"Really?" I ask, not knowing how to react to that.

"Yes, really, tell me what you want to do."

I sigh and thought about it one last time. "Honey, I really would like to have this baby."

"Then *we* are going to have this baby *together*."

"Tyriq, I can't ask you to stop your life to be a father."

"Who said anything about me stopping my life? Life goes on, and I will be there with you while you go through the pregnancy. I'm going to be in Baltimore in just a few weeks. As a matter of fact, I'm going to fly up next week now that I know what's going on."

"You don't have to do that. I'll be fine."

"That's not the point, Denise. That's what you would expect of me. That's what I expect of myself."

"Tyriq, I want you to know, this wasn't planned, honestly. This is not the way I wanted my life to be. I feel like I've dragged you into something that you wouldn't have planned for yourself."

"Listen, Denise, this isn't what I planned for myself, but the way I feel right now, there's no one else I'd rather go into this with other than you." *Oh my god! Where has this man been all my life? Young or old or my age, I don't care anymore. Can I ask for any better? Tell him, Denise. Tell him now. Tell him you love him.*

"Listen, everything is going to be just fine. I'm going to call the airline and try to find a flight out of here next week. Maybe that will be a good time for me to meet your dad, but can we hold off telling him about this until I get moved in, please?"

"Sure. I don't know how he's going to handle this, but the longer we wait, the better."

"I'm going to call about a flight. Are you going to be okay, babe?"

"I'll be fine. Just let me know when your flight comes in. I'll be waiting there when you get off the plane."

"I know you will. Oh, one more thing I forgot to mention. I've been meaning to tell you for a while now, but this seems to be the best time."

"What's that?"

"I love you, Denise."

Well, there it is. Tell him, tell him, TELL HIM! You know you're feeling it. TELL HIM!

My mouth is frozen open, and goose bumps cover my arms at the thought of being in love with someone—really, really in love.

"Denise? Did you hear what I said?"

"Yes, baby, I heard what you said. I know you do."

"Good," he says with a bit of sadness pooling in the bottom of his voice. "I'll see you in a few days."

I hang up the phone feeling as if I have just missed out on a wonderful chance. But can love, true love be a reality after just two months? Two weeks?

You love him, don't you? You should have told him so.

I pick up the phone and dial his number again. I get a busy signal. He is calling the airlines for a ticket.

Yeah, to come see your pregnant ass!

"Damn! I really should have told him how I feel," I say out loud.

Yes, you really should have.

Fifty-Two

I work like a dog at the beginning of the week. I have to; Tyriq calls Sunday to tell me his plane is coming in Thursday afternoon at two thirty. He sounds letdown, and he doesn't talk about love, but I am going to meet him with love on my lips. He will hear it from me for the first time without a doubt. Nothing is going to get in the way of my telling him that I love him and am *in love* with him. It is time for me to stop messing around with my heart and his, and just jump in.

Bruce helps me knock out paperwork for another big government contract. I can take Thursday off.

Before leaving the house, I double-check to make sure it is clean as a five-star hotel room. I am not going to drink anything, but I make sure there is plenty of wine in the fridge. I even look up a gumbo recipe in one of my cookbooks.

Hey, why not learn how to cook some of his favorite food?

On my way to the airport, I grab a huge summer bouquet of flowers at my favorite florist.

It's all right to give a man flowers, isn't it? Well, he's going to get these.

If this is not enough to convince him of my love, I'll just take him home with me and give him some of the same stuff that he had when he was here the last time.

That *should refresh his memory and make a believer out of him.*

Washington National is about as empty as an airport can get in the middle of the day. Tyriq's plane is on time according to the arrival board and is only twenty minutes from landing. I sit smelling the sweet aroma of his flowers and wait. Minutes later, a voice crackles over the public-address speakers.

"Now arriving at gate 15-B, American Airlines flight 69 from New Orleans."

I can see the plane taxiing in. I get up and walk over to the huge picture window to watch the ground crews guide it to the gate. I wonder how much they make. It seems like such a dangerous job out there with big jet engines on even bigger planes. I stand there watching them even as the first passengers begin to deplane. A bit of mischief seeps into me. I stay by the window where I can see Tyriq, but he will not be able to see me. I am going to sneak up behind him and give him one of those big bear hugs he gives me. More people file out of the gate door, parents with children greeted by grandparents, businessmen and businesswomen on their way to K Street lobbyist offices or even to Capitol Hill, even a few college students carrying books with care packages and youthful enthusiasm in their backpacks, but no Tyriq. I move from my hiding place by the window and stand where I can see directly down the walkway where he should emerge. The last few passengers trickle out. After a moment, my heart sinks. Two flight attendants, the pilot and copilot walk past chatting about lunch. I walk over to one of the flight attendants and try not to let panic show on my face.

"Excuse me, but I have a question. Is that the plane from New Orleans?"

"It sure is. It was a direct flight."

"Were there any more passengers still on the plane?"

"No, that's it. When we deplane, the cabin is empty," she says. And I can tell she can see worry settling in on my face. She looks at my flowers, and her voice grows sympathetic.

"Ma'am, do you want me to check the passenger list for you real quick?"

"Do you mind? Maybe I have the wrong flight or wrong time. This has to be a mistake."

We walk over to the customer service desk. The flight attendant's fingers quickly click over the computer keyboard.

"What's the name of the passenger please? This was a full flight. I think everyone who was supposed to be on this flight was on board."

"His name is Tyriq Austin."

"Spell that please."

"t-y-r-i-q a-u-s-t-i-n," I say.

"Aha! There it is." The attendant points to the screen. "We had a full flight all right and one empty seat. Mr. Austin missed the flight."

To say I am pissed is an understatement. How could he miss the flight? Is he pissed at me because I didn't say I love you? I know I should have said it if I felt it. But why play games now? Why make the plane reservations and not get on the flight? Did he have second thoughts about the baby? What's going on? Is he not coming? This is bullshit!

Just chill, Denise. Maybe he did miss the flight. Maybe he got a late start. Maybe traffic was bad. Before you go flying off the handle, wait until you get home. There will be a message from him on your answering machine.

"Yeah, there better be!"

Fifty-Three

Nothing! Absolutely nothing! There is no message on my home answering machine and no voice mail at work. I call Bruce to see if anyone left any messages for me. There are three messages, all them work related. Nothing! I call Tyriq's home number, the phone rings, and then the answering machine picks up.

"This is Tyriq. I'm not home right now, but say what you want, and I'll get back at you. Peace and blessings." *BEEP!*

"Tyriq, this is Denise. Where are you? I waited at the airport for you, and you weren't there. What happened? Are you mad at me? Did you change your mind? Call me, I'm at home."

I call Nightie-Night and expect Ms. Clara to answer, but the phone just rings; then the answering machine picks up. Tyriq's voice is on the message trying to sound sexy but professional.

"You've reached Nightie-Night, New Orleans's finest in ladies' luxury lingerie. We are open Monday through Wednesday from ten to seven, Thursday through Saturday until eleven. Please come and visit us. It's a luxurious experience you won't forget." *BEEP!*

"Ms. Clara, this is Denise Younger calling from Washington, DC. Tyriq was supposed to catch a flight to DC today, and it seems that he missed it. If you hear from him, please have him call me at 202-555-2007, thank you." Now what? I look around my bedroom as if the answer is on the wall somewhere. I look at my watch. It is 4:30 and still no word. This is really inconsiderate. He should have at least called by now. I pick up the phone and call Saundra at work.

"Hey, girl! What's going on? Aren't you supposed to be knee deep in some chocolate man by now?"

"Saundra, that Nee-grow stood me up. Can you believe it?" I complain.

"What do you mean 'stood you up'?"

"I mean, I went to the airport to pick his ass up, and he missed his flight. I had to check with the passenger list to find that out. He didn't have the decency to call me and tell me. He just dumped on me. I'm pissed!"

"You should be! I would be! That's just weird! What time is it? It's about a quarter to five, he should have called by now. Did you try him at home?"

"I sure did and left a message. I don't know what's up."

"Do you want me to stop by after work? I was going to get together with David, but I can stop by if you want."

"No, don't worry about it. You go on and get with your man. I'll just sit here and get more pissed off at mine. Shoot, after tonight, I don't know if I'm going to have a man."

Just then, I hear a beep on the phone.

"Saundra, let me call you back, somebody is trying to call in. It's probably Tyriq with his inconsiderate ass."

"Call me back," Saundra says and hangs up.

I click over. "Hello."

"Denise, is that you?" the voice says.

"Yes, this is me. Who is this?"

"This...is...Clara." Her voice is slow and low, eerily calm, just above a whisper.

"Clara? What's going on? I called the shop earlier and just got the answering machine. Tyriq is supposed to be here in DC, but I haven't heard from him. Have you heard from him?"

"Denise, how soon can you come to New Orleans?" she asks. I can barely understand her.

"What? Why would I need to come to New Orleans now? I'm waiting for Tyriq to come here."

"He's not coming, dear. You need to come to New Orleans right away."

"Ms. Clara, what are you talking about? What happened? Where is Tyriq? Is he all right? Tell me what's going on!"

"Denise—somebody murdered my darling baby boy!"

Fifty-Four

I arrive in New Orleans late-Friday night. I get the last seat on the last flight available before the weekend. I knew I would come back to New Orleans someday soon but not like this. Ms. Clara met me at the airport. We cry as soon as we see each other. On the way to the Garden District and her home above Nightie-Night, she tells me what happened.

"Tyriq never made it to the airport. That morning, he stopped by to say good-bye. He told me he was going to a French Quarter cigar shop to pick up a pack of imported cigarettes before going to meet the plane. I scolded him about smoking, and he said he was trying to quit, but he said he had a lot on his mind. He promised this would be his last pack.

"That was the last time I saw him. I thought he was gone until I got a phone call from the police. Tyriq was mugged only a block from the cigar shop in broad daylight. The police say there was a struggle, and he was stabbed in the chest with a wicked massive thing that looked like a butcher's knife. They caught the man right away. Police thought he was just a middle-aged white man, a drifter who had run-ins police.

"But they discovered he was one of the last of the Mini-Mob, carrying out long-standing code of retribution. It was a crazy, insane vendetta against my baby for the money his father hid when Tyriq was too young to understand the world. "They caught him right away because he was covered with Tyriq's blood. There was nowhere for him to hide."

I cover my face with my hands and pour more tears out. I know from Ms. Clara's description that the same man and the same knife that could have killed me, killed Tyriq. That double mountain tattoo was the mark of the Mini-Mob, still watching, and waiting after all these years. Tyriq didn't heed the same warning he gave me only a few months ago, be careful about your surroundings. If he hadn't gone for the cigarettes, would this still have happened? I can't say. But there is a bitter irony that I can't seem to get out of my head. Even if it's not completely accurate, Tyriq's cigarette habit eventually led him to his death.

I stay with Ms. Clara until the funeral. She refused to have it any other way. Like Tyriq's birthday party, it is a well-attended, lavish affair, one of those traditional New Orleans jazz funerals tourists hear so much about . Ms. Clara says they usually only have them these days for musicians or drug dealers, believe it or not, but on occasion they have them for people who really want to go out in style. If Tyriq had nothing else, he had style.

Ms. Clara writes a check for more than $12,000 to make sure every detail is covered. Everyone who attended his birthday party and many others come out to pay their respects. The mayor and the president of Xavier University walk in the long procession next to Ms. Clara and me. The jazz band plays mournful tunes as the funeral winds its way through the Garden District and past Nightie-Night. It is still very hot in the city, and perspiration runs in my eyes as I stare at the gleaming copper casket resting in the back of a horse-drawn carriage.

When I can't walk another step, Ms. Clara and I sit in a white funeral limousine for the rest of the ride to the Mount Olivet Cemetery in Gentilly. I watch as his closest buddies from college perform pallbearer duties. They slide the casket into one of the many above-ground crypts for which New Orleans is famous. I hear so much about the city burying its dead above ground because the city is really below sea level. I just never expect to see it, not like this.

The whole thing becomes surreal for me as the jazz band picks up the tempo with "When the Saints Go Marching In." It is strange and painful, but in my heart, I believe Tyriq probably would have said something like, "That's really cool."

As the graveside service ends, Ms. Clara hands me an envelope. It has my name on it and several large bloodstains.

"The police gave this to me after they closed their investigation. It's for you, and I think it's important. I think my son was thinking about you, even as he took his last breath." She kisses me on my cheek. "I know you're going home now, but do me a favor, please. Take care of yourself and my grandbaby. I would like to come and see him or her sometime."

I am surprised that Tyriq had mentioned my pregnancy to his mother so soon, but I'm glad he did.

"Of course, Ms. Clara, you are always welcome at my home and around the baby."

I kiss her and give her one of those Tyriq-style bear hugs. I step back into the limousine alone. The driver points its long hood out of the cemetery gates and then on the road to the airport. As if he reads my mind, the driver closes the partition that separates the front seat from the rest of the limo with a flick of a switch.

I reach into my purse and pull out the thick bloodstained envelope Ms. Clara gave me earlier. As I begin to open it, I notice a short slanting cut near the middle of the linen stationary. Almost as heartbreaking as the news of his death was the realization that

Tyriq had the letter inside his suit pocket. The knife of his killer sliced through the letter before inflicting its deadly wound. I take a deep breath and carefully open the letter along the top crease. His warm, wonderful scent brushes at my senses. For a moment, he is alive again and with me. I unfold the fine linen stationary and trace the double-hump crimson stain of half a heart turned on its side. If it weren't so horrible in its creation, I will consider it a gesture of tenderness. I summon up my strength and settle in the leather of the limo seat to read the last words I will ever know from Tyriq.

My Dearest Denise,

When you gave me this pen, I promised I would write many letters to you with it. This is the first one. It is also the most important one. I am telling you, once again, that I love you. Now, you have it in writing.

When I first said those words to you and you didn't respond. I was hurt, and I was worried, about you, about us. You see, baby, in a short, very short time, I gave you my heart, and it was as bare and as open as it could ever be. I thought that I lost or maybe never really had the woman my soul told me was the love of my life. That woman is you, Denise Younger.

For a only a moment, I was willing to give up on us and even believe that true love isn't possible, not the way I wanted it. But even as I listened to your silence and then your last words before our phone call ended, I knew you had fallen in love with me, even if you couldn't speak the words from your lovely lips. Knowing what my heart told me was true, I am willing to wait until you are ready to tell me, until you are ready to be as open and as bare as I am now.

You have changed my life, Denise. If I had never met you, this new, wonderful journey would not be possible. Now we have created a new life together. For that, I can only offer all of me with passionate gratitude.

Our lives are only beginning, and we have all the time in the world. I can wait to hear what I want to hear from you. But know this: I love you now, Denise, and I will love you always.

I thank God for creating you for me!

True love, Tyriq

I can barely read the last few lines. My eyes flood with tears and drip on the stationary. I can hear Tyriq's words in my head and heart.

"I love you too, Tyriq."

Epilogue

Loving Tyriq as quickly and as fiercely as I did was something I never thought would happen to me. It is a fairy tale. I stop believing in them a long time ago. So I am doubly shocked after my son is born. Someone I never ever considered, steps in to help, but eventually steps into my life.

Bruce goes from subordinate to office buddy, to supportive friend, to the guy who is always around when I need something. He doesn't judge me about having a child out of wedlock.

When I discover a flat tire at the end of a long difficult day at the office, Bruce fixes it, dirtying a new shirt and tie in the process. I replace them with a French cuff shirt and a colorful striped silk tie. He remembers my birthday, Saundra's birthday, and always comes to cookouts we have. We are just friends, I think. When I try to date, Bruce babysits little Tyriq Jr.

Why would any man be willing to take on the chore of babysitting a toddler? When I come home from these outings, impatient and unhappy, Bruce gives me a hug, a peck on the cheek, and says, "Call me if you need me."

After barricading my heart against all comers and constantly calling and needing him, Bruce and I start dating. It is awkward at first for me, and both of us have to unpack our baggage about racial prejudice. He also doesn't judge me about it.

Interracial couples are not unusual in DC, so being with him in public isn't a big deal. There *are* times when he makes me tingle, and the sex is pretty good even if it was strange and new for us the first time.

Yeah, but not freaky like you like it. He'll learn. Love has a way of fixing things.

We are together for three years when Bruce asks me to marry him. I say yes without hesitation. Marrying a white guy is something I never thought I would do. Loving a man younger than me was not something I considered, either. In the end, Tyriq and Bruce were different, but they were both good, loving men who changed me forever, and that's the most important thing. We exchange our vows among the late spring azaleas at the National Arboretum in DC. Daddy, Ms. Sadie, Ms. Clara d' Beaux, Saundra, and Bonnie are there to honor the occasion. Bruce's parents and an older brother from Perry, Florida, are there too. They are warm, comfortable, caring people. It is obvious where the seeds of Bruce's loving heart were planted.

Saundra and David tied the knot too. By that time, little Tyriq was twelve years old, and I know it is time for me to *really* tell him all about his father. It's time to go to New Orleans. Bruce thinks it is more than appropriate that I do this with Tyriq, Jr., alone. But our trip had to wait. Hurricane Katrina bullied her way across the Gulf that year, scattering the people of New Orleans and so much of the character and history that took centuries to create. Ms. Clara was also taken from me, swept away in the surge of the storm. Her body was never found.

A year later, little Tyriq and I finally make the journey to the Crescent City. Nightie-Night is still there. But the flamboyant thin man who sold me the beautiful dress for Tyriq's birthday party more than a decade ago owns it now. We go in and walk around. I tell little Tyriq this is where I met his father. The owner looks at me, thinks he recognizes me, but then dismisses it. I don't tell him who I am. For me, seeing the lingerie shop still standing and still beautiful is enough.

We take a cab to the Mt. Olivet Cemetery and walk to the d' Beaux family crypt where Tyriq is buried. But like many of the above-ground tombs after Hurricane Katrina, his is also severely damaged. The tomb lies open; his casket is gone. I shed one last lonely tear and then close the final chapter on my love for Tyriq. I don't even have a photograph of him, but little Tyriq, Jr., looks so much like his father, I know I will never forget.

As we get back into the cab, I hear little Tyriq's stomach growl.

"Are you hungry, or are those monsters in your stomach?" I ask and tickle him with a giggle .

"Yeah, I am hungry, Mama. Can we go get something to eat?"

"Of course, honey," I say. "Let's go get some gumbo. You'll love it, and I know the perfect place."

About the Author

Harold T. Fisher has spent his entire career as a TV news anchor and radio broadcaster. He has always had a passion for poetry and the urban romance-erotica genre. This is his first novel.

He is a native of Washington, DC and has lived all over the eastern United States. He is a graduate of Morgan State University in Baltimore, Maryland where he currently makes his home.